Ashix Rising

Book Two
An AshFieran Duet

K.L. ANDERSEN

Acknowledgments

Thank you to those who took a chance on a brand new author and for motivating me to write this book to finish the story of Raine, Kal, and Zy.

I can't express my gratitude enough to my 'beta' readers, Kelly, Lou, Alicia, Bethany, and Oliver. You five are amazing, and I will forever be thankful for the insight, excitement, and pointers you have given me.

To my mom, thank you for helping mold this story into what it is today and for your help with the plot twists. I am so grateful to have you as my cheerleader and forever reader.

Last but not least, thank you to my husband. Even though you will likely never read my stories, you always encourage me to keep writing and check in to see how my story is going. I'm blessed to have your continued support while I chase my dreams.

Trigger Warning

While there are not many triggers, it is always good to check for your mental well-being. Please note that some trigger warnings could spoil the story. So, if you don't mind them, then skip the rest.

Some scenes include: Kidnapping, verbal abuse from a parent, violence against other individuals, death, loss/grieving, mention of pregnancy, sexually explicit scenes

To those who have ever had to help your furry soulmate cross the rainbow bridge, they will be waiting for you on the other side.

Blurb

After Raine shoves her mother and Kal through a portal back to Earth, she closes it off from her father, who is hellbent on using her mother as leverage while also trying to kill her mate.

After she's drugged with a magic dulling concoction by the irritating male, Zynas, Raine finds herself in a new environment. Now, she fights her father's control over her powers and encounters a chance to free her Ashix, Beauty, and herself. All while dodging advances from the aggravating male, Zynas, and her growing attraction to him.

She must find a way to reunite with Kal, keep her head above water regarding Zynas, and stop her father from continuing to destroy the world she grew up in.

Chapter One

Raine

Dark thoughts of punching the male walking beside me on our way to visit my Ashix consumed me. I couldn't stand being in this bastard's presence, but he insisted he was the only male in AshFiera who could accompany me to the stables on the newly acquired property my father had taken.

Who even knew what that poor soul went through and if they suffered or had to die for us to stay in this lavish mansion and even more luxurious property.

After all the complaining about my situation, I had to admit that it was a beautiful prison. My room was spacious and decorated with the beasts I found myself so entranced with, the Ashix. Everywhere I glanced, there were some figures of vicious beasts adorned beautifully. My headboard was one of my favorites as its intricately carved wooden piece with Ashix flying around each other above waterfalls, representing a mating dance. I assume whoever carved this thought of them as dearly as I did. I knew the females could be territorial against others of the same sex, but the males tended to group and live as a family unit with their one female mate. It was a beautiful concept to be loved by multiple males, but I always wondered if they would get jealous in the end.

With those thoughts, it got me thinking about the situation with Kal and Zy. Even if I didn't want to think about Zy, he was always in the back of my mind, even invading my dreams at times over the past few weeks while holed up in my bedroom. Maybe if the situation was different and Zy hadn't helped my father in capturing and keeping me held in this prison, I could let my feelings run wild for him. But as it was, he was my keeper, guard, and enemy. I had to remind my heart of that fact continuously as it ached for my mind to give in.

"It sure is a beautiful morning. Don't you think, Raine?" asked Zynas, startling me from my inner reflections of none other than the topic of him.

In my peripheral vision, the silhouette of his body turned toward mine, looking, waiting to see if I would give him a flicker of attention when he tried making simple conversation. But I kept facing forward and didn't respond. I never gave him the time of day. My body, on autopilot, kept my pace brisk with determination to reach Beauty in the stables every chance I was able to steal being with her. I didn't understand why he kept trying to garner my time with him. It was useless, and his effort went unanswered every time.

His breathy sigh indicated that he would not continue trying to get me to open up further during our visit with Beauty that day. Internally, I danced because, to me, it was a small victory. Even if it was childish, I couldn't let him wedge his way further into my life than he already had.

The echo of our steps on the brick path, along with our tandem breathing, was the only noise emitted during the walk through the lush gardens of Hydrangeas, Azaleas, and Daylilies.

The combined aromas of the flowers in the gardens gave me joy and contentment when all that was contained in my daily life lately were anger and resentment. I loved these gardens and vowed that when I returned to the human realm, I would plant the flowers that were among us around Gigi and Aunt Sam's home to continue basking in their beauty long after I left this soul-sucking place.

When I reached the stables, I didn't wait for Zynas to lead me inside. Instead, I pushed past him to get to Beauty and ease the lonely ache that usually formed the moment I left her. I couldn't explain it, but ever since she and I bonded weeks ago, I had a sense that she always needed me, and the ache that consumed me was not my own but hers. Of course, she must have been in the grips of insanity being left alone in the stables tied up. Her only other company was the dense males who guarded her and the building surrounding her very own prison.

Those males stayed outside most of the time, though. From what I heard from Astora, if any of them stepped foot inside or even got close enough to her, she would hiss and claw at them, even catching the pants of one male and ripping them off. We giggled when she described how his boxers and cheeks were bright pink, especially when he saw Astora in the gardens, witnessing his embarrassment while running to grab new trousers.

Beauty was in the same spot as usual, casually lying her head down as if she were napping. But once she heard the light crunch of hay under my boots, her head popped up, and her gaze followed my movements toward her.

As I was about to reach my beast, her body stiffened, and her burnt orange orbs brushed past my face to the male behind me, Zynas. A soft coo left my throat to catch her attention back onto me. It worked until the heat of his presence was behind my back.

My body flinched, and Beauty's shallow growl left her at my immediate reaction. She could feel the panic and anxiety coursing through my body while having this male so close behind me. I needed to tone it down for all of our sakes before she decided to lunge and cause more havoc than I needed to deal with.

So, I spoke to Zy for the first time in weeks.

"You need to back off, Zynas. She can feel what I feel, and you're not helping keep her calm," I said through clenched teeth.

"Ah, so is this how I get you to respond to me? I just needed to get too close to you in Beauty's presence to earn your attention." Zy said, with a smugness laced in his alluring, deep, baritone voice that sent shivers down the column of my spine with every rumble as he spoke against my back.

"Don't be silly. As you can see, I'm in between you two, and I would prefer not to be sliced accidentally."

"Hmm, you and I both know that Beauty would never harm you. Regardless of whether or not you are in the way."

"Yes, well. Back the hell up and let me enjoy my time with her. Normally, you stand by the stable doors and let me have the brief moments I'm able to spend with her alone. Why are you in our space today?" I asked, suddenly suspicious of his proximity. *What in the world are you up to, Patches?*

"No particular reason, my lovely little storm. Just assessing something." He answered cryptically.

"And I suppose you won't divulge the reasoning for your assessment?"

My patience was wearing thin with Zynas and his coded quips. He never answered my question that first day I arrived at the mansion. His comment about fitting Kal into the equation still left me puzzled, and if I brought it up again, he always danced his way around the conversation. So, my vow of silence began until he elaborated, but he never did all those weeks.

Zy smiled at me, "You worry too much about what I'm doing. Are you starting to care about me, my precious female?"

I scoffed, "Absolutely not, *Patches*. I could care less if you get hurt. In fact, why don't you step closer and get an even better assessment for your mental records."

The smile he had donned left his lips, and a familiar sneer replaced it.

"I told you before, *female*, not to call me *Patches*."

And with that, Zynas walked away and out of the stable, not lingering around like usual. I must have hit a nerve with him when I call him 'Patches.' I would have to keep that in mind for the next time he pisses me off. It would come in handy when I wanted to get under his skin. My vow of silence against Zy was coming to an end. That conversation was more words than I have had with him since the day I flung my mother and Kal into the portal at my childhood home.

Beauty nuzzled my hand, obviously wanting attention herself. So I turned back to my glorious girl and scratched at her neck. She loved being itched, especially under her chin, where the muzzle they kept on her would rub constantly.

It was easy to tell what she liked and didn't because she conveyed it through the bond. I still had no idea why we had entwined our souls together when I returned to AshFiera and not before I left. But I had a feeling it was because my immature, muted magic all those years ago were missing, stored in the necklace my father gifted me and later on my mother had enchanted. When I reconnected with them as an adult, something clicked, even when I was injected and muted yet again.

The injection didn't last long; I only felt its effects for two weeks. Not only did it diminish my powers but also my strength, and the worst part was the lethargy. I slept most of the time in those two weeks. I'm surprised Kal didn't have the same reaction I did when he was poisoned himself back on Earth, but of course, I think he was only poisoned with ten times less than what I had been.

I missed him like something fierce. When we connected before coming to AshFiera to save my mother, I could feel the bond begin to form. Like how it is with Beauty, I felt brief flashes of his feelings but didn't understand or pay much attention to them until I bonded with Beauty. Then I understood.

Now, it's all I can think about. However, because Kal isn't currently in the same realm, the bond has essentially been quiet. Muted the same way my magic is.

Beauty nuzzled me harder, interrupting my thoughts. She understood that they were turning to darkness before I even did. Smiling, I patted her long, scaled neck and gave her a tight squeeze.

"Don't worry, girl. I will somehow free us from this prison, no matter how long it takes. Just be ready for me when I say it's time," I said softly.

A clearing of a throat came from the stables' entry. Zy was back and ready to escort me to my gilded cage, which he called a bedroom. Following him like the obedient female he wanted, I was surprised when he didn't say a word on our walk back or even when he left me at my door. All I could do was stare at his retreating back before he disappeared, shadow-jumping from my view and leaving my changing emotions a mix of chaotic confusion and hurt.

A week passed, and every day, Zy escorted me to the stables for my daily visit with Beauty but never spoke a word to me. He always left me alone with her when we arrived, unlike before when he would stand in the doorway lingering.

It was a nice change of pace for awhile, but even with his presence right in front of me, I felt oddly lonely. Strangely, for all the times I just wanted him to keep his mouth shut, I missed his attempts at small talk and the confused hurt that started a week ago grew the more the silence did.

One day, I couldn't take the distance from him any longer. It was causing my stomach to bubble with unused and unwanted energy. I stopped in the middle of our walk to the stables, "Zy, what's gotten into you?" I asked. He had kept walking, but once my voice rang out in the silence, his body became motionless, still, facing away from me.

"I can't handle your silence. I know I haven't been very welcoming, but this change from you has me on the edge, and I don't like it."

He turned and gazed into my eyes. There was a strange sadness that flickered across his face, but then he adjusted his stance, and the cocky asshole was back.

"I have no idea what you are talking about, Raine. You didn't wish to speak to me all those weeks before, so I merely acquiesced to your silent treatment. Is that not what you wanted from me?" Zynas asked.

Crossing my arms and tapping my foot, I glared at him, "I was pissed off at you for your role in my imprisonment. How the hell else was I supposed to act? Just accept that I no longer have my freedom and that at any moment, my father would come knocking and demand I use my powers against my wishes."

"So you are no longer pissed at me, then?"

"What? Of course, I'm still pissed at you, Zy."

"But my dear little storm," He started, sauntering in my direction like a predator stalking his prey. "You said 'was,' so that must mean I have grown on you somewhat during our visits with Beauty." He was now standing so close I could feel his body heat seeping itself into me, enveloping safety and comfort from this dangerous male.

I wanted to smack that cocky smirk off his handsome face, *fuck*, what was wrong with me that I let him in just a little bit. No, I needed to rebuild that damn wall and push him back out. Kal was waiting for me to come back to him, and together, we would stop my father and live happily ever after. *Right?*

Merely muttering about stupid males and their stupid egos, I brushed past Zy to continue my walk to see Beauty. I had wasted enough time blabbering to Zy and trying to get him to react.

Practically running into the stables, Beauty was already up and waiting for me instead of sleeping like she usually did when I entered during our morning hangouts.

"Hello, my stunning girl. How are you this morning?" I asked, widely smiling when she seemed more relaxed today than she had been since coming to the mansion on the outskirts of Ozryn.

The air crackled with unnamed tension, and I knew that Zy had decided to join us today instead of skulking around outside the stables. He didn't stop walking and instead stood close behind my back again. I didn't turn to look, instead bracing for Beauty's reaction and growl. But she never let out a sound, and her body remained relaxed.

The heat of Zy's body left my back, and as I kept my focus on Beauty, hers was on Zy's movements, following him around the stables. Oddly enough, she was still calm, and suddenly, the feelings of admiration flowed through the bond as she watched him.

Shocked, I jerked back. My movements caused Beauty to startle slightly, and when she felt my confusion through the bond, she chuffed at me. *Actually, fucking chuffed.* I didn't know what I was missing or was I an idiot for not seeing what she saw?

Turning my head to look over my shoulder, I found Zy leaning up against a post with his arms and one leg crossed over the other. When I slowly looked up to his face, his uncovered eye was staring at my ass, desire swirling within that honey-speckled eye.

I cleared my throat, and his eye snapped up to my face. "Can I help you with something?"

"No, not at all. Just enjoying the view," Zy said, smirking, showing off one sharp fang that had my face flushing briefly. *Who knew fangs could be sexy.* The thought startled me.

Rolling my eyes to hide the fact I had just been checking him out, I turned back around to scratch at Beauty's neck when Zynas' voice lowered and practically whispered, "Roll those eyes at me again, female, and see what happens."

I laughed hysterically and, without looking at him, said, "Touch me, and I will find a way for you to lose a hand. It would go quite well with your missing eye."

"Don't test me, little storm. I–"

Suddenly, the air changed, negative currents and energy flowed around the room, suffocating all that was good. Beauty stiffened and let out a deep, menacing growl while her claws dug themselves into the dirt.

Instantly, I knew that the only person who could emit so much toxic vibrations in the otherwise harmonious morning I was just enjoying could be none other than the last male I wanted to be near.

My father, the despicable male I hated with every fiber of my being, Lazarus Celestine.

Chapter Two

Zynas

The moment Raine's body tensed, I knew someone would be joining us. I would need to find out how she detected it so early. It was an incredible gift because it gave me a few seconds to prepare my instincts not to go into overdrive when the male finally showed himself in the stables' doorway. No matter who it was, my body demanded I protect Raine, and luckily or maybe unluckily, it was only Raine's father. *What an unexpected visit.*

He usually stayed away from here and left Raine for her daily outings with Beauty. He knew the beast would act out of violence if he showed his face.

As the male took another step inside the building, hissing and growling erupted, shaking the post I was leaning against. Stepping away, I headed toward Raine and Beauty, looking over at Lazarus before I spoke.

"Lazarus, I wouldn't come inside further than where you are. We wouldn't want Raine to get hurt in the beast's attempts to reach you." I warned, watching Beauty's body closely. I learned when she was about to lunge since she used to do the same to me a few weeks ago.

Luckily, I gained her trust, and now she lets me come near her. Today, she let me come close in Raine's presence, which I would say is the progress I had hoped for. It will make things easier soon.

"Ah, Zynas. Perfect. I was hoping you would be the male with my daughter here. I will need you as well," Lazarus said.

"Yes, I am the only male who comes here with Raine. I won't permit anyone else to escort my betrothed to visit her beast."

Raine's laughter broke out over the muffled growling Beauty was still emitting—a clear warning to Lazarus to stay far back, away from her bonded master.

"*Father*, you think Zynas would honestly let other males around me? That's hilarious. No, he's a possessive, controlling asshole." Raine seethed. Angry at our earlier exchange before her father interrupted us. If you focused closely enough, you could see the sparks flare within her pupils.

"Raine, how often must I tell you to watch your tongue? No daughter of mine will talk like one of my males. What does that show your betrothed?"

"Does it look like I care what I show my *betrothed?*" She sneered, evident disgust lacing her shaky voice. Even though her wrath was directed toward me, I knew there was no real depth to it.

I stepped further before Raine when the hint of displeasure flashed through Lazarus's eyes. "Don't worry, Laz. I can handle myself where it concerns your daughter. She has spirit, and I prefer her that way. Makes things more interesting." I said, hoping the stifling anger swirling in Lazarus's eyes would diminish.

It worked as his boisterous laugh boomed in the air while he tilted his head back. "I'm glad she amuses you, Zynas. I still prefer the females in my life to watch their language. We are important here in Ozryn and must keep a good impression on others who are also of relevant standing. Isn't that right, my little Ashix?" He asked Raine, directing his gaze onto her.

Raine stood beside Beauty, rubbing a hand along the beast's neck to keep her calm in the face of the male she wanted to burn and devour. She didn't hesitate to answer, because Raine knew if she left her father waiting for a response his temper would flare.

"Yes, father. I apologize for my rude outburst. What is it you want? I would like to hurry this along. As you can see, Beauty is upset with you in her current home."

"I would like you and Zynas to accompany me into the city. I wanted to show you around before we attended to some business that requires merely your presence."

She studied her father for several moments. I could see the gears running through her head about whether or not she would be required to use her magic against another. I knew he wouldn't ask this of her yet. It was coming, though. It wouldn't be much longer, and his patience with his daughter's reluctance to adhere to the new standard would wear out.

"You only require my attendance, nothing else?" She asked, still sceptical and rightfully untrusting of her father's motives. He always garnered some form of manipulation without the person knowing until it was too late.

"Yes, my little Ashix. Your powers are not needed for where we are going. Plus, you have Zynas and me to protect you if we run into any trouble." Lazarus said, his smile widened.

He knew he had her, and she couldn't refuse him unless she wanted to witness his anger again. The first few days she arrived, she saw him for who he was: a short-fused tempered male. He wanted to spar with her like when she was younger and before he had been imprisoned, but she refused. Stomping off to her room and locking herself away aside from leaving to visit Beauty. When she was gone on one of those visits, he destroyed her room and all the Ashix decorations she had admired. The bastard sat on a chair in the middle of her room, smirking and waiting for her to return to witness what he had done.

When she walked in and saw the disarray of her room, she started screaming at him and advanced. Before she could get to her father, I stepped in and stopped her. I remember the whimper and cries she let out when he threatened her privileges to see Beauty. It was crushing to witness, and I struggled to keep a straight face. Not allowing myself to show him the waring emotions just below the surface, as I was also affected by his actions.

The globe I had specially made of Beauty sitting on her boulder back at Raine's childhood home was shattered across the floor. Her bedframe was marred from a blade slashing across several areas. The paintings I picked out for her flung across the room, torn. Anything that had to do with an Ashix was destroyed.

She reluctantly gave in and agreed to spar with him the next day. He didn't go easy on her, and she turned black and blue. Sitting on the sidelines and watching him take his anger further out on her was challenging. But, if I had stepped in, it would have only been far worse for Raine. I wasn't about to allow him to hurt my female any further, so I endured watching her punishments doled out. When she returned to her room that afternoon, I urged her maid, Astora, to take care of the cuts and bruises. Making sure she forced Raine to soak in a hot bath to relax her muscles that would surely ache later on.

I arranged for all the broken decorations to be replaced with new ones while I took her to see Beauty several days later. The headboard turned out even better than the first one. The male I paid to make a new one carved his own magical artistry into the wood, precisely depicted what I wanted him to. I needed her to understand the beauty of multiple loves on a multiplex of levels. But would she recognize the message I wanted to show her in the mere carvings?

Raine cleared her throat, rousing me from thoughts of past events, "I suppose I could come to visit Beauty later and join you, Father. I have been wanting to see the city for a while now."

"Excellent. I will see you in the foyer in half an hour. I suggest you change into something more befitting of your new station. Things are altering around AshFiera, Raine, and I want a united front." Lazarus said, the message loud and clear, just before he shadow-jumped out of the stables leaving us alone.

Turning toward Raine, who was still behind me next to Beauty, I peered deep into those emerald green eyes that shone bright with mischief already brewing.

"I suggest you heed his words, little storm. I know how you like to ruffle feathers, but if you disobey him today, I'm afraid your room won't be the only thing he destroys." I said, allowing my gaze to land on Beauty. She had grown on me over the last few weeks. Even if, at first, she nearly took a hand off. Raine meant the world to me; in return, so did Beauty. I needed to keep Beauty safe just as much as Raine.

Her expression changed from mischievous to something of awe. I didn't know if I had let too many of my feelings show through my face, so I hardened my brows and sneered. "Let's go. If you want to make it in time, we need to get walking now. Unless you wish to stay longer, and I shadow-jump us into your bedroom?"

"No, that's quite all right, Zynas. We can end our visit now and walk back. I prefer the view of the gardens much more than my bedroom." She said, patting Beauty's neck again before wrapping her arms around and squeezing her. "I'll be back later, girl." She whispered, hesitating before moving away from her beast.

Walking out of the stables, Raine stayed by my side as we returned to the mansion. She was quiet for a long while. I'm sure she imagined what her father was up to with this impromptu visit and request. I couldn't help but wonder to myself what the male was up to and what horrors he would show Raine today.

"Tell me your thoughts, Raine."

She glanced over at me briefly before returning to keep walking. "What makes you think I have any thoughts?"

"Everyone has thoughts, little storm. Even you, I'm sure there is a hurricane brewing inside waiting to be set free."

She laughed, "I suppose my head isn't completely blank. But I won't bore you with what is happening up here." She tapped her head, "And don't worry, Zy. I will play the perfect little princess since you and my father are so desperate to have one around. It should be time for me to act like one since my father is determined to turn AshFiera into a kingdom instead of a free world."

"I don't care if you're a perfect little princess. I much prefer you to be your feisty self. This whole demure and meek act isn't like you." I pointed out.

"It's not an act, Zy. I have just given up on leaving here anytime soon, if ever." Sadness encompassed her eyes, even if she tried to hide it behind a fake smile. She wasn't fooling me though, I saw through her facade.

Silence wrapped around us as we continued walking back to Raine's room. Her prison cell, she had called it. When we reached the bedroom, I opened the door for her to walk through first. I shut it, knowing no one could listen in once it was closed.

When my father was still alive, he had a room enchanted by a witch where he would confide in the only males he trusted. It would allow me to drop the act momentarily before we had to be in the foyer.

Stepping up behind Raine, I placed my hands on her upper arms, breathing in the scent of jasmine and honey. She was intoxicating, and I wanted to strip her bare, lay her on the bed, and worship her like the goddess she is. If only she knew how much I wanted and everything I wanted to do to her. I only hoped she would allow me to touch her someday like how I so desired.

"Zy," she whimpered.

The sound went straight to my cock. Hardening in my pants, I stepped closer so she could feel what she did to me, pressing myself into her back further.

"My little tempest. Do you feel what you do to me when we are this close? Mmm, what I wouldn't give to hear you moan my name in passion. Throw you on your bed and show you what a male would do for his female."

Her breathing grew heavy, and she pressed herself back further into me. Growling, my hands roamed down to her waist, squeezing lightly onto those delicious hips. I bent slightly, placing my lips on her neck to speak. "Gods, Raine. I could lose myself in you for days. I vow to free you from your prison, then we can truly explore this connection."

Suddenly, she twirled around and stepped back, one hand on my chest. Determination crossed her face. "Zy," she breathed heavily. "We can't do this. I can't do this with you. I'm in love with Kal; he is mine, and I am his."

"And you forget, little storm. Kalpheus is not currently here, but I am. You. Are. Mine. First." I said, punctuating each word with a growl. "As I am yours." I delicately finished, attempting to ease the growing tension.

"No, I won't allow you to cloud my head with your sexy growling. And stop looking at me like that!" She huffed. Stomping her foot and further pushing at my chest but my body wouldn't budge as I pressed myself further into her.

"Like what, Raine?" I smiled smugly, knowing she couldn't resist the growing desires swirling around our nearness.

"Like–like you're going to devour me. Only Kal is allowed to look at me like that. Why can't you go back to being an asshole? It was so much fucking easier hating you when I believed all you cared about was pleasing my father and helping him with his fucked up plans for me. But today, you stood between us like you were protecting me. And then, just now, making me feel something forbidden that I should only feel with Kal. Whatever secret powers you are wielding, I need you to stop."

"Raine, I have no powers. You can't deny there is a connection between us. I feel it deep within, a bond aching to be touched and caressed." I said, reaching out and stroking a finger along her jaw until I reached her chin, curling one underneath. Ever so gently forcing her face up to lock her eyes with mine. Desire swirled in those beautiful green globes, but then they turned violent, and she ripped her face and body far from mine.

"I don't care what is taking place between us. I won't explore it any further. You need to leave now. There is a pretty little princess dress I have to put on for dear old dad." She sneered. "And if my timing is correct, I have about five minutes before hell breaks loose in the foyer. So, shoo." She motioned her hands, flapping them in the direction of the door.

"This conversation isn't over, Raine. Mark my words. We will revisit this."

"Not a fucking chance, Patches." She hissed.

That goddess forsaken nickname she decided to give me irked my nerves every time she used it, and she knew it too. It reminded me of my shortcomings and the way I lost my eye.

Soon, my pretty little mate, you won't be able to run from these feelings.

Darkness wound it's way around my heart, growing as I fought with myself and how I wanted to force her to love me, desire me. But, I knew this wasn't how I would win her over. No, the way this was going my female would be the death of me first.

Glaring at Raine, I kept silent and hurried out the door, slamming it behind me. A startled squeak came from behind it immediately after. And then shuffling moved around the bedroom, followed by muffled swearing.

Chuckling to myself, all I thought about was that even with being irritated at her, I couldn't stay mad for long. I leaned against the wall to wait for my infuriatingly beautiful female to emerge so we could get this little tour with her father over.

Soon, she would know precisely the male I was, and when we got the chance, I would reunite her with those she loved— even if I had to sacrifice everything to make it happen.

Chapter Three

Raine

I was officially going to strangle Zynas. Fucking arrogant, dickheaded male. I can't believe I let myself enjoy his touch and his dirty words. My center still pulsed with unbidden need as I replayed the moments when his hands held my hips while those lush lips rubbed along my neck as he spoke the filth that affected me. I didn't want them to; I wanted to continue to despise him, but I'm afraid he somehow wiggled his way into my guarded heart.

Shuffling around in my closet, looking for the dress I knew my father would approve of and avoiding his wrath, I cursed under my breath. All the words I knew I wanted to call Zy and my father. Two bastards in a pod, as their intentions were similar, just in different ways. Where my father was a selfish prick wanting to use and control my powers for evil, Zy was a nuisance for all his control throughout my life, threatening any male who dared talk to me—and continued to control when and where I walked by myself in the mansion.

Finding the perfect dress in my father's eyes didn't take

long, and my inner thoughts ran wild. It was beautiful but not something I would typically wear. It was a light lavender with subtle vines adorned at the bottom, and when I put it on, those vines practically touched the floor while I was barefoot. Looking into the mirror, I gazed at myself smiling. The top was form-fitting and helped boost my breasts to be enticing while billowing out in a lovely flow from my hips to my toes.

Will the extra lift to the girls distract Zy long enough for me to snag one of the many daggers he constantly wears slung around his waist and chest in his many straps? I wasn't allowed weapons for obvious reasons. *There's only one way to find out. I must hurry to the foyer before Father rips the mansion apart.*

I was startled by Zy's big, broad body standing directly in the middle of the door once I opened it to leave. His brows were drawn together, wrinkling his forehead while his lips, those kiss-able lips, were scowling instead of his typical cocky grin.

"You're about one minute from being late. Are you done cussing like an unhinged warrior before we meet your father?" Zy asked, irritated.

"Yes, Master Zynas, I'm done cussing for now." I snarked. Letting the sarcasm roll off my tongue.

"Perfect, my little *pet*. No time for walking. We need to shadow-jump now."

Zy slung his arms around my waist and pulled me into his body, but before he jumped with both of us, his eyes lingered downward, right where I knew they would go. Smirking, I slowly inched my hand to the nearest dagger on his waist when we jumped.

We landed in the foyer, my father stood waiting for us, impatiently tapping his foot and looking at his wrist like he had an invisible watch just waiting to be examined.

I quickly snapped my hand away from the dagger when I realized we were no longer alone. I would have been so close to snatching it if only Zy had given me a moment longer in the doorway to remove it from the sheath.

"There's my beautiful daughter and her soon-to-be mate," Father said, clapping his hands together. "You are a vision, my little Ashix. I do love the dress you have picked out for our outing today. So much better than those fighting leathers you constantly wear around the mansion."

"I'm glad you like it, Father. I hoped it would be appropriate for where you want to take me and that it would please you." I lied. Secretly, I hated wearing any kind of dress he wanted, even if it was beautiful.

"It is marvelous. You look just like your mother." He said wistfully.

"So, where are you taking me? Somewhere fun, I hope?" I asked, knowing this likely wouldn't end up fun at all considering it was my father who was the one escorting me through the city.

"No, my little Ashix. It's no fun this time, I'm afraid, but I would like to show you a few shops, and you can tell me if they appeal to you. Then we can come back together another day." He said, his previous impatience seemed to have disappeared from our ongoing conversation. I didn't want to linger longer than necessary; I craved for this trip to be over.

"Right, shall we go? Are we shadow-jumping or walking?"

"We will shadow-jump a few blocks from the shop we will visit today. Zynas," he glanced at the male behind me. "I need you to jump in with Raine and always stick by her side. There is word that the resistance has some Shadow Assassins hiding in Ozryn. I want them to double-think that trying to kidnap my daughter again would be a perilous idea."

Shocked, I stared at my father, "What do you mean kidnap me? What is going on?"

"Nothing for you to worry about, my little Ashix. We handled it long ago." Father said.

"Handled it? Don't you think you should have told me I was in danger? Father, please, take these bracelets off. I can defend myself if something happens. Haven't I proven myself to you yet?" I pleaded, but his following answer would convince me he would never release me from my prison or the hold on my magic.

"No, Raine. I am afraid you have yet to convince me you are truly here to be a family. It hasn't been long enough anyway, and your mouth has gotten you into more trouble than I care lately."

Beside me, Zy remained quiet. *Bastard.* Apparently, he couldn't stick up for me here when it mattered and involved my powers. I guess I was right to continue to guard myself. Even if it was tough while he was so close, his musk of sandalwood and leather drew me in. With Zy's aroma rolling around me, clouding my judgement, clearly I couldn't consider anyone in AshFiera an ally, and I could only count on myself.

If only Kal had figured out how to open the portal and get me out already. I shouldn't have been so foolish to think that Theo could figure out another way to open the gateways into our world when I rendered them useless, even with his warning that it wouldn't be easy to come up with another spell that would override the closure.

Zy pressed the front of his body into my back, wrapped an arm around my waist, and laid his hand on my stomach. His other hand engulfed mine into his, and we shadow-jumped without saying another word.

Shadow-jumping had gotten easier the more I experienced it. Zy always jumped with me; he stuck to his word, and no other males came near. So the more he used the ability with me, the less dizzy and nauseous I felt coming out on the other end.

My gaze swept around the spot we were currently rooted to. It was marvelous, and my mouth gaped in awe at the beauty surrounding me. A long, wide, cobbled path went as far as the eye could see, with buildings on either side. Those buildings were massive and interconnected. Only sparingly did I see an opening between them that held massive trees and a garden of hedges and flowers surrounding them as if they were the center piece to the nature laying within those spaces.

Before I could ask to look at the gardens, Zy's hand lightly touched the small of my back and encouraged me to move forward. I realized then that my father was waiting for us to join him. So I cleared my throat, stood straighter, and walked toward the male who held my true freedom in his hands.

When I reached my father, he held his arm for me to take, and I did. As Father had instructed back at the mansion, I left Zynas to walk behind us to keep guard.

Walking along the cobbled path, several children ran out, giggling and chasing each other. It reminded me of the day I first ran into Zynas in Martslocke with the children running around the beautiful Ashix water fountain. It wasn't entirely a happy memory either, he was such an asshole, and I couldn't understand why he didn't introduce himself. We had known each other previously when we were younger. Although, I suppose it would have ruined his plans the next day when he was instructed to snatch me from my home without so many witnesses around.

The stores along the cobbled path had large windows that made it easy to view the contents, which the owners proudly displayed. My eyes snagged on a display with several sparkling crystals, casting rainbows from the sun's rays that hit them just right. I stumbled slightly, and Father took notice of what my eyes regarded.

Chuckling, he said, "We can come back on a different day and visit that shop if you would like, Raine?"

"I would love to see what they offer. Their window display is beautiful," I said, trying to peer further into the store as we continued walking.

"Kojax, remember this store, The Serenity Crystals. I would like to bring Raine back here another day." He ordered. Kojax nodded and briefly met my stare before he continued to take in our surroundings, also keeping guard alongside Zy.

A delicious roasted nutty aroma and the sounds of chatter made their way toward us. It was divine, and I wanted to know if we had time to grab a quick drink. I opened my mouth to ask, but my father quickly turned me down.

"Next time, my little Ashix. The coffee smells enticing, but we have a special place to be, and it's right there." He said, pointing to a shop just a few doors from the coffee place. "This shouldn't take long, and then we can be on our way back home."

The shop's doors were encased in glass, and when I peered through the windows, I could see several shelves holding books of different sizes and colors. We were at a bookshop. Growing up, I was rarely allowed to consume books unless they related to my mom's teachings, which sometimes disappointed me. But then, I would get distracted by my daily lessons with Uncle Cass. Looking up at the sign, which read 'Bookings,' it was apparent what they sold.

Ding–The doorbell rang out as we entered the shop. An older gentleman was behind a counter toward the back, and before he looked up, he kindly greeted us. "Welcome to–" He stopped, eyes growing wide when he took in my father, who still held onto my arm with his. Then, the shopkeeper glanced my way briefly before my father's growl erupted, making me jump.

"Jull, have you been avoiding me? Whenever I show up, your store seems to be closed during regular business hours. And it seems that happens every time I mention I'm coming here. So, I have an informant of yours in the mix, and I want to know who it is." Father growled, tightening his hold on me.

Gritting my teeth, I waited patiently for the shopkeeper, Jull, to answer my father. I hoped the male's answer would appease him and he would let up on the bruising pressure.

"L-Lazarus, so good to see you. Unfortunately, I have no idea what you are talking about. If my shop has been closed during business hours, it is likely due to my daughter going out to lunch or running an errand and not having anyone here to keep it open." Jull stuttered, fidgeting with a pen he was holding while a fake smile crossed his face.

His gaze met mine, and something flashed through them like recognition. But that couldn't be right. I had never been any further than the mansion, which sat on the edge of Ozryn. Being here, in the city, was the first outing my father allowed since I had been brought back to my prison after the events that happened several weeks ago at my home.

"This must be your daughter I have heard rumors about. It is good of you to bring her into my shop. May I interest her in some light reading? Maybe a fictional story of her choosing? On the house, of course."

"No," Father seethed. "Cut the bullshit, Jull, and stop trying to distract us. You're an intelligent male, you must have some kind of knowledge as to what I am inquiring about. I am told that several Shadow Assassins had come through this shop a few weeks before my daughter had left AshFiera. And again, right before she came back home." Father paused, waiting for an answer, and when none was given, he continued, "A single name, that's all you need to give. It will help, and then I will leave you alone."

Father smiled at the shopkeeper, and we watched his mouth open and close several times. My father's grip on my arm loosened, and he stepped forward, leaving me to stand several feet from the counter.

"So, what will it be, Jull? Will you give up just one name and save yourself the trouble, or will we have to raise the stakes?"

"I'm sorry, Lazarus, I have no idea what you are talking about. I can't be of any help." Jull answered, still jittery as my father continued to approach the shopkeeper.

The moment he finished, I could swear my father had steam billowing out from his ears. Like lightening his hand wrapped around the male's throat, his choking was the only sound in the shop. No one dared move or breathe.

My hands instinctively gripped my own throat, watching the poor male struggle for air.

"I won't repeat myself. Give me a name or watch your precious books burn."

"No–" The male tried speaking, but that was all he could manage. His face began turning purple as he struggled to catch his breath.

Suddenly, the air in the shop changed from a cool, comfortable autumn to a stifling, searing magma, instantly making sweat bead on my forehead. I tensed, and then a swirling of sandalwood and leather was behind me as Zy approached to protect me. Someone else was here, and they were powerful.

A moment later, a woman who appeared to be close to my age revealed herself in the back doorway behind the counter. "STOP!" she screamed.

My father's head snapped up, and he loosened his grip on the male, letting him gather some air in his lungs. The color returned to his face, and he was no longer purple or on the verge of passing out.

"Jull, is this your daughter?" Father asked, finally letting the shopkeeper's neck go fully.

The female ran out of the doorway and up to her father, assessing the damage my own father had inflicted upon his neck. It was already beginning to bruise, and the female glared at the male who had just moments ago encased his grip around the other's throat.

"Yes, I am his daughter. What is it you want so badly you resort to nearly killing an innocent male?" She asked. Hatred filled her eyes as she took him in.

Coughing, the male, Jull, gripped his throat and spoke, "I already told you, Lazarus, I don't have any information on any of these males you wish to be named. The only Shadow Assassins that have come into my shop have been you all today."

Father tsked, "It's too bad you want to continue playing this game. So, if we are to play, we will simply take your *Seer* daughter. I'm sure there is some use for her. What is your name, dear?"

The female's eyes grew wide, and she shook her head.

"My name is Andromeda, but you should know I will not be coming with you this day or any other, " she said, glancing over her shoulder and looking directly at me. Her eyes bore into mine, and a sense of ease brushed my mind as if she were somehow looking into my thoughts and soothing my rushing heart.

Father saw where she was looking, and as if he was reminded that I was there, he reached over and gripped her arm. She cried out as his grip tightened, dragging her out from behind the counter and away from the male that was left behind on the floor.

I couldn't just stand by and watch him harm this female. She was innocent, and so was her father. I was sure of it. Zy's hand gripped the back of my dress, and I shot him a glare that I had hoped would tell him to let me go. When I felt his hand relax, I stepped out of his reach and toward the two.

When I reached my father, I lightly gripped the arm holding Andromeda's. I needed to speak softly to calm the tension in the room, it was nearly choking my emotions.

"Father, please. I believe they are telling the truth. I would feel their deception; all I can feel is their fear of you. The room is stifling with it. Please, let her go. We don't need a Seer." I pleaded.

He knew I spoke the truth, as my empathic abilities have skyrocketed in recent weeks. I began to feel others' emotions in the air, similar to how I could feel Beauty, but with her, it was different and more complex since we were bonded.

When we figured out my talents grew, my father was torturing a male in the foyer, not bothering to hide him. The fear, shame, and anger swirled around the open room, and I screamed for him to stop. I nearly tore apart the furniture when he wouldn't listen to my pleas, leaving Zynas to step in and take me away. When we were far from the mansion, I was able to breathe again, and the uncontrollable destruction of my insides dropped. Zy had figured out what happened, and of course, the jerk reported it to my father. But, I do have to say there were no other torturing incidents around the mansion. I had been at least thankful for that reprieve.

"My little Ashix, you are just as soft as your mother. Sometimes, I loathe that about you. But, if you feel they are not harboring any deception, I must listen. I know how right that intuition of yours can be." He said, letting the female's arm go.

She hesitantly backed away from us, keeping her gaze locked on my father. Waiting for him to change his mind, she grabbed the shopkeeper when she was far enough away.

"Is this interrogation over then? I need to get my father to a healer to make sure no permanent damage has been done." Andromeda sneered.

Father waved at them, "Yes, we are done here. We will leave. But, female, you should know that someone might just drop in and check on things for me at any time."

The smile he gave her made me want to punch him. So, he would just torture them differently. I would have to see that wouldn't happen, but it would have to wait until we left. There was no way I wanted to make anything worse than what it already was with my wild attitude toward the male I had to call my father.

"Let's go. I'm ready to spar with one of you males. Kojax, will you be the first to take me on?" He laughed, jovial and unfazed by what he just did to an innocent male.

"Yes, my lord. I would be honored to spar with you," Kojax responded as they walked out the door and stood on the cobbled pathway.

Zy had been quiet while we were here, especially when he snuck up on me again to place his warm hand on my back, gently pressing me to exit the shop. I glanced back over my shoulder and caught Andromeda's stare. Her furrowed brows relaxed, letting a smile grace her lips. She nodded and then turned her back on me to bring her focus where it mattered most to her.

Zynas and I exited the shop, and Father approached us with a wide grin.

"I'm very proud of you, my daughter. You showed restraint and used your gift to access the truth."

"Wait, is that why you asked me to come along so that you could use my abilities on these people?"

"Yes, of course, Raine. I had my doubts of this establishment being involved in the resistance, and I needed you to either confirm or squash those suspicions."

"What the f–," I started, but Zy's fingers dug themselves into my side, reminding me to watch my tongue.

"Now, I have some other matters that don't involve you. However, I would like you to join me for dinner tonight. I have someone I want you to meet." Father said and then turned toward the male who kept his tigh grip latched onto my side. "Zynas, take your betrothed and show her around Ozryn for a few hours. I'm sure she would love to return to that crystal shop we passed by earlier."

"Of course, Lazarus. Any opportunity to spend time with my betrothed is my pleasure."

"Excellent. As an added precaution, I will leave a few males with you." Father raised his hand to brush a stray hair away from my face as he spoke. "I will take you to the coffee shop in a few days, and we can try a few of their drinks. See what you prefer, and then have it shipped to the mansion to enjoy when you want."

The smile he gave me almost seemed genuine. Like he loved me as his daughter and not just a pawn in whatever game he thought he would win. Biting my tongue until pain radiated and I tasted the tangy copper of my blood, I smiled back at him. And then I watched him shadow-jump with several males while a few others stuck behind with Zynas and me.

Chapter Four

Raine

"Shall we head to the crystal shop, my little storm?" Zynas asked, a smile playing across his lips. His arm was held out as he waited for me to take it.

I turned toward him, crossing my arms, and glared. Was he just going to ignore everything that happened today? *What the actual hell!*

"We will in a minute, but I have a bone to pick with you. Why didn't you say anything in the foyer before we left?"

"About what, darling?"

"Don't darling me *Zy*, and you know what. You stuck up for me earlier in the stables against my father. So, what's the difference when it comes to my magic? Are you too afraid that if I have my powers back, I will use them against you?" I asked, quirking an eyebrow and tapping my foot impatiently, waiting for whatever excuse he would come up with.

Instead of answering, he sauntered up to my body, touching his hard abs to my chest. His finger crooked under my chin and lifted my face, making me stare directly into his beautiful honey-speckled eye. The remaining globe reminded me so much of Kal's I had to bite my tongue and cause pain to keep me from doing something stupid like kissing the idiot. There was only one male who held my heart. *Right?*

"I'm not afraid of you, little storm. You enrapture me. If I held any sway with your father regarding your powers, do you not think I would have already tried? He's a very untrusting male, and with good reason." His thumb touched my bottom lip lightly while staring into my soul. "Don't you know there isn't anything I wouldn't do for you, my tempest? If you told me to rip my heart out, I wouldn't hesitate, and I would serve it up to you on a golden platter."

"Don't tempt me, Zy."

He chuckled a low rumble that vibrated from my chest downward, swirling toward my center with a flicker of need. This male was dangerous on all levels. Especially when it came to my heart because it had already been claimed, hadn't it? My mind whirled with so much confusion and questions. Would it be wrong to love two males and be loved by them in return? Would either of them object to sharing a life with me? I shouldn't be thinking about these questions. They were wrong and made me despise myself for even considering it. The guilt and betrayal of Kal crept in slowly, squeezing my heart so painfully I had to swallow the lump forming in my throat.

"Enough talk of your powers and your father. Would you like to check out the crystal shop? Otherwise, I can jump us straight to the mansion so you can enjoy a few hours before meeting with your father and his *guest.*" He said, sneering at the word guest as if he already knew who would be joining us for dinner.

I was just about to ask him who it was when he slightly shook his head. It was almost nonexistent if I wasn't already staring at him. The other Shadow Assassins my father attached to our entourage shifted around, waiting for us to move. And I knew then that something else was going on, and I wasn't privy to what it was.

"No, I would like to browse the shop before dealing with whatever my father has in store for me later. It will help keep my mind off of the unfortunate hand I have been dealt with."

When Zy stepped away, the cold seeped into my body. I hadn't realized how warm I was with him so close. Shivering, I took hold of his arm, which he had held back out for me. Then, silently, we walked a few shops down to The Serenity Crystals.

When I entered the establishment, a wave of aromatic florals floated around the crystals, glinting with any touch of light that hit them. Taking a deep breath, I released it slowly, along with the tension that had wound tightly in my limbs.

Shortly after entering, a shopkeeper greeted us. While Zy chatted with them, I meandered through the neatly organized shelves, which held crystals of all shapes, sizes, and colors.

I stopped before a display of necklaces, fingering them and letting them tinkle against each other. One necklace captured my attention when the sunlight caught the beautiful orange flame-colored gem. Holding it while still hung up, I gazed at it harder. It was almost identical to the color of Beauty's burnt orange eyes.

The gem called to me, silent words whispered in the wind. *Yes, choose me. I will help harness the power in your soul. Choose me. Let me help free you from the shadows.*

"That's a fire opal," Zy said, startling me. I dropped the necklace, looking around for the unknown whisper that faded away. No one was near but Zy. That was odd. I could have sworn someone was in my ear, coaxing me to pick the necklace. Of course, I didn't have any funds, so it would have to wait another time before I could purchase it, if ever.

"Raine?"

"What Zy?"

"Did you not hear me? I said it's beautiful, isn't it? It matches perfectly to Beauty's eyes. Shall I get it for you, my little storm?" The tenderness with which he inquired about his purchase for me made my heart skip a beat while warmth wrapped itself tightly around my throat before I could speak.

"Uh, no, that's alright. I don't need it," I said, moving away from the display and walking over to the globes. When I reached them, I noticed their style looked familiar—like the Ashix globe my father had smashed and replaced.

Thinking about my father only led me down roads of boiling anger. I didn't want to go back to the mansion or have dinner with him that evening. He drew out the worst in me.

I wasn't paying attention when Zy snuck up behind me again. The heat of his body, along with his scent, was beginning to become increasingly familiar. I didn't turn around; instead, I touched one of the globes and spoke.

"You know, when I woke up in my bedroom at the mansion, the first thing that caught my eye was this beautiful globe of an Ashix. My Ashix, to be exact, was sitting on the same moss-covered boulder that sat outside my home. It made everything that happened feel so insignificant for a few moments. And then everything came crashing down when you came to retrieve me, and my father revealed he had Beauty." Letting out a sigh, I closed my eyes. "It was you, wasn't it? The globe, both of them. My father would have never smashed something he gave me. He would have taken it away as a punishment like he took Beauty from me."

"Yes, my storm. I acquired both globes because I know how much the beast means to you. I wanted you to have something to look at when you couldn't be with her in the stables."

Letting out a ragged breath, I said, "Zy, you make it extremely hard to continue to hate you. And I want to continue hating you. It would make everything easier." The growing confusion of my feelings split me apart. I needed a reprieve soon. If only Kal would hurry and find a way back to AshFiera and rescue me from my unending fate.

Zy grunted, "I don't want you to hate me, Raine. I have felt drawn to you since that first day we met, right before the hunting incident. Deep in my very soul, I knew we were destined for one another. Watching you grow up and never being able to come near was the hardest thing to endure. All I wanted to do was wrap you up in my arms and tell you everything would be okay on the bad days. But I didn't because I was terrified you would remember the pain and would associate me with it. I wouldn't have been able to live with myself if all you remembered of me was pain and not the young teenage male who desired to make his betrothed happy."

I studied the male before me. How he was just now reminded me so much of that teenage male I had been alright with being betrothed to. Even if I hadn't known a single thing about him, everything he pushed forth was warmth and kindness until my father got ahold of him as an adult.

"I do remember that day. And I can say that my memories of you were only of compassion and consideration." Looking down at the shelf in front of me, I leaned forward to avoid his presence. I wanted to lean back but willed myself away from those thoughts. "The Zy I knew back then wouldn't have helped my father and wouldn't have drugged me either. The male I was betrothed to would have stuck up for me, especially against my father, no matter the circumstances."

"Raine, you have no idea how much I want to tell you. How much you don't understand." Zy whispered in my ear, his breath hot against the shell.

"Then tell me, Zy, I want to know and understand. I can handle it." I said, breathlessly.

35

His whispers trailed down my neck as he said, "Not here, my beautiful mate. Maybe one day, but there are ears everywhere, and I'm afraid nothing is private now."

"Then take me somewhere private. Help me better understand why you did the things you did." I pleaded.

"So impatient, my little storm. In due time, but first, I have a gift for you." He said. I turned around, but he tsked, "Stay facing the other way. It will be easier for me to clasp this."

Tilting my head and looking over my shoulder slightly, I saw Zy's smirk grace his lips as he pulled a chain out from behind him. It was the fire opal necklace I had been drawn to. He lifted it and placed it around my neck, clasping it together, and before he let go of the chains he laid against my collarbones, he brushed his fingers against my skin, skimming them up and along my shoulders.

The contact was electric, and prickles ran up my spine. Goosebumps erupted along my arms, making my hair stand on end.

"Zy," I breathed out the singular word, his name. My tongue was tied for words that I couldn't produce. It seemed Zy was brilliant at eliciting this reaction out of me. Everything he had done the last few hours was not the same Zy that drugged me the day I saved my mother and Kal.

"It suits you, Raine. A beautiful piece of jewelry for an alluring tempest." He smiled.

"It is beautiful, but I can't take this. I don't have any money to pay for it."

"You don't need to worry about paying for it. I have already taken care of it with the shopkeeper. Are you ready to return home, or would you like to continue browsing?"

"Thank you for the gift. It's quite thoughtful of you," I said, smiling and finally turning toward Zy. Gasping, I took in how incredibly handsome he was, still smiling. I rarely, if ever, saw him smile, and it was so disarming that my jaw dropped slightly.

"What is it, little storm? Are you alright?"

"Um, y-yes. Yes, I'm okay. You know, you should smile more. It's a good look on you and makes you look less like an asshole and more approachable."

His booming laughter filled the shop before responding, "Well, being an asshole is the goal now, isn't it? If I walked around with a smile on my face, other males might think it's okay to make me a target. We wouldn't want that, especially when I must keep you safe."

"Ya, I suppose. Well, maybe you could smile more around me. Then, I wouldn't be so difficult to deal with, and it would be a nice change of scenery." What in the world was I saying? Had I lost my mind?

Before I could say or think anything further, Zy stepped closer to me. Wrapping his arms around my waist as he held me tightly. "We need to go out front and let the males waiting for us know we are heading back. I will bring you to your room to prepare for dinner."

"Ya, mhm, that works." I stammered out. This male made me lose all sense of control when he practically smothered his body into mine.

He guided me to the front, said goodbye to the owner, and turned to reach for the door. I also waved goodbye before we exited, facing several males who stood on guard, silently chasing away any patrons who wanted to enter the shop.

"Raine and I are headed back to the mansion. Once I jump, you males will be relieved of duty for the rest of the day, " he instructed. Several males nodded, and a few glowered at him. I couldn't tell what the dynamic of his leadership was with the males, but it would appear a few didn't care for him.

Zy held out his hand toward me to take before pulling me

into his body again. He was beginning to make a habit of this that I would have to squash if I wanted my sanity to remain intact. But he didn't give me much time to think as he shadow-jumped into my bedroom.

Blowing out a breath, I walked out of his embrace and over to the window near my bed, looking out. It was a habit I picked up since being here to gaze outside to see where everyone was and what they were doing.

After a short while, I turned back around and saw Zy still in the room, staring at me intently.

"Raine, I need you to listen to me and wait until I'm finished. We are safe to speak freely in this room only. Nothing is kept secret when we go outside of here, especially from your father." He paused, running his hands through his neatly kept hair, messing it up. "There is going to be a powerful male who joins you and your father for dinner tonight. Heed my warning when I tell you to tread carefully. Your snark and attitude might get you into trouble as your father believes this male to be incredibly important to his plans."

He closed the distance between us, one hand gripping my waist while the other dove into my hair at the back of my head. "Promise me you will be on your best behavior. I won't be able to interfere, which will only further anger you. But please, my little storm, bite your tongue if you have to."

Silently nodding my head, I just stared at him. *Who is this male, and what happened to the asshole Zynas I knew who was willing to help my father?*

Before I knew it, Zy closed the distance, and our lips collided. A moan escaped my throat, and his echoed in response. The feel of his soft lips against mine was so wrong but so right. And as I gasped, it allowed his tongue to invade my mouth, finding mine and entangling together.

Our bodies moved, and my back gently hit the wall behind

me. Zy took the opportunity to grip onto one leg, hitching it to the side of his waist while his body wedged further between my thighs. Giving me the perfect pressure of his erection against my clit. His moan deepened, and he started to grind himself into me slowly.

It was heaven and hell as I lost myself in the sensations he pulled forth. He continued to move his body against mine while our tongues danced erotically. And then his lips left mine and began exploring my neck with nibbling and soothing kisses.

"I want to strip you bare and fuck you until you can't walk and can't think about anything but my cock filling your cunt and stretching you like the good girl you are. Fuck, you're all I think about every day, my little tempest." He breathed heavily against my throat.

I knew what we were doing was wrong, but I wanted him to continue. That little voice in the back of my mind was blaring her siren, waking me up from the lust-driven ecstasy.

Kal. I'm with Kal. I had to stop this before we went any further and did something I would genuinely regret. I wouldn't forgive myself if I betrayed Kal further, even though my body still screamed to give in to Zy. Why was this so complex, and when was it going to stop?

"Zy, we can't. We need to stop." I shook my head and pushed lightly on his chest. "I'm sorry, I can't do this. Even if I'm trapped here, I'm with Kal. I love him."

Zy glared at me with his eye and growled, "Gods, Raine. Don't you think I know you are with Kal and that you love him? But would it be so wrong for you also to love another?"

"Why are you okay with sharing me? I don't understand why you are pushing this."

"Because deep down you know that I am yours and you are mine, regardless if you share those sentiments with another. All those years I spent away from you tore me apart like my soul was ripped in half. I refuse to allow myself to continue to be ripped apart. You are the air I breathe. My heart beats only for you. Please, don't shut me out, little storm."

Our heavy breathing mingled together, and Zy lowered his face to mine. His lips touched lightly when a knock on my bedroom door roused us from our little bubble.

Pulling away from his hold, I called out quickly, "Come in." It was Astora, and she had another female with her. She stopped inside the bedroom and glanced back and forth between Zy and me. I'm sure she saw our ruffled clothing and how close our bodies were to each other.

"I apologize. Am I interrupting?" She asked.

"No, Astora, you are fine. Zy was just leaving, weren't you?" I asked, glancing up at him. He looked back down and frowned.

"Yes, I have somewhere I need to be. I will see you at dinner, Raine." He stepped back and shadow-jumped, leaving me with the females who were now giggling after Zy had left.

"Don't even think about saying a word Astora." I glared at her.

"Don't worry, princess, I won't," She teased. Causing me to frown even more at her. It was the title my father requested all the staff and his Shadow Assassins call me. He considered himself the new lord or king or whatever the hell he declared.

Turning toward the new female, I tried to smile and greet her, "You're new. What's your name?"

"My name's Iriel. I am shadowing Astora, learning the ropes to take over for her when she leaves."

Glancing at Astora, my eyes widened, "Astora, is everything okay?" My heart thumped wildly, thinking my father had something to do with her departure.

"Yes, yes. Everything is fine, Raine. Your father instructed me to train Iriel here since my father's debt is almost paid. I have another few days before I have completed his obligations."

"Tell me you are running away from your father as far as possible. Oh, I know! You met a rugged Shadow Assassin, and he's going to sweep you off your feet and take you to the countryside where you pop out little Astora's and live happily ever after?" I asked, ecstatic to have some girl time with her and this new female Iriel after such a long, eventful day that wasn't over yet.

"Well, I guess you could say a certain Shadow Assassin has asked me to come with him on his next assignment so I wouldn't have to go home to my father." Astora gushed, her cheeks turning a rosy pink hue.

"STOP! Oh my goddess, do I know him? Please tell me who it is!"

"I can't. My male made me promise not to tell a soul. He doesn't want your father to know he is leaving with a female."

"Okay, *fine*, don't tell me. It's not very fun, but I get it. I don't want whoever the male is to get into trouble. So, tell me one thing, then. What are you two females doing in my room?"

Iriel clapped her hands loudly and excitedly said, "We are here to help you prepare for the dinner with your father and his very important guest."

Looking at the new attendant, I frowned. "I don't need help getting ready; I can do it myself. You two are welcome to stay and hang out, though."

"I'm sorry, Raine. Unfortunately, we do have to help you with this. Your father instructed us on what dress he wanted you to wear and how he envisioned styling your hair." Astora winced, waiting for my tantrum to flare up.

Instead, I groaned and sat at my vanity, placing my face into my hands and breathing in and out deeply.

"I'm in deep shit, aren't I? This 'guest' my father has joining us is bad, isn't he?"

Both women nodded and looked at each other solemnly. "It

will be okay. Just let us work our magic. I promise we won't do anything overly dramatic; it will all be subtle."

I just nodded and let them get to work. While my friend Astora took over my makeup, my newly acquired friend Iriel handled my hair. We giggled, and the two females told stories of some Shadow Assassin males who had made fools of themselves to garner their attention.

They took my mind off the dinner looming over my head and what had transpired between Zynas and me just a short time ago. He was determined to change my mind and be with him, but I needed to know how Kal felt before that could happen. His feelings were my priority. I just needed to figure out how to get out of here with Beauty and avoid my father's wrath once I did escape.

Chapter Five

Raine

Zynas wasn't outside my bedroom door like I hoped he would have been. Weirdly enough, I needed his presence before joining my father and the guest he wanted me to meet.

Something shifted between Zy and me earlier today. I didn't know if it was the calmness Beauty held around him this morning in the stables. The tender way he draped the beautiful fire opal around my neck in the shop. Or the brief make-out session in my bedroom before Astora and Iriel knocked on the door interrupting us.

Biting my bottom lip as I walked toward the dining room. All I could think about was that kiss and the way his body moved against mine, as if we were made to be molded around one another. It had been easy getting into that position with Zy and so incredibly hard to pull away when I knew it was wrong to want him.

When I entered the room, my father was already sitting at

the table with another male who looked to be around his age. Their attention was drawn to me as I entered through the doorway loudly. The clacking of my low-heeled shoes echoed, and I had to be careful not to step on the bottom of my floral evening dress as I reached the table.

My gaze darted around for the most suitable seat, as far away from both males as possible. But Father stopped me when I walked further down the large table.

"Raine, my beautiful little Ashix. Why don't you have a seat across from our guest this evening? No need for you to sit down there when you will be involved in our discussions tonight." His threat was subtle but very much there. He wanted me to sit near them so this male could get a good look at me. I just hoped whatever role my father required of me was small and quick.

Walking back to the other end of the table with the mystery male sitting to my father's right, I sat to the left while my father led the table at the head.

Smoothing my dress down, I folded my hands into my lap and waited for the food to be served. Wanting to avoid eye contact with the male, I started to fidget with my fingers until my father spoke again.

"Raine, this is Darrem. He is the wealthiest male in all of AshFiera. He controls most food growth and distribution, owning most of the land scattered worldwide."

I looked up at the male, giving him a small smile, "Interesting. I wasn't sure who my father wanted me to meet, and your profession was certainly not what I had imagined." I said, looking over the handsome male. His hair was light brown with streaks of gray along his temples, allowing me to guess he was an older male. His bright hazel eyes bore into mine, and he smirked, opening his mouth to begin speaking, but I interrupted him, "And although I'm sure looks can be deceiving, I am not sure I am the female or person who can help you with whatever it is you require of me. I'm unsure what my father told you, but I don't play nice."

My father's hand slammed down on the table causing me to jump in my seat while he stood staring at me, burning anger lighting his eyes. His nostrils flared out, and speaking to me took him a moment. He likely tried to reign in his temper in front of our current guest.

"Raine Samara Celestine, you will mind yourself before our guest. You will sit there and listen to what Darrem requires, and then you will agree whether you like it or not." He sneered. His fury was getting the best of him, and his control was almost at its wits' end. I really should be careful, but I just couldn't find myself to care.

"Now," my father began again, displeasure still laced in his voice but much more controlled. "From my understanding and what has been presented, Darrem will require your magic and strength against someone threatening his operations. We need to ensure that whatever resistance has begun is squashed and that our continued control over the food distribution is regulated so no one thinks they are above what we are trying to achieve."

Glaring at my father, I said, "What are you trying to achieve, father? Don't you think the people of AshFiera have suffered enough, especially in the bigger villages and cities where you seem to leave them hungry?"

"My little Ashix, we are trying to achieve compliance. When someone tries to undermine what we have started to build, it needs to be righted. It is for the people's good. This world has gone on long enough without the proper leadership, not just little segments here and there. That is what I am doing and what Darrem is helping me achieve."

My mouth dropped open as my gaze refused to leave my father's. He was earnest about turning this into his kingdom, not a free world like it had been before I was born. Dread formed in the pit of my stomach as I thought about all the people who had been suffering over the last several years. Had he already been working on diminishing the people's food source before he came to retrieve me?

Anyone who couldn't grow their crops had always relied on this person, Darrem, who I thought was a generous male who had the means to help those less fortunate. Was that all a lie growing up? Was this male in front of me deliberately responsible for the males who became thieves and beggars?

My indignation began its slow boil in my veins and only intensified when Darrem spoke for the first time.

"If I may, Lazarus, I would like to discuss the situation further with your lovely daughter myself," Darrem said, folding his hands and smiling widely at me.

I shifted slightly in my seat and was saved momentarily by our food arriving before the male could continue.

The meal we were served was lavish beyond anything I had consumed while growing up in AshFiera. Even with my mother's gift of growth and my father's hunting skills, we usually only ate the vegetables harvested from her gardens and the meat from the deer or boar my father or Uncle Cassius had slain.

Steam curled up from my plate as I was presented with the most extravagant, juiciest steak I had ever seen. It was adorned with seasoned vegetables, and a brownish sauce drizzled over everything on my plate. Raising an eyebrow, I hesitated to grab my fork even though my mouth watered from the delicious aroma drifting into my face.

"Go on, Raine. Eat up while I explain my situation," Darrem said, his broad grin watching my face closely.

I picked up my fork and hesitated again, clearing my throat, "I need a knife to cut this."

One of the 'servants' my father employed hurried up to my side and, with precision, cut my steak into perfect bite-size pieces. I snorted at the absurd circumstances. I was being treated like a child. Either that or my father decided he couldn't trust me with a knife around our guest which he was right to do as I didn't know if my actions or my tongue for that matter could be held.

"What is so funny, my darling daughter?"

Swiping my hand toward the servant, scurrying away, I replied, "Don't you think that's a little ridiculous, Father? I'm old enough to cut my steak without the need for help. I am, after all, an adult and no longer a child."

"Ah, yes, about that. I am afraid that while I am certain Darrem can handle himself against your muted strength, I didn't wish to risk you with a weapon quite yet." Father said smugly, answering exactly what I had predicted.

I wanted to punch the smile off his face. Gripping the fork so forcefully that it bent, I began digging into my food. While I stuffed my face irritably with a small slice of meat, Darrem cleared his throat to bring my attention back to him.

"As you know, I own most of the land in AshFiera for farming and provide for most of the AshFierans worldwide." He paused, taking a bite of his food. "I would like to think I can ensure no citizen goes hungry. But, as it would seem, there are males out there who are trying to overthrow your father's efforts to make AshFiera a better, more complacent place. And those males have disrupted my deliveries to those who need that food desperately."

The disruption to deliveries certainly had my attention. But I couldn't understand where I came in, seeing as my father couldn't even trust me with a knife. He wouldn't trust I wouldn't run or shadow-jump and use my powers against anyone who got in my way.

"I propose you help me obtain information from a few individuals we have apprehended. Your lightning powers could prove useful when wielded properly. I have someone who could help you train to ensure we don't make unnecessary messes," Darrem said. Did he know about the incident I had as a child with my training dummies? I had recollections of blowing one up before my father disappeared the day I met Zy.

Thinking about Zy, I glanced around the room and noticed he wasn't present. His absence was odd. He was always existing in the span of my space, so if there was any sort of interaction that involved venturing outside of my bedroom, I could count on him to be there.

"So, Raine, what do you say about helping?" Darrem leaned back in his chair, wiping his face with the cloth napkin, waiting for my reply.

Quickly, I shoved a few more bites into my mouth before answering because I knew my father would be furious as soon as the words left my mouth. And I didn't know when I would be brought food the next time. Typically, Astora brought the nourishing meals to my room, so I wasn't around other males eating in the main dining area apart from this formal one.

Gulping the food down, I swallowed some water and replied with slow, vicious rage burning deep inside, "I'm going to have to decline your proposal. I don't use my magic on others unless it is to defend myself or those more vulnerable to males such as you."

"Raine, darling." My father's warning told me to stop where I was, but I had already had enough of this conversation and dinner.

"What, *father?*" I seethed at him.

"Don't you get an attitude with me, young lady. You will help Darrem with what he is asking. Or did you forget who has graciously allowed that beast of yours to stay on the mansion grounds alive?" Father threatened.

His threats enraged me even further, spilling out words I

hadn't meant to speak, "You honestly think I'm going to play the good daughter and do as I am told? No, I don't think so. The moment you take these shackles off of me," I paused, thrusting my hands toward my father to show the beautiful bangles still adorned on my wrists. "The moment you take these off, I won't hesitate to use my powers against you or any male who dares to keep me from my Ashix. Do not threaten me again or that of Beauty's life."

Quickly turning my attention back to the male who sat across from me, his smile was more expansive now, and it just pissed me off further.

"And you," pointing my finger at Darrem, my voice dripping with menace, "I am not helping you cause harm to another AshFieran. Over my dead body. I would rather use my lightning to light a fire under your ass to get you the hell out of my sight."

"ENOUGH!" My father stood abruptly from his chair, glaring red fire dancing in his eyes. His booming voice echoed in the dining room, making me jump from my chair. I started backing away from him to escape the room and his reach.

He began to advance toward me, fists clenched. My heart pounded viciously in my chest. I thought it was going to jump out and onto the floor. Suddenly, Zy shadow-jumped in front of my body. *Where the hell did he come from?*

I took a deep breath, tried to steady myself, and slow my heartbeat. Zy's presence was like a soothing balm on a sunburn.

"Lazarus! Don't you dare touch my mate!" He warned, pushing my body further behind his.

"She isn't your mate, yet Zynas! Move so I might teach this disobedient female a lesson on how to talk and act around males properly."

"Raine has been considered my mate since the day you and my father decided to betroth us to one another." Zy stood taller as Father continued to get into his face. "Let me deal with my female and punish her my way. I will straighten her up and get her to comply. Give me a few days, and she will come willingly to Darrem's request."

Father glanced back and forth between Zy and me. What felt like forever was only mere moments when he nodded his head. His face was, at first, a mask of pure rage, but it smoothed out, and he smiled. Clapping Zy on the shoulder.

"Very well, do what you must, but do not draw blood. I would hate for you to ruin my daughter's beautiful face before your expected wedding in a few weeks."

My eyes widened, "What the hell? What wedding, and what do you mean in a few weeks?"

Father's stare snapped back to my face, "That mouth of yours will get you further into trouble, my darling Ashix. I suggest you hold off on your questions until your soon-to-be husband has finished dealing with you."

I couldn't help myself. I went to open my mouth again when Zy's hand clamped down hard on mine. That was my cue to shut up, so I did. It was probably for the best since my father was being subdued in front of our guest.

The male, Darrem, quietly watched the whole exchange with a beaming smile. That amusement was disturbing, considering my father almost just beat me in front of him.

He clapped his hands, emitting a sharp echo, "Raine, it was a pleasure to meet you. I hope our next meeting will make you more agreeable to my proposal."

Zy glanced over to the male and, through clenched teeth, spoke to him, "I will see to it, Darrem. Now, if you two males don't mind, I will take my mate back to her room to deal with her little outburst."

Father waved his hands and ushered us out of the dining room, saying, "See to it, Zynas."

Zynas wrapped his arms around my waist, and without

saying another word or even looking at me, he clenched his jaw together, shadow-jumping us out of the dining room. Surprisingly, he took us outside of the stables where Beauty was held. A question was on the tip of my tongue, but before I could ask, he ushered me inside, where Beauty perked up at our presence.

Chapter Six

Zy

Whisking Raine to the stables instead of directly to her room, I already knew I would defy 'Lord Lazarus' desires to see her punished. He would never know if I did indeed punish my beautifully spirited mate.

She was fearless in facing her father and the male who held the world's food supply in his hands. When I found out who would attend the dinner with Raine and her father, I shadow-jumped around frantically, setting things into a faster motion than I had planned.

Tomorrow. Tomorrow would be the day I created chaos, and everything would change. I wasn't sure if the change would be for the better initially, but I knew that with time, if we were allowed that time, it would work out, and AshFiera and Raine would be free.

Beauty became alert as soon as she saw Raine and me enter the stables, and her excitement was palpable in the atmosphere. It was infectious, but it was slightly clouded with the looming anxiety I was trying to hide from the two females.

Raine practically slammed her body into Beauty's, and I silently watched as her body relaxed while she pressed her nose into the beast's scales, inhaling her scent.

"I'm so glad to see you before bed, Beauty. You wouldn't believe the crazy day I've had since I left you this morning." She whispered. Nuzzling further into Beauty's body. The beast's claw came around and encircled Raine's body protectively and lovingly.

Beauty's love for Raine was vibrant, like neon lights that shone through the darkness in the human's incredibly crowded cities on Earth.

I had only been there a handful of times for various jobs my father sent me on before he was brutally murdered. I didn't enjoy all the technology they had, it was too noisy, and the smell was horrendous, like shit and a suffocating smog. Preferring our limited technology world to the humans, I had tended to slough off my jobs onto other males more willing and excited to see Earth themselves.

Raine had been whispering more to Beauty, but I tuned them out as I gazed around the stables, ensuring the females had a sense of privacy.

Speaking of privacy, I really should get Raine back to her room so I can finish everything I need to accomplish before the morning hours hit. I was usually left alone at night, no one followed me, especially after Raine went to bed when she no longer needed to be guarded.

I don't think I will be getting any rest tonight because of how much I have left to do, but the results would be worth it. I couldn't wait to see the look on 'Lord Lazarus' face when he discovered what I had done.

It would take hours before he discovered what I enacted, and hopefully, two females would be gone long enough that their scents would be masked by a few of the males I trusted to help me.

"Zy," Raine roused me from my deep thoughts, "Where are Beauty's chains? There seems to be a significant amount missing." She inquired, her voice slightly higher, giving away some semblance of excitement.

I knew damn well what happened to Beauty's chains, but I wasn't about to disclose anything to her while we were still being closely monitored.

Lazarus had stopped me a few days ago to express his growing concern with how Raine continued to defy me. Someone disclosed that my fiery female wasn't acting like someone who was about to be mated to a male, this made the assassins uneasy. Lazarus indicated he would see to her being more welcoming, but I brushed it off, telling him that her fire was an entertaining challenge and that I was up to taming her. The disgust I felt afterward left me to harbor my anger on the males who were training in the designated area that day. Several of them had to be brought to a healer along with myself.

I tilted my head slightly, answering, "I'm not sure what you are talking about, little storm. All of her chains are as they should be. No male would dare take any off, let alone come into the stables."

"It's odd, though, Zy. I could have sworn there were more chains on her earlier this morning. She also looks more calm and relaxed. Usually, she's somewhat tense since some males like to come in and get a look at her, which agitates her, by the way." Her eyebrow raised, peering over her shoulder at me. It was adorable how her body seemed to angle itself slightly with attitude whenever she did this.

Goddess above her fire lit my body up, and I couldn't help but let loose a low growl, which she remarkably heard from across the stables.

"Did you just growl at me, Zynas?"

"You heard that?" I asked, stunned it was audible.

"Ya, of course, I heard it."

Interesting, "How long have you been able to hear like that? All of your powers should be muted with those bangles still attached." I pointed to her wrist as a reminder they remained. Could she overcome the magic that bound hers? She shouldn't be able to hear like a Shadow Assassin. I wonder if the witch that cast the spell on the bangles was careless or if she is more powerful than her father understood.

"Huh, I guess it just started today. Weird. Anyway, don't change the subject. What makes you so moody that you need to growl at me like an animal?" Raine asked, now fully turned around and leaning her back against Beauty's front.

"I'm not moody, my little storm. I couldn't help the noise coming out when I get the pleasure to sit here and stare at your beautiful body."

She rolled her eyes at me, "Oh please, save the dirty talk for someone else."

"Never."

"Well, we certainly are not having a repeat of earlier. So keep your words and your hands, for that matter, to yourself." Raine sneered. Her anger was beginning to show, and I knew if I continued pushing, I would see that inferno explode. Did I like provoking my female to see her eyes flash with fire? *Absolutely.* I couldn't help it. It gave me a thrill to push her.

Before I could press her any further, I knew our time was coming to an end in the stables before her father decided to see why I hadn't punished her yet.

"Are you finished with your visit this evening? I know your father is expecting me to punish you. He will wonder why I rewarded you with a night visit instead of taking you straight to your room."

She huffed, "I suppose we should get back there. I'm guessing we have to shadow-jump in, and I don't get to enjoy the evening walk through the gardens?"

"No, I'm sorry, my tempest. It would be unwise to take longer getting back."

"Alright, give me a few more moments."

While she was busy hugging and soothingly speaking to Beauty, I peeked out of the doors just to make sure no other males were beginning to make their rounds to the stables for the last time this evening.

I didn't see anyone or feel any presence, so I let her have a few moments longer before I strode up to her back. "Come, the last check will be happening soon."

Raine stepped back into my body, kissed her hand, and laid it against Beauty's chest. "Good night, girl. I will see you tomorrow. Sleep tight, and don't let the hay bugs bite." Beauty tilted down, pressing her forehead to Raine's. As Raine giggled in contentment Beauty began to back off, the beast directed her focus on me.

"What are you so amused about?" I asked. Raine could feel Beauty's emotions, but I wasn't sure if they could speak to each other in their minds. I would only understand their bond if Raine opened up to me about it. But I still had yet to question her on the kinship she shared.

"Beauty is smitten with you. I have no idea how you managed it, but it made me laugh because I'm sure if you were a male Ashix, she would claim you as her mate." She said this, giggling once again.

Wincing, I wrapped my arms around Raine tighter. "Sorry, Beauty, but there is only one mate for me, and it is your lovely bondmaster." Footsteps sounded outside, and our time ran out. So I quickly jumped without further warning.

In most cases if you weren't experienced in jumping, especially leaving so abruptly, it left you dizzy and nauseous, but since she had jumped dozens of times with me already, those lingering effects should no longer bother her.

And I was correct as she stepped away immediately and spun around, glaring at me. "You could have at least let me say 'goodbye'."

"I did let you say goodbye. We couldn't linger around much longer. A male was approaching the stables, and if he saw I took you there instead of straight to your room to discipline you, the news would have reached your father. I'm sure you wouldn't want him to punish you instead of me just leaving you to your evening now, would you?" Crossing my arms, I waited for her reply. Her face expressed different emotions that rolled over her quickly before she let a smile slip on her lips, which only left me confused.

Raine sighed and slowly approached me. "You're right, Zy. I did say goodbye. I was just hoping to linger a little more with Beauty. I feel like lately, I haven't been able to spend as much time with her as I would have liked." She shifted on her feet and placed her hand on my still-crossed forearm.

"Thank you for today. Not only for helping me keep my cool but for the necklace," Raine's other hand came up to her chest, rubbing the fire opal between her fingers. "Something called me to it, and I wasn't sure if I would have been able to leave there without it, so I am grateful you bought it for me. I also want to say thank you for coming to my rescue at dinner this evening. I was losing it, and I didn't know how much longer it would have been before my father struck me. The dinner could have turned disastrous, especially with Darrem in our presence."

Her eyes grew distant as she stared into my chest, lost in her thoughts about gods only knew what. I wanted to know what was going on in her head, but I knew I had to leave it alone for now.

Uncrossing my arms, I gripped Raine's wrist before she could pull away from me. I needed her close, in my space. I desired her like I needed air to breathe, food to sustain my strength, and blood pumping throughout my body to keep me alive. She was everything to me and more.

I ensured she looked directly into my uncovered eye, "There is no need to thank me, little storm. I only wish to see you happy, and if those small things are the only way I can do them for now, I will do it willingly and without thought."

"Zy, I do have to thank you, though. You have been different today." Tilting my head, I must have given away that I wanted to question her as she continued, "Not in a bad way. It's like when we were younger and that first day we met. You make me feel safe and cared for. I didn't think you had it in you, considering how our reunion and the following weeks have been."

That gave me pause. Of course, my brilliant mate didn't understand why I had helped her father in the first place. I didn't think this moment was the appropriate time to tell her what he blackmailed me with. She needed to be away from the mansion, and my plans were enacted before I could tell her why I had helped him. I needed to change the subject quickly; it would be a long night, and she needed her sleep for tomorrow. If I told her everything now, I knew she wouldn't leave willingly and she would want to stick around to help make sure I also left. But, I knew once everything fell into place my departure would be swift.

"Well, if you need to thank me, then so be it. But I should get going. It will be a long day for you tomorrow, Raine, and I think you should get as much rest as possible."

"Wait, Zy, we need to talk more about what you said earlier before you know." Her cheeks heated, and she looked away from me. I knew what she was talking about, but I loved watching her squirm. She was about to say before I kissed her and made her feel things she didn't think she could feel with me while also in love with another male. But I wouldn't push her to admit she felt something for me, not yet.

"I'm not sure I know what you are talking about, Raine," I smirked, watching as her eyes narrowed.

"You know what I'm talking about. But, anyway, are you sure we can speak freely here?"

I nodded. I wasn't sure what she was thinking but it must have been something she knew not to ask me outside of here. Because anything she said or did was reported directly to me and her father.

"I need you to help Beauty and me escape. And soon."

Did she already know what I had planned? No, there was no way she could have any idea what would happen.

"I'm working on it, little storm. Have patience." It was all I would give away, but I knew her persistence would soon melt my resolve and the barriers of my secrets would crack away.

"Wait, what? It's that easy?"

Staring at her longer than I intended, my body started buzzing, and I looked down to see her hands, which had the lightest purple glow to them. They were resting on my chest. *When did they get there?* Was she trying to shock me? But it didn't hurt, and she wasn't paying any attention to where she was touching me as she kept her beautiful eyes on mine.

I leaned down and captured her lips in a slow, tantalizing kiss. Her eyes closed as if to take in the sensations that she would pull away from soon. I just needed to be the one to do it first so that it would leave her wanting more.

A moan escaped her throat, and I deepened the kiss, pushing my needy tongue into her mouth to taste her and consume those moans and lovely whimpers she let loose.

Growling, I lifted my lips from hers, and surprisingly, she tried following my movements as if to prevent it from ending so soon this time.

So, I whispered against her lips, "My little storm. Be ready at a moment's notice."

Stepping away from Raine, she faltered and then narrowed her eyes angrily as if to say something, but I was too quick and shadow-jumped from her room.

I ended up at the stables again, I needed to get away. I couldn't linger much longer around Raine without losing control over my instincts. I was so close to stripping her naked and making her see stars using my body against her. But I knew she wasn't ready for that yet. First, I needed to get Kal back here somehow.

Did I know how to do that? Absolutely not. I wasn't a witch or a warlock. And they were few and far between in AshFiera, more prominent in the human world, and some more powerful and feared than Shadow Assassins were.

The stables were slightly darker, which benefitted me tremendously as I approached Beauty, who was sleeping.

She stirred and saw that I approached, which caused her excitement to flare, "Shh, Beauty, we have to be silent. I know you understand me. Be patient, my mate's little beast, and prepare for tomorrow. I am getting you and your bondmaster, my beautiful little hurricane, out of here."

Chapter Seven

Kal

It had been several weeks, and I wasn't sure if we were any closer to opening up a portal that would lead us back to AshFiera to save Raine and end her father's existence.

My heart ached thinking about my beautiful Enayah and how much I craved being beside her. My soul was restless and empty without being near what I had deemed its other half. The only solace I could find was that the bond we formed was still there—although barely.

Every witch or warlock I encountered told me the same thing: there was very little information on bonds. Some of the magic wielders looked at me like I was crazy and that such a thing had never been heard of. But there had to be something out there. The need for more information and understanding drove me mad.

Pandora thought her friend Maggie would have the answers, but she did not. The female said she would dig and ask other people in her community. That was several weeks ago, and nothing had dredged up from that either.

The hunger pangs reared up, and my stomach growled, leaving me to groan. I could barely eat, barely think, and barely sleep. *What the hell was that anyway?* I had to force myself to leave my room and head for the kitchen to get food down my throat, even when I didn't want to.

Gigi and Samara graciously let me stay with them in Raine's bedroom. I tried staying in my own home, which wasn't far from here, but I couldn't bring myself to be alone.

Walking through the living room, I turned the corner and entered the kitchen, but then I stopped dead. Pandora and Cassius were just separating from a kiss that I likely wasn't supposed to walk in on. Seeing as Pandora's cheeks were bright red and Cassius was glaring daggers. If looks could kill, I knew I would be one dead male.

Clearing my throat, I cautiously approached the cabinet, "Whatever is going on between the two of you is none of my business. But I suggest you stop sneaking around and acting like you got caught doing something you weren't supposed to do."

I waved my hand between the two and continued, "I'm sincerely happy for you both. Pandora, I know you didn't have it easy, and Raine would also want you to be happy. Please don't feel you need to hide your relationship any longer."

Did I have an inkling they had been having a fling for a while? Of course, but I wasn't going to be the one to spill it to Raine if she didn't already know herself. I'm sure she wouldn't care that her mother has no love left for her father. After all, the bastard is why I am here and not with my mate.

My lovely new mother, Pandora, stared blankly at me while Cassius said, "Thanks, Kal. We weren't sure how to approach or if we should broach the subject of our relationship."

"I suggest you not hide it from Raine once we ensure her safety," I warned. I didn't think Raine would care to have further information hidden from her. She was likely still pissed off about her mother hiding her father's disappearance.

"We won't Kal. She deserves all the honesty I can give her now. I know that I haven't been truthful about her father, but I did what I thought was right by keeping it from her to keep her safe. And he still ended up with her." Pandora said, unshed tears forming in the corners of her eyes. Cassius, sensing her distress, took her into his arms, shielding her from the pain of the past. He glanced back up at me again and scowled.

Shrugging my shoulders, I resumed searching for food when my stomach gurgled its displeasure again at being so empty. Pandora pushed away from Cassius' hold and peered over at me. The sadness in her face dropped, and her smile shone brightly. Glimpsing at the older female before me made my heart ache again. Raine and her were so identical that I missed my mate even more.

"Are you hungry, Kal?" Pandora asked.

"Of course. I'm after something to quiet down my loud ass stomach. It will grow louder if I don't put something in it. Just like Raine's stomach usually does." The ache in my heart increased more. *Gods above strike me where I am. This longing will kill me one day before I have my female back in my arms if it isn't soon.*

I was a lovesick fool, and anything I did or said reminded me of my beautiful Enayah. I needed to see Theo soon. I could shadow-jump over there today and see if he has made any progress. Waiting around for him was getting on my nerves, and there were only so many males at Gage's boxing club that I could pummel into the mat before they all stopped letting me fight them.

Just then, Gigi and Samara walked into the house, and the aroma they carried with them made my mouth water.

Samara held up several bags and shook them with a

delightful expression. "Kal! Perfect, just the man I was hoping would be home."

"Hello, Samara. You were hoping I was here?"

"Yes! I have some news from Theo. Well, actually, from Maggie. While grabbing lunch, she called Gigi and me and said that Theo might have something put together, but you guys need to be there in case something goes wrong. You know, like if he accidentally summons a bunch of Shadow Assassins." She said, laughing nervously.

Theo had been working on part of the spell that would open another portal to AshFiera. He was trying to figure out if it could be contained better than when Pandora opened it all those years ago. He wanted to control the radius of where a portal could be used to prevent any unwanted assassins from coming to Earth and retaking Pandora.

This was perfect timing because I had grown impatient for the male to contact us.

"Perfect, I will head over there as soon as I have had something to eat." I eyed the bags Samara was holding. She noticed where they were glued and shook them again.

"Gigi figured everyone would be hungry, so we picked up some burgers from Burgers N' More. Here," she thrust a bag into my arms. "We asked for separate bags, as yours and Cassius's have more food. No idea where you men put all that, but we got extras for you both."

Her grin was infectious. All the females of this family had the most contagious emotions, and I felt my body lighten after the dreary thoughts that clouded most of the morning and early afternoon.

I had taken my time eating, enjoying the tastes of the diner's burgers and fries. It would likely be the last time I enjoyed the food Raine had loved to devour during her time here. When I was finished eating, I decided that a shower was in order. I wanted to ensure I smelt as good as possible for my mate when I saw her again.

She would likely tell me to bathe if she knew how bad I had smelt earlier. Surprisingly, none of the females ever commented on it, but I occasionally got a whiff of myself, and it would get out of hand. I hadn't been very good at caring for basic needs the past week. It felt like a chore to eat, bathe, socialize, and all I wanted to do was curl up in Raine's bed and wrap my arms around the pillows that still had her lingering aroma. It was the only thing that seemed to keep my sanity.

The news that Theo might have a working solution brightened my mood, as well as whatever those females did. Gigi had explained what she and Samara could do with emotions. Those two meddled in my mental state often because, at any opportunity, when my thoughts turned dark or melancholy, they were there to ease them. I was grateful, though, and for everything they had done for me, but sometimes, I just needed to feel the grief I had attempted to hide beneath the surface for my Enayah.

Wiping the steam from the mirror, I stared at myself. I had let my beard grow out, and it was beginning to look wild and out of control, like how I felt every day I was separated from Raine. Would my little star be opposed to seeing my face clean shaved, or would she prefer my neatly trimmed beard?

She had never seen me without facial hair; it had been years since I had been clean shaven. *Now was a good time for a fresh start, it would grow back eventually if she didn't like it.*

Gripping the razor, I slowly shaved the hair, starting at my cheeks and finishing along my collar. A few times, I nicked myself, and small trickles of blood rolled down the side of my neck. I knew it wouldn't take long, and the wound would be closed, so I left it until my entire face was complete.

I made sure to clean up after myself in the bathroom. There were females in the house that would ring my neck if I left all that hair along the sink and floor. One morning, Samara had been scolding Gage after he had shaved at the sink. He left the hair and, unfortunately, received the wrath of his female. I knew I didn't want anything to do with being punished like an adolescent, so I learned from the male's mistakes.

Entering Raine's bedroom, I found my leathers on a chair in the corner, the same place they had been in for weeks, just waiting for me to put them on. Most of the time I wore comfortable clothes, shorts and plain T-shirts but today I wouldn't wear anything leisurely. Today, I would wear my Shadow Assassin leathers and gear up with all my weaponry, preparing for anything that would unexpectedly come our way.

I was ready to see my pretty little mate and prepared to bring her home.

"Kal," Samara's soft voice called from the other side of the door before she knocked lightly. "Can I come in?"

"Of course, Samara." I was just finishing attaching the last blade to my many straps when she hesitantly opened the door, peeking around the corner.

"Oh, you're ready to go, huh?"

"Yes, I'm ready to see Raine."

She walked further into the room, and when she reached where I was standing, she wrapped her arms around my torso. "Bring her home to us, Kalpheus. And if you have to kill that bastard so he can't ever touch Raine or my sister again, do it, don't hesitate."

Returning the hug, I breathed deeply, grounding myself

before chaos broke the calm. "I will not fail to bring my mate home. It won't be quick, but I will succeed."

"I know you will. Pandora is beside herself since Cassius is going with you."

"Cassius can certainly handle himself." Ending the hug, I grabbed the tiny box I purchased shortly after being forcibly returned to Earth. Access to my human funds was beneficial, especially when the item currently occupying the small box caught my attention one day.

I had been traveling with Samara in her truck into Lunaris Falls. She wanted to check out this new shop that opened up. It held crystals and smelt strongly of herbs. I didn't want to enter the shop, but Samara dragged me along the pavement.

She was fierce and stubborn, just like her niece. So I appeased her and joined. It wasn't long, and I stood staring into a glass case at what I knew would be the perfect gift for my stunning mate, I didn't know how but deep down I felt she would love it.

"Hello? Earth to Kal." Samara's voice floated around a memory's swirling fog, and I shook my head to clear it.

"Sorry, Samara. Just thinking about–" I didn't finish my sentence when Cassius and Pandora appeared in the doorway.

Pandora's eyes were bloodshot, and her cheeks still held dampness that I knew were tears. She sniffled and embraced Cassius tightly. "Pandi, my darling. Everything will be okay. Kal and I will get Raine back home, and you can rest easy when I take care of that piece of shit."

"I know." She whispered into his chest. I watched Cassius draw Pandora in further and kiss her openly, no longer hiding their relationship. My heart further ached, not only for my own longing but also because he had to leave her behind.

She wasn't safe anywhere near AshFiera. If she came along and Lazarus found out she returned, he would find a way to get to Pandora and use her against Raine. My little spitfire was likely giving them all hell. She wouldn't surrender the kindness that encased her heart for anything and would fight for what was right.

"We have to go now. I will be back as soon as possible. Stay here where it is safe. Maggie will come to stay with you while we are gone, " he said, holding her face in his hands and staring intensely into her soul.

I cleared my throat. "We should go now to Maggie's home. Theo will be impatiently waiting for us."

Cassius nodded and pulled away from Pandora. Then, we both shadow-jumped to the outside of Maggie, Theo, and the asshole Marcus' home.

Marcus still didn't care for my presence, so whenever I came to the home, he would quickly disappear—leaving me to deal with business peacefully without his hindering existence.

"There you two are. What took so long?" Theo appeared in the entry to the mansion, arms folded and leaning against the doorway.

I grunted in annoyance. Didn't he understand I needed to look and smell my best for my Enayah? Those things did take up my precious time, but I needed to do right by her, my little star.

"Relax, Theo. We are here now, are we not?" Cassius said, clearly just as annoyed with the male as I was.

"Yes, yes. I just figured the lover boy over here would have been clawing at the chance to reach the beautiful, luscious, totally delectable Raine."

This time I growled and Theo's cocky smile was wiped from his punchable face. He liked to tiptoe along a thin line whenever he spoke about her in interest. He knew I didn't care for his lusting over my mate, and I had made it clear he would never get the chance to woo her.

Cassius grunted and walked to Theo. I stayed rooted for a

few moments but then followed, knowing this male would help me return to my mate.

We followed Theo through the mansion and into the back gardens. He led us to an enormous waterfall, almost identical to the one Raine had fallen into.

Clapping his hands together, Theo looked at Cassius and me, asking his question, for he only wanted my answer. "Are you ready to get back to AshFiera, Kal?"

"Yes."

The echo of my answer ricocheted across the open petals of the flowers that surrounded us and amplified further down into the cave below the flowing falls. It held the anticipation of being reunited with my Enayah and the chance at revenge against the males who dared to keep her from me.

I was ready. The wait was over, and soon, I would feel the warmth of my mate seep into my body again.

Chapter Eight

Raine

The lingering anger followed me out of my dreams. Zy was a sneaky bastard. Not once but twice did he lay those inviting lips onto mine, which caused me to feel things I should only be feeling for Kal. *Ugh! Why couldn't I get Zy out of my head and heart?* He wiggled his way in, and it was tough not to fall for him.

It was forbidden, *right?* I had heard of females and males falling for multiple partners, and no one batted an eye at those who chose to love more than one person. But could I not allow myself to hope and dream that I would be allowed to do the same?

No. Focus, Raine. We need to be ready at a moment's notice. That is what Zy said last night before he up and shadow-jumped out of my room after that last kiss. *Jackass.*

I would have to yell at him for being so incredibly irresistible yet again. Of course, he couldn't honestly know he was working his way in.

Once I saw Kal again, I needed to let him know what

happened. That would be something that would eat at my heart and soul if I kept it from him. I just hoped that he would be able to forgive me on my part. Zy taking the lead wasn't my fault. But you know what it was? Enjoying and continuing the kiss not once but twice! *I should have slapped his rugged, gorgeous, one-eyed face instead.*

Suddenly, there was a knock on the door. It was odd. Usually, Zy shadow-jumped into my room without caring about my privacy. The sun was just peaking past the horizon, giving off yellowish-pink hues, indicating the start of the day.

Astora wasn't due to come with breakfast since it was still so early. Since arriving in Ozryn, I had told her a while ago not to come in until the sun was fully up, choosing to sleep in most days. There wasn't much to do during the long boring waking hours, besides sleep late and visit Beauty. If I was lucky and Zy was in a good mood, he would take me on a tour of the mansion or the surrounding grounds.

"Just a moment!" I hollered. Wiping the sleep from my eyes, I was still in the early stages of waking up and needed to get ready for the day. Quickly, I put on my signature black leggings and a plain white T-shirt. They were comfortable and practical, and after protesting about all the pretty dresses I chose not to wear, I had a whole wardrobe filled with them.

Once finished, I decided I was decent enough to check on whoever still lingered outside of my bedroom. "Come in," I yelled and waited for the door to open while I pulled my hair into a loose bun on top of my head.

Whoever was in the hall decided to stay out there and didn't enter, so I was left with no choice but to open my door. When I peered into the hallway, I was surprised to see that it was Kojax, another one of my father's best and closest males.

"Oh, I wasn't expecting you, Kojax," I said, staring at the male who stood with his arms crossed over one another. His long blonde hair was pulled up into a man bun, and I laughed thinking about the time when Zy had long hair the first time I met him. I had snickered at Zy as well. It was always odd seeing males around AshFiera wear their hair long, but it seemed to be a style they were starting to like and take part in. Kojax wasn't the only male around the property who grew his hair long.

I looked out and down the hallway, noticing there was no one else around; in fact, it was empty. Looking back at the male, I met his bright blue eyes and waited for him to speak. When he didn't, I filled the silence by asking, "Can I help you with something? If you are looking for Zynas, he isn't here yet."

Kojax grunted, "I'm not looking for Zynas, Princess."

My eyes narrowed, "Don't call me princess, you know I hate that shit." The venom dripped from my voice. I had yelled at any males who decided to use the title my 'self-appointed ruler' of a father demanded they all call me. It pissed me off, we weren't royalty. Never have been and never will be. That's not how AshFiera worked.

Our world was meant to be a free one, where the people chose who was in control. My father murdered the person they had chosen so he could change it.

Kojax stood still, staring at me silently. *What the fuck?* "Well? What do you want?"

"I'm here to take you to the stables today. Let's go." He said, abruptly turning around and walking away.

"Hey, wait! Kojax!" I said, running after the male who it would seem is my escort for today instead of Zy.

What was going on, and where was he? Zy told me long ago that he would be the only male to escort me anywhere. That none of the males were allowed to be alone with me. What changed?

The questions swirled around in my head as Kojax walked alongside me through the gardens to the stables. It was a slight reprieve that he didn't insist we shadow-jump, allowing me to enjoy the gardens like I usually did. However, something felt off with the male in my presence. He seemed almost nervous and was extremely alert to our surroundings. His gaze kept straying in every direction, and wherever he looked, I followed with my own eyes but never observed anything out of the ordinary.

I couldn't stand the silence any longer, and I needed answers about Zy's whereabouts. I had things to discuss with him, and I needed to put my foot down on his wandering hands and lips.

So I broke the silence in hopes Kojax would divulge what was going on. "Kojax." I called out.

"Yes, Princess." His use of the label again was like nails to a chalkboard and fired up my irritation. So he wanted to continue to call me princess? Well, then, I guess I need to act like one now, don't I?

"I demand you tell me where Zynas is," I said, stopping in the middle of the walkway and stomping my foot like a spoiled child. Internally, I giggled at the absurd and over-the-top performance I was presenting. But on the outside, I kept my face a mask of annoyance.

When Kojax turned to stare at me with an eyebrow raised, I had to control my face from smiling. Obviously, my little outburst surprised him, and I'm sure he was trying to figure out my game. But I wouldn't relent, so I frowned and crossed my arms, stomping my foot again.

"Zynas said I was never allowed to be alone with other males, and I see he hasn't kept his promises. So I'm demanding to know where my bastard betrothed is to give him a piece of my mind."

He shook his head and chuckled, "Seems I have underestimated your persistence to know where your male is."

I rolled my eyes. I couldn't very well deny that Zynas was

my male since I did just call him my betrothed. "Well?" I asked again.

"He had some things to take care of that needed to be addressed this morning. I don't know when he will be back, but I don't think you need to worry about that right now." Kojax still didn't answer my question, instead skirting around the subject and completely ignoring it.

Whatever. I will likely have to sulk in my anger for however long it takes for Zy to come back to the property.

"Fine, don't answer me then," I said and began to walk to the stables. I paused briefly with a smile on my face, turning back to Kojax, "Just so you know, your stupid man bun looks ridiculous on you, you know, with having blonde hair and all. You could maybe pull it off if you had darker hair like Zy, but I doubt it. I would cut it if I were you, especially if you have a lady friend you're interested in."

Why in the world did I mention Zy at all? He was consuming my mind, and I needed to pluck him out like an irritating ingrown hair. *Ugh, irritating was an understatement. He was a real pain in my ass.*

It wasn't much further to the building that held my companion prisoner. We were just at the edge of the garden. The walk had remained silent after my snarky comment. I had a feeling that Kojax wasn't too happy with my attitude, but I didn't care. Since no one would heed to my questions and let me know where the hell Zy was, I wasn't going to play nice.

I was just about to go inside when I noticed Kojax leaning up against the side of the stable's wall, peering out into the open again with an unreadable expression that briefly crossed his face. Looking over my shoulder to where his eyes were glued proved nothing was amiss. I wasn't sure why he was standing guard outside when someone had to always be inside with me.

"Aren't you coming in?" I asked.

"No, the beast doesn't particularly like me. And I would rather be out here anyway while you visit your pet." He said, not looking in my direction.

"So, are you one of the males who likes to antagonize her when I'm not here then?"

I needed to know if this male had any good in him. Deep down in the pit of my stomach, my emotions turned and rolled. Something was going on, and I needed to be on my guard. The air was electrified, and it made my pulse pound in tune with its own set of beating drums.

"Of course not," He said, finally looking away from whatever had his attention. "I admire the Ashix and all their deadly beauty. When I was younger, I had a good relationship with them, but your female doesn't seem to like me. So, I stay out of her way as not to upset her."

It was actually kind of him to do that. However, he was still a male who was here under my father's orders—following him mindlessly.

"It's probably because you're helping my father, and she can tell what sort of male you are. You are no longer a mere child nor innocent by any means."

His eyes flashed with outrage and hurt all at once before he turned his back to me to watch the side woods. Shaking my head, I couldn't help that my heart squeezed with guilt after the things I just said to him.

Did I feel remorse for someone who decided to follow the devil himself? My father was a lousy male, and all the males that followed him had to be deplorable to some degree, right?

As more questions remained unanswered, my hands landed on the stable doors, yanking them open. It was dark inside, and my alarm bells went off until I felt Beauty's excitement ripple through the bond. Letting out the breath I had been holding, I walked in and closed the doors behind me. *Clink.*

The doors had never latched before, and if Beauty's excitement and energy weren't distracting me, I think I would have felt more frightened that this was a trap.

My eyes had begun to adjust to the darkness when I noticed a sliver of light coming from the back of the room. There was another door leading to the back woods. They had always remained closed and locked tight. Today, that wasn't the case, and it was startling to see them cracked open. When a gust of wind blew them ajar even further, I noticed Beauty wasn't in her usual spot.

Not only that, but she was completely free of her chains.

Was this what Zy had meant when he said to be ready at a moment's notice? Did he somehow set all of this up? I still wasn't sure where that male's head was, but I wasn't going to kick a gift to the curb. Not if it meant Beauty and I could be free from this place. I would have to find someone to help me get these bangles off, though, so I could jump with Beauty in an emergency.

For now, we would have to do this the old-fashioned way, and I hoped that she would let me ride her. It would be a first for both of us. But I knew one thing for sure: She trusted me, and I trusted her. I had to believe that this would work out.

Beauty's small leaps shook the floor, and I had to hush her excitement. "Shh, Beauty. Easy girl, let's get out of here, shall we?" Her huff was loud enough that it had me looking back toward the front of the stables. The doors remained shut, and the male, Kojax, who was on guard, didn't come barging in to see what all the commotion was.

Silently, I let my fear show through my bond with Beauty. She needed to understand the dread because, in the very next moments, we would be free from this place, but we would be on the run.

She placed her head to mine and dimmed her excitement,

only leaving a calming happiness in the echo of her soul connecting to mine.

Now we were ready. I spoke softly to her in case Kojax was listening: "When we get outside, you need to fly as low as you comfortably can. Once we get far enough away, we can go higher to find a place to stay. We need to stay as silent as possible, okay, Beauty?"

She huffed a trundle of smoke and then tilted her head toward a table next to the cracked door. I hadn't noticed it before, but on top was a dagger in a sheath. I picked it up, and my body began shaking as I realized what I held in my hand. It was Zy's dagger. The one I tried taking from his strap before we left for Ozryn. *Goddess above, this male made it so difficult to distance myself.* Would he find me once I left?

If it were meant to be, then he would find me. But now I can get away and try to find some semblance of escape towards Kal. First, it was time to fly from this prison and get the hell out of here.

After strapping the dagger to my leg, I slowly opened the unlocked doors just enough to get Beauty's body through. And before she could walk out, I hopped onto her back, sending a silent prayer to the goddess that I wouldn't fall off to my death while she carried me high above the ground.

"Spread those wings, Beauty, and let us soar the skies free females." I urged her. It didn't take much to convince her to go, and when she leapt into the air, I let out an involuntary squeak.

Nobody could prepare me for the exhilarating feeling of being in the air with the wind blowing around my body. Or the rush of blood that went to my head, causing tingles to tickle the back of my skull down to the base of my spine.

It was freeing and absolutely terrifying being so far off the ground while Beauty flew through the tree line.

We spent the next hour in the air, getting as far away as we could. We were in the clear and would be able to see where we should land.

"Go higher, Beauty. I want to see if we can find a safe enough spot to stay for a while."

She obeyed my request and flew high above the trees. It was a good thing I wasn't afraid of heights. Otherwise, I would have ended up getting sick or passing out. Flying with Beauty was freeing, and I imagined I was an Ashix flying along with her.

The wind whipped around my body in a caress, pushing and pulling. Some threads of hair escaped my bun and floated around without a care that they weren't tucked neatly together with the rest. I wanted to pull it free, but I didn't want to hinder my view of the land in front of us.

Looking around, I knew we were far enough away from Ozryn and even further from my home outside of Martslocke. The mountains rose so high in the sky that they still blocked some of the morning sun, which had only just begun to touch the darkest parts of the forest below.

Ahead, I spotted a glittering glare, and soon, the sounds of rushing water filled my ears. *A waterfall!* There may have been a cave hidden around or behind the falls that would shelter us.

Yes, go there. There, we will find salvation and replenish our strength, begin to create our balance, and open our minds to possibilities.

The strange voice called out to me again from the necklace, which was still wrapped around my neck from the day before. I had usually taken jewelry off before bed, but I had forgotten last night and didn't even think about it this morning.

My instincts told me to trust the strange voice that was rattling around in my head. I had a good feeling about the falls in general. They were beckoning me to come closer, drawing me in the same way the falls outside my home had.

So, I pointed in the direction I saw the glittering sparkles from the sunlight, "Over there, Beauty, there's a waterfall."

Through the bond, her excitement increased, and when we were in sight of the falls, she dived. My throat burned from screaming as I latched on tighter to her neck. Her unexpected dive sent a thrill down my spine. After the initial rush was over, laughter bubbled up, and I couldn't contain the smile that spread across my face.

Beauty's happiness radiated brightly, like a star shining in the black abyss of the skies above. It only intensified my joy, and the fear of being found dissipated slowly.

As we got closer, there was a small grass clearing that I could see she was headed for, and I braced myself for her landing. When she arrived, I was jarred slightly, but Beauty settled onto the grass with an effortless grace.

Several male Ashix that had been near the falls growled at us, and when they saw there was a female among them, they immediately took off. None of them stuck around, and if one did, it would be because they were ready to find a mate with my female companion. But it seemed these males weren't interested in that.

Climbing off my Ashix's back was easy enough. But when I landed on the ground, my legs gave out, and my ass landed on the hard terrain with a thump. "Haha, oops. Guess I should have realized my legs would go numb." I said while Beauty's head tilted down to nuzzle me, checking to make sure I was okay.

It was nothing I couldn't handle. I just needed to stretch my legs out before me.

"I'm fine. Go on, check out the area. I'm going to sit here for a bit before I get up again." She hesitated, watching me closely, and decided that whatever I had been emitting over our bond indicated I was indeed okay. She sniffed the air before trotting off to forage for food or whatever she had a desire to do now.

Taking a deep breath in, I held it and then let it all out slowly. We were free, but for how long? There wasn't an answer to this question because, at any moment, someone could come along and find us. But, the blessing for the time being was that I didn't see any signs of a village or city nearby.

And while Beauty was gone, all was silent around me except for the rush of the falls, which gave me time to think about what was going to happen next.

I knew what needed to happen. It was critical Beauty get as far away from me as possible. We gained our freedom for now, and it would devastate me if she were captured again. I had no idea if I would be able to control myself or my emotions if that did happen.

Luckily, or maybe unlucky, my powers were muted, and I couldn't hurt anyone accidentally. With the faint buzz of electricity slithering beneath the surface of my skin, I had slowly been feeling them come back. There was an inkling in the back of my mind that the fire opal was part of the reason, if not the whole reason, that the bangles were failing. I just wished it would hurry up and render them utterly useless if that was the case, but I would take any little scrap I could get. It could come in handy in a pinch.

The sun was shining down in the small clearing, allowing me to tilt my head back to soak up the warmth as it caressed my face. When Beauty came back, I decided she needed to leave to find safety away from me, for I would only cause pain and imprisonment until my father was stopped.

Now, I wait. Wait for her, my first friend. I want to say goodbye and then find my way back to Kal.

Chapter Nine

Raine

Several hours later, Beauty was returning, her calmness and drowsiness flooding down the bond toward me. I still had yet to see her, but she must have had a good meal if she was already sleepy. Of course, after weeks of not flying or getting any kind of exercise, suddenly having to fly for over an hour would tire anyone out as well.

She was close, and I anticipated convincing her to leave me behind and flee for her safety. While I waited to spot her in the sky, my right leg bounced. The urge to move and expel the anxious energy was almost involuntary, making sitting still, tricky.

Finally, Beauty came into view, and I stood. She landed next to me, and the ground shook. Her sudden weight collided with the earth.

I smiled and reached my hand to pat the side of her neck, "Did you have a good meal, my beautiful girl?"

Her chuff followed, and my stomach felt full, but I knew it was from our bond, and I smiled.

"Good, I'm glad you were able to fill your belly."

I dropped my smile and hugged her around the neck, squeezing, "Beauty," a sob choked out, and I had to breathe deeply before continuing, swallowing the lump forming in my throat. "You need to leave me. If you stick around, I'm afraid I could get you hurt, or worse, you could die because of me."

Her sadness filled the bond, and an ache in my heart pounded, "I need you to go. Before Father finds us both, I can handle myself, but soon, I will have to find a way back to Earth. You can't come with me to that world. And It's no longer safe here for me. If you are with me, it will no longer be safe for you either, but if you go far, far from here, Father will never be able to find you."

Still holding on tight to her neck, Beauty nuzzled my body, and a claw came around my waist like she was hugging me back. I sobbed harder into her, letting all the hurt escape. We sat like that for moments and then down the bond; instead of her sadness clouding us, a determination shone through the thick fog that was building.

"No, Beauty, I have a feeling I know what you are thinking, and you can't stick with me. You need to go, get out of here, and find a mate to keep you company. Have lots of Ashix babies and be free."

I was smacked with more determination, and then a sassy, giddy, no-nonsense tingling circled us, and I had to step back. My hands fell to my hips.

"Beauty–"

Snap.

The sound of a branch brought both of our gazes toward dense woods. A male stood staring at Beauty and me, his jaw slack open and his eyes wide. He looked familiar, but I had never seen him before. His short blonde hair was mismatched to his darker beard, but those eyes were the brightest blue and shone brightly with brief relief.

That was until Beauty growled low and deep, smoke billowing out of her nostrils, and she stalked slowly forward to get in between me and this unknown male.

Suddenly, her body lurched forward, tackling him to the ground. Her claws caged him beneath her, and when her mouth opened and descended to the male's head, he let out panicked words, "Wait! I know Cassius!"

Gasping, I willed Beauty to stop with my panic radiating down the bond. Finally, I found my voice, "Beauty, don't bite his head off yet. Let me speak with him."

The male squeaked, "Yet?"

"I have to determine what kind of threat you are before I decide," I said as I walked toward them. "If you promise to behave, I can make sure she lets you up so we can speak properly. Do you agree with this?"

"Y-yes." The male answered. His jittery response told me he was scared shitless, and that's how I wanted him to remain.

"Let him up, Beauty."

At my command, she stepped backward toward me, keeping her eyes trained on the male. When she reached my side, she lay her body down and hooked her claw once again around my waist, repositioning where I stood.

She had me directly between her claws, and I laughed, "It's alright, girl, with you by my side, this male wouldn't think of doing anything nefarious. Would you?" I asked, gazing back to the male who surprisingly stood in the same spot he had been tackled, silently watching Beauty and me.

"So, are you going to give me your name, or should I keep calling you male?"

"Ahem, yes, sorry. My name is Gezr. I know I have said this already, but I know Cassius and your mom, Pandora."

I froze. The male's mention of my mother shook me. Was he helping my father? I had assumed that by now, my father knew I was gone. But if he was a part of my father's group of Shadow Assassins, how did he find me so quickly?

He must have known what I was thinking as he stared at me, explaining himself.

"Apologies, I only know your mother because of Cassius. They both tasked me with finding a suitable male to guard you months ago."

Looking at him, it clicked who that male was, "Wait, are you the one who asked Kal to watch over me?"

His eyes lit up, "Kal? Yes, he is a friend of mine and fellow Shadow Assassin. So he did find you in the human realm, then? I mean, I suspected he did since Cassius had come back to AshFiera to rally our comrades."

"Find? Yes, I suppose you could call the stalking he did for weeks before he had to intervene when my father's assassins found me at my grandmother's home as 'finding' me." I blurted out fast, laughing and forgetting about the most important thing I needed to know.

"So, you're not helping my father currently look for me, then?"

He shook his head, "Definitely not. I was actually just coming here to meet with my brother and, coincidentally, get an update on your situation. But, surprise, surprise, I found you instead of my brother."

His brother? I wonder who that could be, especially if he was one of the males at the mansion keeping watch over me. Did I know who it was? Did I have any interactions with his brother? Too many questions, as usual, rolled around in my head, leaving the beginnings of a slight headache to form.

But first, I would ask this male to bring me to my uncle. He would know who could get these bangles off and how to find one of the few witches that resided in AshFiera. "Do you know where I can find my Uncle Cassius?"

He looked at me strangely and then with pity. "I'm sorry, Raine. Cassius hasn't been back here since he left for Earth to warn you that something was amiss. We have no idea where he is now."

My eyes widened. *Oh no.* Uncle Cass must have been stuck in the human realm after I closed the portals. *Shit.* This wasn't good. He was the one male I trusted and knew would keep me safe. I didn't doubt that Gezr would do the same as well, but I wasn't familiar with the male, and the unspoken and unanswered question that kept popping up remained. Who was his brother, and did I know him from my time spent at the mansion?

"I think Uncle Cass is still stuck on Earth. I didn't know he came to warn Kal and me. He told me not to go to come here, and I wasn't going to just sit idly by while my father held my mother captive. So I didn't listen."

I started picking at my fingernails, a nervous habit I had picked up while on Earth, during all the uncertainty about who had been after me. Even now, knowing it was my father and having spent several weeks here, the habit never left me.

"I didn't know. After I shoved Kal and my mother through the portal and back to the human realm, I closed it. Closed the ability for anyone to come or go to that world. I had to ensure my mom and Kal were kept safe from my father. He would have gone after both of them. He would have killed Kal and then made my mother a pawn to control me. Just like he made Beauty that pawn for all the weeks he kept me at his mansion."

A silent tear rolled down my cheek. I brushed it away quickly and recentered myself. I had to be strong. If Uncle Cass weren't able to help, maybe the male Gezr would. He had helped Uncle Cassius and my mom before. He would help me too, wouldn't he?

"Well, that explains where he has been, then. We were worried Lazarus had gotten to him and speculated the worst." Gezr shrugged his shoulders and visibly relaxed, seemingly forgetting that he was almost eaten by my Ashix only moments ago.

Beauty, not wanting to be left out, nudged my arm slightly to get my attention. Her eyes sparkled, and warmth surrounded my heart. Her ease seeped into my body. I had to take that as a good sign that she trusted this male had only good intentions. So, I would ask for the help that I knew both Beauty and I would need.

"Gezr?"

"Hm?"

"With Uncle Cass on Earth, I don't have anyone I know here that can help me." Holding my hands out in front of my body, I showed him the bangles that my father had placed on me. "Do you know any witches that can help get these off? And, do you maybe have a place we could stay?"

He crossed his arms and brought one hand up to his face, petting his beard in contemplation.

"I do have a place we could go that would be safe for both you and your beast. As for a witch, I'm afraid that is an area of expertise through Cassius."

My disappointment must have shown on my face. "But, I can ask around to see if anyone knows who Cassius used to speak with, and that would help." He smiled, easing the sting of how important Cassius must have been in their group to be the only one who knew a witch who would help.

Before I could open my mouth and ask more questions, like who his brother was, Beauty's head perked up, and moments later, the distant echoes of deep male voices were heard through the trees. Beauty started to growl but was quickly silenced when I hushed her, both through the bond and out loud.

Gezr looked over his shoulder and then turned back to me. "Those are not any male voices I recognize. We should get out of here quickly."

Nodding my head, I stepped out of Beauty's embrace. "You're right. We need to get out of here, but I think if Beauty flies, it will draw attention to us. You said you're a Shadow Assassin as well, correct?"

"Yes, of course I am."

"Perfect, can you shadow-jump both me and Beauty out of here?" I asked, hoping it wouldn't be too straining to haul not only me but an Ashix as well.

He hesitated, drawing up the courage to step closer to us. When Beauty didn't growl or blow smoke at him, he relaxed slightly. "I have never shadow-jumped with an Ashix before, but I don't see why it would be hard to do. Can you make sure the female won't bite my head off mid-jump?"

"She won't; don't worry," I assured him as the voices grew louder in the distance. They were closing in on us fast. "Please, we need to hurry."

Gezr nodded, walking hesitantly up to us, placing one hand flat on Beauty's side and with his other gently gripping onto my upper arm. Then, we shadow-jumped before the males reached our location and discovered where we were going.

Chapter Ten

Zy

After leaving Raine to fume about yet another kiss, I went to find one of my most trusted males. Kojax.

Tomorrow had to be the day that I helped free Raine and her beast, Beauty.

Luckily, I arrived at dinner on time to placate her father's anger. He had been about to strike her, and I wouldn't allow such an act of violence toward a female, especially against my mate. The male was spinning out of control and needed to be stopped. It was becoming dangerous and worrisome.

Then, when I saw the male who had been seated at the table with them, I had to stop myself from reacting.

Even without being a Shadow Assassin, Darrem was a dangerous and powerful male. He was known for being ruthless against those who opposed the control he had over most of the world's food supply. This male was vying for control over Raine's powers to use against whatever unfortunate soul was in his path. I knew it was time to get her out of there. Consequences be damned at the rushed approach.

So, instead of going to sleep, I enacted the plans I had been making for the last several weeks since Raine joined us at the mansion.

Firstly, I was to meet with Kojax. He was one of the males I trusted to be alone with my mate. He would protect her at all costs.

It didn't take long to locate him outside of the stables, sitting in the grass with his legs crossed over one another and his eyes closed.

Meditating is what the male called it, to ground himself further with nature and things no male could see with the naked eye. A slight twitch of his lips gave away that he knew I was present, and it wasn't a hardship to interrupt my closest ally.

"Good evening, Kojax. What a surprise that you should be sitting outside of the place where my female's beast slumbers. What brings you to meditate near such an uncontrollable animal?"

"I am at peace being near her, even if she doesn't trust me. But I have been waiting for you to arrive so we can discuss Lazarus' actions earlier. I knew you would come here."

Nodding my head, I walked toward the stable doors and began opening them. Inside, Beauty had been sleeping, her dazed blink taking in who would disturb her. Once she saw it was me, she instantly perked up and was no longer in her bouts of sleep.

Her liveliness was short-lived when she spotted the male entering behind me. Growling tumbled out of her snout, and Kojax stiffened, sticking near the wall opposite her.

"Oh hush, Beauty. Kojax is a good male. He wouldn't harm you like the others." I placated her. And the low rumbles of growls followed until she calmed when Kojax remained where he stood.

Turning toward the male, I smiled and clapped my hands

together, "We need to move fast to get Raine and Beauty out of here." At the sound of her name, Beauty huffed but remained lying on the hay beneath her. "Lazarus had Darrem here at the mansion for dinner tonight."

Kojax visibly stiffened, and a sneer crossed his face, "That good-for-nothing male was here?"

"He was, and he is here to request the use of Raine's magic. Although, I'm not sure he understands how much my feisty female will rebel at any chance and won't be a willing participant in whatever he needs."

Kojax's gaze bore into mine, and his lingering anger flared even more within his blue orbs, "I take it you have no idea what he wants with your female's powers?"

Shaking my head, I huffed out a breath, "Unfortunately, I wasn't privy to that information or if they even disclosed that with Raine herself. I would assume that Lazarus would keep that a surprise until the very last minute, the sadistic male that he is."

As far as anyone knew, Darrem was not a male you wanted to cross, and I was afraid that Raine's attitude and rebellious streak against her father would get her hurt. I wasn't about to sit around and watch that happen to the female that had so enraptured my heart. So it would seem a few things needed to be laid out, and her escape was number one.

"Kojax, you know that we need to get the females out of here. And it has to be tomorrow. I don't want to risk her safety for another day. I need to know that you will help me get them out." My voice shook. I was terrified for my mate, and the carefully laid out plan could go to shit if things were accelerated, but we didn't have a choice. Not when Raine's safety was in dire peril.

He must have seen the panic shooting through my body

when he nodded his head, "Alright, Zynas. Tell me what I need to do, and it will be done."

"Your job will be to escort Raine to the stables. It has to be early in the morning before the sun has risen above the horizon. I will take care of the rest. Just leave her to go inside alone, and she will figure out the remainder."

"Will you leave her with something to protect herself out there?" He asked, making a good point that I almost looked over. I was getting sloppy about the accelerated timeline, and I was glad to have a male who could look at things without the haze of a mate.

"I will leave her with the dagger she attempted to swipe off of my body. That should be a clear enough message for her to grab it and go."

Kojax leaned away from the wall and headed for the doors. It was getting late, and if he were to escort Raine to the stables early and watch the chaos unfold himself, he would need to get to sleep soon.

"Once she is gone, I will ensure that my brother protects her with his life until I can leave here with my female, " he said, giving me pause. I stared at him, and a smile spread across my face.

"So, you have also found your mate?"

The shuffle of his shifting feet was all that I needed, but he still answered nonetheless.

"Yes, she was brought here against her will as well. Her bastard father owed Lazarus a favor and used her to squash his debt. But, I am taking her far from this place and further from her father."

"I only hope the best for you and your female, my friend. I will see you soon, and we will reconvene with your brother in a few days."

With that, Kojax left without another word. I turned toward the beast, who only just a few short weeks ago, wanted to snap a hand off and swallow it whole. Today, though, that was much different as I approached her.

Beauty's body vibrated, and a cooing trill escaped her throat. It would seem she was happy to see me this evening.

Did she have some premonition that tomorrow would be the start of freedom? It was at the back of my mind, their release from Lazarus' hold. I would ensure that both of them remained that way if it cost me everything, even my own life.

"Alright, Beauty. I'm going to take these chains off. You need to remain in the stables until Raine comes in the morning. She will help get you out, but you need to wait for her. Can you do that?" I asked. It was silly to talk with an animal like she could understand me, but I knew better. She was clever. I had watched the way she reacted to Raine when my mate whispered to her.

Her breath huffed out in reply, and I smiled, knowing full well that, yes, she did indeed understand.

The chains clinked on the ground of the stables, and I ensured that no others were

attached to her hind legs. Walking to the back door, I unlocked and unlatched it as well. Then, I left my dagger on a nearby table just for Raine to find. Everything in here was ready.

My strides were slow as I walked back up to Beauty. I reached out my hand and patted her neck, "Take care of my female tomorrow, beast. Both of your freedoms depend on how far you can get her away from here. When you can't fly anymore, find the nearest waterfall. She will be safe there."

Before I could walk away, Beauty's claw wrapped around my body, and she hugged me back. This beast was too bright, but it would aid them both well in the next few days.

This would work, it had to, and before long, I would be the ruin of Lazarus' short reign. Beauty and my female would be safe and free from the rising mad-male.

The following day, I woke early and decided that I would rather spend my time sparring with other males. This would give me a good excuse for my whereabouts when Lazarus found out Raine was no longer on the property.

So, I made my way to the training grounds, which were on the other side of the estate from the stables.

A few males were already taking laps around the field when I joined them. I recognized a few as close allies in the resistance against 'Lord Lazarus.' I smiled to myself, knowing this was perfect, and I couldn't wait to see the chaos break in a few hours.

We passed the time, running, hitting each other with long sticks, wrestling and pinning one another to the ground, and finally, shadow-jumping and coming out of it fighting. Some of the males were bloody by the end, and we all laughed at how dirty we had gotten when the sun was high in the sky.

Time had passed quickly, and it was likely nearing the lunch hour. I knew at this point Raine had been gone for hours.

So, when shouting and a roar came from the mansion, I knew I needed to brace myself quickly.

Lazarus shadow-jumped into the middle of our group, and his focus glued to the males around. They looked for me, and when they narrowed in, I saw he was furious, but I stood my ground.

He stomped over, his hand immediately finding my neck, and his grip tightened. I didn't flinch or move and didn't speak until he finally calmed himself enough to spit words into my face.

"WHERE IS MY DAUGHTER?" His shout rang in my ears. It took me a moment to answer since he was still gripping hard onto my throat hard.

"I assume she will be in her room, Lazarus. I haven't gone to see her yet today. I have been here busy with the males training."

"Don't give me that bullshit, Zynas. You have eyes on her at all times. I'm not going to repeat myself, so I will ask once more. Where is Raine?"

"I. Don't. Know." He gripped my throat harder, and the pressure caused me to choke, but still, I didn't budge.

Another male, one loyal to Lazarus, spoke up, "Lord Lazarus, Zynas has been here with us since well before the sun rose. I do not think he knows where the female is since she doesn't like to get out of bed until nearly the afternoon, most days."

Lazarus glanced over at the male, and for a moment, I thought he wasn't going to let go of me. But, he relinquished his hold and stepped back.

"Very, well. It would seem your mate has run." He looked over at another male and gestured for him to approach. "Ready the beast. When we find Raine, she will regret that she ever tried to run from me again."

"Yes, sir." The male said and shadow-jumped out of the training grounds.

The other males started to fidget as they waited for what their 'Lord' would do next. But what they weren't expecting was the male who had just left to arrive back so soon.

"Lord Lazarus," He was out of breath as if he had run around the stables and the surrounding area, quickly looking for the Ashix that I knew was no longer there. "The beast is gone.

Sh-she isn't in the stables, and her chains are lying in the hay. The back door toward the forest is wide open as well."

"WHAT!?" Lazarus growled loudly. His hand then clamped around the male's throat at the news. "You're telling me the only leverage I have against my daughter, her beast, is not here either?"

"I'm sorry, sir," he started choking out. "I ran around looking and figured I would come back and tell you right away." His words were gurgled just before Lazarus began to tighten his hold further. His face turned a purplish blue as he tried to suck in the air that was being kept from him.

And then, he suddenly let go. The male lay on the ground coughing, clutching his throat while angrily looking up at Lazarus. *Oh, this was perfect. With that outburst, he would turn his loyal males against him in no time.*

Lazarus turned back to me with darkness in his eyes and his fists clenching at his sides. I stood rooted to where I was, daring him to come closer and rechallenge me. I allowed his violent actions to show that I was compliant with the other males, but deep down, it took everything I had to keep my composure.

"My males," he bellowed out as some of the other Shadow Assassins who had heard the commotion started coming over to where we stood. Soon, a large group formed, and a mixture of the males I trusted and the ones who were loyal to Lazarus loomed around.

"It seems my little Ashix has decided to make a run for it with her beast. You are to subdue my daughter and chain the beast. I will be the one to end her companion. She will wish she had never run from me. The best places to begin looking are around waterfalls. Not only are the Ashix drawn to them, but so is my daughter." His smile turned sinister as he glanced back at me.

I knew I made a mistake telling the beast to look for waterfalls as a safe place to lay low. I could only hope my mate was smart enough to figure out her father would look for her there. Angry at myself for not realizing he knew where they were headed, I leveled my emotions to play a scorned male whose mate just took off on him.

"And you, Zynas, will not be able to save your mate from the punishment she so deserves this time. If you dare stop me, I will gut you."

I sneered at the male, showing my distaste for the unfolding events. I would play his accomplice until I could get away myself without being followed. I had proven my loyalty to him—at least, I had in the last few weeks. The males who had been following me at every step had gone away.

Now, I would continue that false compliance.

"Don't worry, Lazarus. What she has done today certainly won't go unpunished, not only by you but by myself. She runs from me as well. Or did you forget her resistance to our betrothal?" I asked, smirking when I realized I had him right where I wanted. He smiled back menacingly.

"Of course, I haven't forgotten. After I have served her punishment, you may do what you wish to her." Lazarus paused and looked back at the males who gathered. "I believe she has a few hours on us. Spread out, males, and find my treacherous daughter."

With that, Lazarus shadow-jumped out of the training grounds, and several Shadow-Assassins followed his lead.

It didn't take long for me and a few of my loyal males to be left, and when it was just us, I only left them with a simple nod and shadow-jumped myself to my room.

Everything was lining up perfectly. I just needed to bide my time for a few days before I rejoined my mate and kept her safe from her father. If I left now, his suspicions would be heightened, and anyone he knew I had spoken to would also be under scrutiny.

Closing my eyes, I sent up a silent prayer to the Goddess. *Protect my mate and her beast from harm. She is all I have left in this world. May her storms shelter her until I can wrap my arms around her again and finally claim what is mine.*

Chapter Eleven

Raine

When Gezr's swirling darkness of a shadow-jump let up, Beauty and I stood before an exquisite large waterfall. It was slightly larger than the one near my home but so similar, with a large ledge that hung over a plummeting drop into an underground lake and cave.

I stifled a sob when the overwhelming surge of energy from the falls pushed into me. It felt like home, and all I wanted was my mom and Kal to wrap me up in their arms and tell me everything was alright and that I was safe.

But I wasn't out of the woods yet.

Not with my father, who I had to guess was throwing an adult-size temper tantrum right about now. He knew I was gone. There was no doubt of that, seeing as the Shadow Assassins had already been looking around the nearby waterfalls.

Was I safe here? He would be looking for me anywhere near the falls. He knew I loved them, and he knew the Ashix were drawn to them as well.

Turning toward Gezr, I glanced at him questioningly before speaking. "I'm assuming this is your place?"

He brightened while looking around at his home, "Yes, this is the home my brother and I grew up in with my mother and father." His once bright smile faded slightly as he mentioned his parents. Sadness brushed across his features quickly before he recollected himself.

"What happened to them?" I asked, knowing that it might bring old wounds, but I was curious about his background and why his family had chosen to be so close to the falls, knowing Ashix would linger around.

His hesitation was heartbreaking, and I was about to tell him never mind when he revealed what had happened to them. "Father was on an assignment in another world. It was only supposed to be a simple rescue mission. The world he went to was riddled with powerful storms that just kept building. He was successful in rescuing several people, but on his last jump, something happened, and he was swept up into the storm, never to be seen again."

His throat bobbed before he continued, "Mother passed shortly after that. The healer said she died of a broken heart when Father had perished. They loved each other so incredibly much that it echoed down to my brother and me. We had grown up encased in that love that when they died, we both felt it."

I reached forward and gripped Gezr's arm, "I'm sorry for your loss. To both you and your brother."

He nodded and turned away from me toward the home nestled in the surrounding trees. It was a stunning log cabin larger than the home I grew up in. In front was a wraparound porch that reminded me of the home Kal had on Earth. It had a swing on one end and some wicker furniture on the other.

From the outside, it looked cozy and inviting.

After following Gezr up the steps, he sat down on one of

two chairs with a glass table between them. He gestured for me to sit, and we looked back toward the falls, where Beauty was having the time of her life flying around.

Down the bond, I could feel her happiness and contentment. I felt the same, being so near the flowing waters that gave off hints of power that my body craved.

Yes, not much longer now, little Storm Surge. Soon, your mates will join you, and you will be entirely free of your bonds. I will do all I can to keep you safe until then.

That voice, again, was surging up through my necklace and was an enthusiastic feminine ring instead of a blank, listless tone like before. I gripped the pendant in my hand and smiled. It didn't frighten me to hear such a soft voice now calling out to me. In fact, it made my lingering unease loosen further while I was sitting here with Gezr outside his serene home.

"Gezr," My voice, loud in the silence that we had been sitting in, startled him, causing laughter to bubble up. "Sorry, I didn't mean to scare you. But I was curious. What made your parents choose this spot to build their home? It's awfully close to the falls, the Ashix's normal home." My gaze lifted to the sky as I saw Beauty circling along with a few other Ashix that, judging by their colors, were male.

Gezr glanced up and smiled, noticing the same dance I was seeing between the beasts that called these forests their home.

"My mother was a witch from an outlying village called Tallens, and my father was a Shadow Assassin from Ozryn. One day, my mother went to Ozryn because she was called to heal a child in dire need. That child turned out to be my father's sister, and when my father laid eyes on my mother, it was instant. They were drawn to one another. He vowed to give her anything she wanted so long as she stayed with him." He chuckled, glancing back toward me.

"So, she told him to find a waterfall near the city for them to build their home together because she needed the energy of the water to connect to. And that's when he stumbled upon this place. And the rest is history. They built and lived here, raised my brother and me, and then died loving each other fiercely."

I smiled back at him. It was a lovely story, and it made sense that she wanted to be near the falls. I glanced over at him with my head against the side of the home.

"So, if your mom was a witch, does that mean you and your brother inherited her powers as well?" I asked, curious if Gezr was just like me.

Shaking his head, he let out a trembling breath, "No, we never got my mother's powers. Only our father's shadow-jumping abilities. Although, my brother does feel close to the falls and the Ashix that roam the forest. We leave them alone, and they leave us alone. It's a harmony we don't disturb."

"So you said your mother healed your father's sister. Is that what her powers consisted of?"

"You have an awful lot of questions, Raine."

"You could say I'm curious. My mother is a witch from Earth. I'm trying to figure out if there is much of a difference in the human's magic compared to here in AshFiera. It seems like there isn't, but I'm just wondering if I am the only one like myself. A witch and Shadow Assassin."

He shook his head, leaning forward, laying his arms to rest on his thighs. "As far as I know, you are the first to have both. Anyone else who is a witch or warlock mated to a Shadow Assassin has children who usually only inherit one of the parents' abilities. I think that's why Lazarus is now keen on keeping you for himself. You possess a lot of power for such a small female."

"Hey! I'm not that small. I can handle myself plenty. Especially against you silly shadow males." Laughter peeled out of me at the glare Gezr gave me.

"I don't think so, princess." A low, grumbly voice spoke from inside the house just before a Shadow Assassin stepped out onto the porch.

Already irked at the name my father made the males use, a gasp left my throat when I saw it was Kojax. Oh shit, did my father find me here too? What the hell was Kojax doing here? Before I could voice my question, Gezr stood from his chair, walked over to the male I had just been with earlier this morning, and hugged him tightly.

"Brother."

Wait what? Brother? "Wait, Gezr. You're telling me your brother is Kojax?"

"Yup, he's my little brother." He stood back from him slightly and slapped his hand on his shoulder. "You know, we were supposed to meet at the other falls. Not here, right? Anyone could have followed you."

Kojax peered at his brother and then glanced at me. "I know that, brother. However, I thought it smarter to come here and let you know that Lazarus and a few of his loyal males are headed this way. They are checking all homes near waterfalls. I suggest we get the two females into hiding."

Panic raced through my spine, leaving unwanted tingling that made my limbs weak and sluggish. *Swoosh.* Beauty landed near the porch, fury running through her eyes and our bond. She must have felt my panic while flying around and came to my side right away. Seeing her, my limbs finally obeyed my silent plea to move, and I got up off the chair and headed for her.

"It's okay, girl. We will get to safety." Turning back toward Gezr and Kojax, I looked at them both blurrily. "Can you help hide us? Is there somewhere big enough for Beauty?"

Gezr nodded. "Yes, I can take you to the cave hidden behind the falls at the bottom."

Kojax stepped off the steps, and a growl left Beauty as he

approached both of us. I placed my hand on her side and rubbed it, trying to soothe her. Down the bond, I projected that I wasn't afraid of the male who approached us. I knew once she received it, her growls stopped, and she huffed her smoke in his direction.

"Gezr, I can take them both down below. Lazarus and his males will be here soon, and you, brother, need to be present when they come." Kojax said.

Gezr glanced at both Beauty and me, "Are you okay with my brother taking you down?"

"We don't have much of a choice, but that would be fine with me." Turning my head, I looked at Beauty and quirked an eyebrow. "Are you going to behave, my beautiful beast? Long enough for this male to take us to safety?"

The only answer I got was a chuff and nudge. Smiling, I looked back at Kojax and said, "Yup, good to go. She won't be any trouble and will be the most polite Ashix she can be." I said this with a fake smile, not knowing if she would actually keep out of mischief, but I could say for sure she wouldn't risk our safety.

He eyed Beauty for a moment before putting his hands on her. Before he could touch me, we shadow-jumped to the very bottom of the cave's lake.

Coming out of the short shadow-jump, the roar of the falls was deafening, and I had to look around for Beauty and Kojax. They hadn't been too far from me, but I was puzzled about why I wasn't near them. Hadn't Kojax shadow-jumped with me? I could have sworn he touched me before we disappeared. Kojax shook his head and waved a hand for us to follow.

"Those bangles must be wearing off. You shadow-jumped before I could touch your arm and take you with us." He said, assessing me before he led us around the rushing water. Well, that answered my unspoken question and left me elated. Soon I would feel back to myself again.

He brought us to a ledge wide enough for Beauty to walk, bringing us behind the falls without getting wet. My eyes widened, and my neck craned back, taking in the tall ceiling above us. Glancing around, it was large enough that you could fit at least twenty or more Ashix comfortably.

Our shuffling echoed lightly while moving further into the cave.

Kojax turned to me and whispered, "My mother enchanted the cave to help hide those who needed to be hidden. I never understood if my mother was a seer. She never spoke to Gezr or me about it, but the cave hasn't been needed until now." His gaze was far off as he spoke about his mother. The sadness swirling around him as he bowed his head before speaking again, "I would like to think she knew what was coming. Your father is taking AshFiera hostage for his gain. Maybe she saw you needing protection in the form of my brother and me and then, in return, made this cave a safe place."

His throat bobbed, and his head snapped toward the opening of the cave. "Keep quiet. They won't be here long. I do need to go and join them so they don't suspect I am helping aid you. Be well, Princess." He smirked before shadow-jumping.

He must enjoy getting under my skin like several males I knew in my life because that damned nickname 'princess' came out not once but twice since he showed up at Gezr's. Well, I suppose this would be his place as well.

The urge to pummel Zy, Kojax and Gezr was strong. Gezr was only on the list because, well, as they say, he was guilty by association, and he was absolutely affiliated.

Several deep voices sounded out above the cave, and I snuck closer to the opening so I could hear better. Even with the raging water falling from above, I could overhear my father and Gezr's voices.

"Gezr, is this where you have been hiding?" my father asked, his voice irritation-filled.

"I haven't been hiding, Lazarus. I am enjoying some time to myself before I need to start my assigned job in a few weeks. You know where I have been. It shouldn't be a surprise that I enjoy my solitude without other males crawling over each other." Gezr retorted.

"Yes, I suppose it is getting quite crowded in the city. However, I still expect to see you every so often."

"I can make more of an effort to come to the city after I have enjoyed my time here." Gezr's defiance was evident in his voice, and my father must have noticed because I suddenly heard him choking.

Holding back my gasp, I waited, clasping my palms to my throat as if I could ease the discomfort I knew the male was going through at the hands of my father.

"Now, now, Gezr. I would hate for your time to be cut short and for you to start your new life with the Goddess with that attitude. I'm here for more important matters than your attendance."

"What–ah, what can I help you with?" Gezr managed to stifle out even while still being choked. I shook my head at the stubborn male but was grateful when his intake of air was finally audible.

"My daughter, Raine, has decided to run along with her beast, an Ashix. Have you seen her?" Holding my breath, I waited to see if Gezr would give us up or if he was true to his word on keeping us safe. It would be easy for the male to do away with us and be free from that burden.

"No, sir. I'm sorry I haven't seen a young female and an Ashix traveling together." Gezr paused briefly. "If I do happen to run into them, I will notify you immediately. If you choose, I can end the beast and keep the female captive. It might be easier."

"No, I would like to do that myself. Teach my lovely daughter a lesson she soon won't forget."

Beauty growled low, and I ran over to her quickly, patting her neck and shushing her, knowing that Gezr was playing a part. I wasn't sure if she knew or if she was just reacting to my father's words.

When I thought all was clear and confident I had caught her growl in time, believing they were dispersing soon. I was wrong.

I had been too late, and while Kojax said that the cave was enchanted, I still held my breath. Throwing every caution down the bond to Beauty to remain quiet, an unknown Shadow Assassin walked around outside of our hiding spot, leaving crunching steps in his wake.

Then, when I thought he had left, he appeared at the entrance. I froze. Fear radiated from my shaking body, but I kept myself composed enough to remain silent.

His gaze raked over Beauty and mine, but he didn't indicate that he could see us.

The agonizing minutes passed slowly as he continued exploring the seemingly empty cave before he decided to jump back to the top.

Slowly, I stepped back to the cave entrance and listened as the male told my father he found nothing.

I silently thanked the Goddess and then Gezr and Kojax's mother for our hiding spot.

My father's voice boomed as he grew increasingly frustrated that I hadn't been found yet. "See to it that you keep an eye out for my daughter and her beast. I want you to report to me in a few days. If I don't hear from you, I will assume you are going rogue like some other Shadow Assassins I have had to take care of today."

Was he talking about Zynas? Did he know that Zy had spoken to me about being ready at a moment's notice? Was it actually Zy who helped me, or was it the work of other Shadow Assassins who knew Cassius, Gezr, and Kojax?

Several minutes passed when Gezr finally came down.

"Raine?"

I stepped out of the cave and onto the ledge so he could see me.

"Are you going to be okay if you stay down here for a little longer? I don't want to take you out and then have your father show up again and defeat the purpose of hiding you in the first place."

"Ya, we should be good to sit for a little longer." I took a good look at the male in front of me and smiled, "Thank you for not giving us up to him. I'm afraid if he gets a hold of either of us, we will be joining the Goddess ourselves."

Shrugging, he took a step toward me, clasping a hand on my shoulder like I saw some of the males do to each other at the mansion. A sort of commodore. "It's no sweat, Raine. Cassius would have my balls if I didn't protect someone he loves. I'm sure Kalpheus would hang me from my dick as well."

This time, I let myself laugh loudly and looked back over my shoulder toward Beauty, who had come out of the cave to make sure I was unharmed.

"Well, thank you again. But are you okay? Did he hurt you too badly?" I asked, eyeing his throat, that still had red marks all along the front.

"Eh, nothing I can't handle. I will be fine in an hour or less. Shadow Assassin healing and all that." His gaze went above and then back to Beauty and me. "My brother will be returning shortly. I will be back soon."

After Gezr shadow-jumped back up to the top, I turned

around to Beauty. "Come on, girl. Let's get back into the cave in case they come back."

As we walked back into our magical hiding place, Beauty led me first. She circled the cave before plopping down and making herself comfortable. Her gaze landed on me, and down the bond, I could feel her tugging my body to come closer to her, to take comfort in her warmth while we waited for the all-clear.

I settled in next to her and laid my head against her side, drifting off to sleep in her warmth and the safety of her big body cradling mine. Dreaming of a time when we would be free and I would be with Kal again, maybe even Zy as well.

Chapter Twelve

Raine

The ground beneath my body shifted, and I bolted upright, heart pounding wildly, while my brain caught up to what was going on. What I had thought was a shifting ground was actually Beauty moving. I had fallen asleep nestled into her side while waiting for Gezr to come back. Beauty's gaze was glued to the front of the cave while her mouth shifted into a silent snarl, showing her sharp teeth. She was ready to spring into action against whoever was lurking around outside.

We didn't dare make a sound in fear that my father had returned. Down the bond, the anxious anticipation was radiating from not only myself but also Beauty. The silence was loud. The drumming of my heart echoed in my head as the seconds ticked by.

"Raine?" Gezr's voice carried over the rocks and water into the large cave. Letting out the breath that I had been holding, the stiffness in my body relaxed, and I got up from where I had been lying quietly with Beauty.

"Hey Gezr, everything good now?"

"Ya, it's been long enough, and I have seen no signs of any males being left behind. You and Beauty can come out."

When I turned to look at Beauty, her eyes twinkled with mischief. Then, she was suddenly up, galloping toward the entrance. She took to the air, straight through the falls and zipping up toward the sky.

Giggling escaped from my lips as I watched her joy soar as high as the clouds she was now reaching.

The delight was infectious through our bond, and I couldn't help but jog out of the cave toward Gezr, who stood at the bottom of the ledge. He gawked where Beauty was soaring while a smile spread onto his face. It would appear that Beauty could elicit happiness in someone after such a stressful few hours.

Gezr looked at me, still smiling, and held out his hand. "Here, let me help you up top. We can put Beauty in the stables for the evening and get you settled into your room."

Walking the last few steps toward him, I eyed the gash that was located just below his left eye. It was already beginning to heal, so I could only imagine how bad it had been prior to him coming to get us. My father was a ruthless male and was far from gentle. Especially when it came to getting information about those he 'loved' or, more accurately, wanted to control.

Wincing at the brutality, I grabbed his hand as we shadow-jumped to the top.

"I'm sorry for all the trouble we have caused you, Gezr. If you feel we need to find somewhere else to stay, please let me know. We are happy you have helped keep us hidden for as long as you have."

He shook his head, "No, Raine. Please, you are not a burden if that's what you are thinking."

It was exactly what I was thinking. I didn't want anyone else to get hurt because of my actions and the male who claimed to be a loving father. It wasn't fair to involve anyone in my problems. I had a hard enough time thinking about Kal and how far away he was. But at the same time, I was relieved I had sent him and my mother back to Earth, closing any portals to and from and keeping them safe.

"When a male such as myself, a Shadow Assassin, gives his word, he keeps it. Especially since the word I gave was to Cassius and your mother." Gezr said, reaching his hand out to mine. I took it while his other one covered the top of my palm. "I swear to you, I will protect you as will my brother, Kojax. We will treat you just as brothers would treat their sisters. You are important, Raine. And I believe that you will save AshFiera from your father."

I smiled tentatively, squeezing his hand, "Thank you, Gezr. You have no idea what this means to me. For years, it was just my mom and me. Now, it seems my small family has grown more in the last few months."

He smiled back before responding, "Do you want to get your beast down here so we can show her where she will be sleeping?" He asked.

"Ya, hold on. I can feel her distantly. It seems she is distracted currently with a male Ashix." I said, closing my eyes and reaching out to her, calling her back and showing her that there was a safe place to lay down for the night.

She was stubborn, though, and while I still kept my eyes closed trying to convince her to come back, Gezr's soft voice spoke in awe, "You can call her back? Wow, I didn't think the rumors were real, that you truly did bond with an Ashix. Raine, you have no idea the power you possess by the Goddess."

Opening my eyes, I looked at Gezr, "What do you mean?"

His cheeks turned pink, and his gaze shifted elsewhere, "It is said the Goddess possessed the power to bond with the creatures in the forest, but more importantly, the Ashix and she could control them. She never used them for nefarious reasons, of course, but to keep the peace between the wild forest and the AshFierans that lived among them."

My eyes widened. I had never heard that story before. My mother had told me many things about the Goddess and the powers she was thought to possess, but that was one of the things she never disclosed. I wondered if she didn't tell me because we both held the same powers.

"I never knew that about the Goddess. Both my mother and I can connect to the fauna. My mother had told me all about the Goddess of AshFiera but left that part out, apparently." I grumbled. What more did she hide knowingly from me? I loved my mother fiercely, but everything that has happened in the last few months has left me wondering if I could trust her again.

Finally, Beauty drifted down slowly, and when she landed, her ire was beaming. She huffed a trundle of smoke in our direction, and I rolled my eyes. "Goddess, Beauty, you are so dramatic. It's just for the evenings. You can go back to flirting around with your Ashix male in the morning."

She perked up at the mention of the male, and I let out an exasperated sigh. I didn't know if I would get her to come back to the stables after tonight if she spent more time with the Ashix male who had decided to stick around.

Our gazes drifted upward when movement caught our eyes. It was the male circling, trying to entice her to come back and join him. He was beautiful from this far away, with glimmering shades of purple tapering out to bright blues. It was like a mix of twilight and sunny blue skies clashing perfectly together. He was mesmerizing, and I only hoped he would get comfortable enough to approach me and see I wasn't a threat. Beauty was the only Ashix that I had ever encountered, so I was curious if I could gain the trust of another deadly, beautiful creature.

"In you go, girl. I will see you in the morning." Hugging Beauty around the neck, I ushered her inside Gezr's stables that sat beside his home. It was smaller than the building back at the mansion but large enough to ensure she was comfortable for sleep only. I would make sure that come morning, she was let out before the sun rose.

She lazily walked into the stables, taking her sweet time, extending the inevitable of her being shut in for the night. I knew it wasn't right to lock her back up, but just for this night, I needed to know she was safe. After tonight, if she wanted to fly away with the male Ashix, I wouldn't protest. I still felt she needed to get as far away from me as possible.

After shutting the doors, I turned toward Gezr, who had gone to the porch and waited for me.

"Come, I will show you to your room. Tomorrow, I can show you more of the house if you'd like."

Nodding, I followed him inside, where most of the home was large and open-concept. Stairs led up to a second floor located next to a large fireplace. I had to guess that's where the bedrooms were. As he led me through the home, I guessed correctly.

He left me at one of the doors, saying goodnight, and then entered another room further down the hall.

When I opened the door to the bedroom, it was mostly plain. There was a single dresser opposite of a small bedside table and a large queen-size bed that called my name.

The exhaustion of the day was catching up to me, and a yawn escaped. First thing was first, though, before I could chase those dreams, I needed to shower desperately.

I found the bathroom through another door attached to my room. I showered, did my business, and then dove under the covers. As I was getting comfortable, I remembered the necklace that was still nestled against my chest.

Gripping onto the latch, I took it off and placed it on top of the bedside table. When my hands left the necklace, all of the power I had started to feel again zapped away, leaving me scrambling for a gasp of air.

I snatched the necklace off the table quickly and placed it back around my neck. The absence of my powers, even just having a small fraction back, left me feeling empty inside. Now that I had the necklace back on, everything felt better but less than before. *Note to self: don't take the jewelry off until I can get these shackles off my wrist.*

While lying down, my mind wandered to Kal and how he was doing. Was he close to getting back to me, or would we forever be separated? My heart ached at the possibility, but I knew one thing: When I saw him again, I would jump his bones. Another ache deep within pounded through my most intimate parts as memories of his hands roaming my body ran through my mind.

While thinking about his hands, I swear I could feel them gripping onto my body, like he was holding me tight to his chest. The overwhelming feeling of being cuddled overtook my active mind, and while I wished they were real, they helped me doze into the dark abyss of my dreams.

Several days had passed, and things were quiet. Beauty had grudgingly slept in the stables every night, each time throwing her sassy attitude my way. But I think she kept sleeping in there because of the anxiety I couldn't keep contained from our bond.

It made me feel better, knowing she was out of sight of any Shadow Assassin and my father if they happened to come back to Gezr's.

It was an extremely hot day out, and I was itching to swim in the lake below. I just couldn't get there without Gezr shadow-jumping me down. I had tried to jump on my own, but it seemed my powers were once again hidden beneath the surface.

Unfortunately, Gezr wasn't around to help. So, I called Beauty down through the bond as she had been away for most of the morning. She was likely chasing around the male Ashix, who refused to leave her, aside from nighttime when she went into the stables.

The male kept his distance from us, but slowly, he joined Beauty when she decided to give me her presence instead of frolicking with him. At first, he stayed far away, only observing how I interacted with his female. Then, yesterday, he surprised me by laying down next to Beauty while I lay on her belly gazing up at the sky. A smile slipped past my lips as I kept still and admired his beautiful purple and blue scales. As I glanced at him, I decided he should have a name. Kovidar had sounded like it fit him. He was so beautiful, just like the purple orchid trees, that I remembered Aunt Samara and Gigi speaking about and showing me where they had planned to plant around the yard before they left on their cruise.

Beauty appeared just above the trees, taking me out of my thoughts. I smiled when Kovidar followed closely behind her.

She landed hard next to me, causing the ground to shake, and my balance slipped slightly. My eyes widened, giggling. I couldn't contain the tease that was on the top of my tongue. "Beauty, what the fuck? You brazen female! I could have fallen on my ass and bruised it."

She just stomped around, happy as a clam.

"Alright, you shit. Want to take me down to the lake and go for a swim?"

Her stomping stopped, and she turned toward me with a

mischievous look in her eye. She walked over and allowed me to climb on her back.

Without warning, she took off into the sky, and a squeal left my throat at the unexpected departure. She usually let me get my bearings before taking off, but this time, she just zoomed right up and then took a dive toward the lake at the bottom of the falls. On the dive, my laughter bubbled out of me, and I loved the thrill of her sudden drop.

She didn't land on the edge like I thought she would, but instead flew low over the lake and barrel-rolled several times until my grip on her slipped, and I fell a short distance to the water.

Coming up for air, I sputtered water from my mouth and hollered at Beauty, "Goddess, Beauty. What has gotten into you?" She, of course, ignored me in favor of playing in the air with her male.

Swimming to the shore, I got out and stripped my now-soaked clothes, leaving on my bra and underwear, which served as a bathing suit. Laying the clothes on a large rock to dry, I dove back into the water to have fun and cool off from the heat above.

I watched as Beauty and Kovidar flew in and out of the dropping water from the falls in a dance above me. Floating, I was weightless as I admired them, and the love Beauty was flaring to life being with him.

While I was happy my beast had found her mate, I couldn't help but think of my own. Kal. It was hard to imagine my life without him in it, but there was a possibility that neither one of us would ever reach the other. I only hoped he would find happiness in the human realm. I would forever pine for the male I already had such a strong connection to.

Then, my mind twisted to Zy. And once again, my infatuation with the male caused my heart to rip in two as guilt and anger at my body's betrayal sunk in. Would I ever just have a moment's peace thinking about Kal without also immediately thinking about the devilish one-eyed male?

It was as if thinking about the male had conjured him up when a deep growl rumbled from the shore behind me.

Turning slowly, I saw that Zy had, in fact, been summoned. My gaze darted around the large cave and above, looking for Beauty and Kovidar. Neither was in sight, and the slight panic ebbed as my mind raced that Zy had found me while I was vulnerable.

"Zy," I whispered, my voice not sounding like my own as I took in his appearance. He was decked out in his assassin get-up, armed like no other with blades of all sizes, along with the concoction he had used on me months ago. I eyed those vials, and my anger rolled around in my head before finally snapping.

"What the fuck are you doing here?" I asked, seething and glaring daggers at the male who had my emotions rolling in and out of confused hatred and love. *Wait, love?* No, I didn't love this male. It was only my body's reaction to his handsome face and gorgeous physique. The way he had treated me most of the time in captivity was benevolent, and he had confused my mind or tricked it those last few days before I escaped. He couldn't have been the one to help me leave the mansion. There was no way he would betray my father's trust.

"I'm here for you, Raine."

The smirk that crossed his face was cocky, while lusty eyes bore into my body while I was still floating in the water.

My panic rose, and my heart started thudding violently. My breathing picked up, and I drew in short pants. *Where the hell was Beauty, and why wasn't she responding to my panic?*

"Uh, that's great, but I think you need to leave."

"Why?" The question interrupted my all-consuming panic.

"You're kidding, right? Why? I will tell you why, *Zynas*, you are not welcome here. If you think for one second that you came to retrieve me for my father, I have news for you. I'm not coming with you. I will claw, kick, and bite my way out if I have to."

His head tilted slightly, and he crossed his arms, "I'm not here to bring you back to your father, Raine. Now, instead of acting like a brat, why don't you come to the shore? You can dry off, and we can talk about everything."

Oh, I would show him a brat, alright. Fucking bastard male and his assured attitude that I would just comply with his commands. Ya, I don't think so.

I needed to get to the shore and run like hell to the cave, where I hoped Gezr and Kojax's mother's magic would work to hide me from Zy.

My eyes remained glued to the male who was waiting for me near the shore. He was far enough away that I would have a head start when I reached land. I just needed to ensure that my intentions weren't clearly written across my face.

"Alright, fine." Rolling my eyes, "I will come out. Although you rudely interrupted my swim, I will *obey*. I was trying to cool off from the heat."

He continued to remain where he was, with his arms still plastered across his chest. His eyes glittered with longing as he took in my nearly naked body when I emerged from the water. Those delicious muscular arms raised and lowered with the heavy breathing that began. Then, his hands clenched into fists, and I knew it was now or never.

So, I bolted the other way, not daring to look back. I knew he was already after me; the thudding crunch of rocks was enough to indicate that he was quick to act. But then the crunching stopped, and suddenly, Zy was coming at me from in front instead of behind me.

Before I could curse in my mind, Zy was tackling me to the ground. His big body landed on top of mine, and he was effort-lessly wedged in between my thighs. I began to lift my fist to punch him in the throat when he gripped both hands together and raised them above my head. He adjusted himself, and his one hand now held onto both wrists while the other braced himself up slightly.

An angry scream tore from my throat, and I tried thrashing my body around to get him off. The efforts were useless, though. He was too heavy in this position. I cursed these bangles for shorting out my powers again. If I hadn't taken off the fire opal, I would have been able to kick his ass off me.

FUCK, I was screwed, and not the good way either.

Chapter Thirteen

Zy

This female would be my death, especially since I have her legs spread and her body pinned beneath mine. She was a tempting morsel, and I could get myself lost in her body.

I would have her in this position again very soon but in a more fun manner. However, as I see fit, it would serve to tame my beautiful storm until I could let her up. She tried running from me. After everything I had done for her, she acted scared and possibly thought I was there to take her back to her father. Since I'm sure that's who she associated me with.

Not happening.

In fact, I couldn't go back to the mansion either. Lazarus had been suspicious of me at first until another male, one he trusted more than me, stuck up for my presence. It had been a good decision to start training earlier that morning, and it served my purpose of an alibi.

My female's wiggling drew my attention back to her, and I

couldn't help the groan that escaped. She was making things complicated, and I had no intention to act on them just yet.

"Stop moving, little storm, unless you wish to take care of a problem that is starting to arise." Quirking my eyebrow, grinning villianously when her eyes widened.

She attempted to gaze down toward where our bodies were connected intimately. Her eyes snapped back toward mine, and she scowled, "Get off me, you big doofus."

"No. You need to calm yourself, female, before I will let you up. We can talk this way for now until you are less apt to run off again."

She scoffed, "Calm myself? Are you fucking kidding me, Zy? Fuck. You."

"Mmm, maybe later, my perfect little hurricane, but right now, we need to talk."

The light shone down from above entirely onto Raine's face, and her beauty was illuminated. She took my breath away every time I gazed upon her, but at this very moment, she looked like a Goddess.

Her dark chocolate curls were spread out on the ground below us, and her honeyed highlights glowed brightly like a halo on an angel's head. Her beautiful emerald eyes glared at me with such defiance that it was intoxicating.

I would take this female's ire; anything she gave me, I would take. She was mine from the moment I laid eyes on her, and that was the day she was also taken from me. Raine had to realize that she would be mine, and in return, I would be hers; that would never change. She had my beating heart in her grips to do with as she pleased. I just hoped one day, she would caress my heart instead of crushing it in her fists.

Her breathing became labored as she continued to thrash around underneath me. It just made my grin wider, but then she rubbed her lower half just right, and another growl left my throat along with her sudden gasp.

She could obviously feel what she did to me. My cock was so hard that it could have broken free of its restraints to seek the wet warmth of her cunt that it so desired to sink into.

Raine was alluring and desirable, but she was currently unreachable. I would never take my beautiful female without her consent. My only desire was to have a willing partner, and I knew that if I were patient enough, that day would come. Having Kal here would speed things up, but the male still had yet to figure out how to reach AshFiera again from Earth.

"Zy, I said get the fuck off me."

"No. I told you, little storm, we need to talk. You are so keen on running from me. This is the only way I know you will listen and, well, not run."

"I think if you want to speak with me, we shouldn't be in this position, Zy. I'm practically naked." She seethed, breathing heavily, which caused her breasts to brush against my chest as I slowly lowered my body closer toward hers.

"This is perfect, Raine. Because, at least with us being so close, maybe you will listen to me and stop being so stubborn." She rolled her eyes, and I was about to retort that if she rolled them any harder, they would get stuck, but I just couldn't bring myself to say it.

"Raine, I promise whatever you are thinking about me right now. And, I think I have a good idea it has to do with your father. It's not true. I'm not here to take you back to him if that's what you are assuming."

This stopped her further wiggling, and she stared widely at me.

"So, you're not taking me back to my father?"

"No, I'm the one who helped you escape him. And, I also caused some distractions to help further your escape so you had some time to find a place to hide before he searched for you."

"What?" She asked. The anger her voice twinged with a moment ago turned to awe as the fight left her rigid body relaxing below mine.

"You didn't think I would just leave you there to face your father's wrath when you eventually fucked up again, did you?"

She really looked at me. Or maybe she was looking into me. "I thought you were playing a part. You acted one way alone with me and then another in front of everyone else. How was I supposed to know which version of you was true?"

"I suppose I didn't give you much choice to trust me enough to follow through with what I said in your bedroom."

Her eyebrows drew down into a frown, and then she moved her face to the side, not looking at me. "Why would you help me, Zy?"

"Why?" Did she truly not understand the depths of my feelings for her? I would give anything to see her elated. Including my own life, if it meant she was happy and safe.

"Because, my sweet storm. When I looked at you, and I saw you were beginning to lose your light, I couldn't just sit back and watch you dim. I wasn't going to stand to see my mate go through the heartache of being trapped. Not only were you kept prisoner by your father, but you were also kept from your other mate, Kal."

Raine turned her head to look back at me, and tears began to well up and pool in her lids. She bit her bottom lip, breathing heavily. So, I released her bound wrists and, with my thumb, forced her lip free from her teeth.

Her gasp was like music to my ears. She closed her eyes and let me continue to caress her lips. I couldn't help myself as my hand drifted lightly to her cheek, and my fingers wound their way into her hair loosely.

Slowly, I lowered my face down to hers. Our breaths were entangled, our lips barely touching, but something in the back of my mind was telling me not to take something she wasn't actively seeking yet.

Even though I had taken her lips with mine twice before, my body was shouting to hold out and wait.

So, instead, I lifted myself from hers. It pained me to lose that intimacy, but it wasn't freely given, and all I wanted was for her to choose me as I had chosen her. I made some serious mistakes while she was kept as a prisoner at the mansion, and now that she was away from there, I needed to do right by her.

Raine's eyes opened, and she lifted herself onto her elbows, looking at me differently than she had before. Just that look made me want to go right back on top of her and give her every-thing that was going through my mind.

"What happened, Zy? I was expecting–actually, never mind, I don't know what I was expecting." Raine stood and hesi-tantly walked over to the rock that held her clothes, keeping me within her peripheral vision. Her clothes looked a little damp, and I had to wonder what happened to them. Before I could ask the question, she turned back around and began dressing.

"First, you show up here after the last few days have been quiet and then tackle me–"

"Now, hold on, Raine. Let's get one thing straight. I tackled you because you ran from me and didn't give me a chance to explain why I was here. You're so stubborn sometimes, female, that I have to take drastic measures with you."

"Well, excuse me, mister, but what else am I supposed to do and think when you show up out of nowhere with a sinister look in your eye when I'm half naked? Hmm?" She hummed.

Laughter broke from my lips in the silence before I answered her, "Raine, how else am I supposed to look when the female I love is not only wet but half naked? Did you expect a male just to look the other way? I couldn't help it, especially when said female is so deliciously alluring."

It took her a moment to respond. Her mouth opened and closed several times like a fish out of water. It was adorable on those pouty lips that I was craving to take with mine.

Her words were but a whisper, but with my increased hearing, I heard her perfectly.

"Did you just say you loved me?"

"Of course. Is it so hard to believe that I do? Regardless of my past actions, I had a part to play in order to keep suspicions off of me from what I had been planning to do. So, any act I brought on in front of other males was just that—an act. I never wanted you to doubt my feelings, but if I had let myself show through, your father would have kept his males on my ass, trailing me wherever I went. You and Beauty wouldn't be free now if I never played along."

"Look, Zy, I–"

"Don't, Raine, I don't need you to say anything about it. When you are ready to accept your feelings for me, I will be here." Brushing my fingers through my hair, I placed my other hand in my pocket and walked further from her. "But, it's important that you know I don't plan to leave your side anytime soon. And I need you to accept that. You are safer with me around. After all, the seer I went and visited let that little bit slip when she helped me locate you."

Her eyebrows drew down into yet another frown, and she folded her arms, backing further away from me. The distance she was creating was frustrating, but I had to remember to go at her pace from here on out.

"So, anyone could find me then if they asked a seer?"

"Yes and no. Your father, I'm sure, has already attempted to threaten the few seers that are in Ozryn, but none of them will give you up. I know all of them, and they agree that they would rather have everything bad done to them before they give up your whereabouts." I smirked, thinking of the three seers who met with me over a year ago. They sought me out and pledged their fealty to Raine and me.

One in particular had sought me out several times over months. Andromeda had urged me to heed her warnings about Lazarus. And when the time came for Raine to be reunited with her father, Andromeda became more adamant. Especially the day she had officially met Raine.

I remember her visit clearly. She had found me patrolling the city with a few of my trusted males after I had dropped Raine off in her bedroom.

"Zynas, you must get her out of there. Her father has untold plans that will kill her if she is forced to use her magic." Andromeda's *panic stuttered out, and she gripped my arm painfully. How in the world was such a tiny seer so strong?*

"Andromeda, I am working on it as fast as I can without drawing attention to myself. I just got Lazarus to trust me enough for him to call his watchdogs off my back. Things will line up, and I will get my mate out safely."

"No, you need to up your timeline." Her eyes pleaded with *mine, and something in the back of my mind was pushing the urgency forward now that Andromeda insisted on it. I nodded and began to pull away from her.*

"There's something else you need to know."

"If there is such an urgency, don't you think I should get back to my plans?"

"You have time for this." She paused, her eyes going white, *and she uttered the words that would alter my world. "Your brother isn't dead. And Lazarus was the one who killed your mother and ordered his males to have your brother kidnapped. You have already met him, and he has already met your mate."*

"WHAT? Who—who is the male?" I shook her slightly, not

enough to jostle her but enough for her to snap out of her trance. "Andromeda, tell me who the male is?"

"I'm sorry, Zynas, I can't. If you knew right now, it would change the future. You will know soon enough, but you can't know today. There is so much more to it, but things need to fall into place first."

A memory from a short time ago surfaced, and I knew I had to disclose the information in the hopes that Raine would list all the males she had been in contact with.

"I'm sure you remember the seer from Ozryn? Andromeda?"

Realization dawned on her face, and she nodded.

"She told me something that has been at the forefront of my mind, aside from you."

Slowly, I crept along the cave's stone floor and stood in front of Raine. Her scent mingled in the wet air, causing me to clench my hands into fists, preventing my body from automatically reaching for her.

"Will you tell me what she said to you?"

"So impatient. I'm getting there, little storm." Chuckling, I lifted my hand and tucked a stray hair behind her ear even though moments ago; I promised myself I wouldn't caress any part of her. I couldn't help that I needed to touch her, ground myself, and prepare for the heartache I had lived with every day since my mother was killed and my brother was never found.

"When I was younger, my mother was slain in her bed, and my younger brother was taken. We had thought that whoever had killed my mother also killed my brother, but we never found his body." Raine took a step further into me and gripped my hand into hers.

"I'm so sorry, Zy. That is an awful way to not only lose your mom and not know what happened to your brother as well. Did you ever find out what happened to him or who did it?" Her

127

concern and empathy spurred me on to tell her exactly who the culprit was, and I knew once I uttered his name, her smoldered fury would once again ignite.

"Yes, actually. Andromeda, the seer you saved, approached me and told me." I gripped her hand tighter in mine, looking down into her beautiful green globes before dropping the devastating news I received just a few days ago. "Your father was the one who killed my mother and ordered my brother to be kidnapped. My father and I had thought he was dead for years because he never turned up. But, it seems that not only have I met him, but so have you."

Raine's eyes widened, and her mouth fell open. She shook her head, furrowing her brows, "That good-for-nothing poor excuse of a male had your mother killed? I'm so sorry, Zy. If you would have asked me if I thought he was capable of such acts when I was younger, I would have said no. But today–today is a much different story." Her grip tightened on my arm, and she brought herself into me, leaning her head against my chest. "Andromeda didn't tell you who your brother is, did she?"

"No, she said that if I knew right then the future would be altered. And I have a feeling that it wouldn't have been in our favor either. Can you think of any males that stick out to you?" I asked. The question couldn't be helped. Even if it was a long shot, I had to know if anyone felt familiar.

But she shook her head. Then, she surprised me when she wrapped her arms around my waist next, squeezing tightly. She muffled into my chest, "I'm so sorry, Zy, there have been so many males in and out while I was at the mansion that it all blurred together. But I'm so heartbroken about your mom and your brother. I know that one day you will find him again. And, when the time comes, I will help you get revenge against my father for what he has done to you."

Wrapping my arms around Raine, her warmth leached into

my body. A sigh left my mouth. We both had been through so much at the hands of her father. Soon, he would pay, and retribution would be in order. Not just for myself but primarily for my mate because she was so much more significant than the revenge I so wished to seek in the name of my family.

We held each other for so long that the sun had begun to set, and I shadow-jumped with her above to Gezr's home. I knew the male well. After all, his brother, Kojax, was one of the few males I trusted alone with my mate.

Gezr had taken care of Raine the last few days, and I would forever be grateful for his assistance. I would repay him when I took back what was rightfully mine.

Raine and I talked for hours inside the home, and it was easy for us to get lost in each other. When she began yawning, I escorted her to the room she had been staying in.

"You know, I don't need a babysitter to take me to my bedroom, Zy," she giggled. The sound went straight to my cock, and all I thought about was our encounter earlier in the day when I had been between her wet thighs in the cave.

A groan left my throat, "Humor me, little storm. It appeases something inside, being able to ensure your safety. Even if it is to your bedroom."

"If you say so, Zy." Her laughter died down into a breathless murmur, "I'll see you in the morning, goodnight." She closed the door before I could utter a response. Her footsteps thumped as she readied for bed. Then, all was silent.

And so, I stood facing her door for a long while, contemplating whether I should just barge in and join her in bed or if I should walk away and find my room for the night.

I reminded myself that she needed to choose to come to me or give me a clear sign that she was ready to be mine, so I walked away. But instead of walking to an empty bedroom, I made my way back outside and leaned against the railing on the front porch.

Looking toward the sky, watching as the colorful lights danced across, I smiled and promised that while we were here, I would train with my mate and help her regain her strength. If I had discovered anything tonight, it was that her time with her father at the mansion had left her weak because she had not kept up with physical activity.

If she was going to use all of her assets once the seer broke her free from the bangles, I was going to ensure that if her magic failed her, she could rely on her strength yet again.

Chapter Fourteen

Kal

"Did you bring it?" Theo's gaze was intense toward Cassius. His hand stretched out, waiting for my friend to give him whatever it was he asked for.

"Ya, I brought it. Pandora was hesitant even to let this leave her home, so I would suggest you make sure that Maggie brings it back with her to Gigi and Sam's when she comes to stay with the three females." Cassius pulled out Raine's family's ancestral book, handing it over to the infuriating male.

I still wanted to punch him in the throat for all his lusting after my female and that cocky grin he always carried around everywhere he went.

His grin widened as he gazed at and caressed the Celestine family book. His fascination with it was engrossing, but given its magic, I didn't believe he had any ill intent.

"Perfect, this is exactly what I was missing, and I knew it would be here." Theo pointed at something on one of the pages and spoke with himself, not directing his conversation to either Cassius or me.

I needed to interrupt the male and hurry him along. My skin crawled with how close I was to being reunited with my mate–my Enayah, once again.

"Well, can you do it now or not? I have been more than patient with waiting on you these last few months. Anything could have happened to Raine between then and now." My anger was slowly simmering beneath the surface, and I let him see a fraction.

"Yes–yes, loverboy. There's no need to get your panties in a twist. Now that I have this, combined with the spell I came up with, the missing pieces are now connected. In just a few short minutes, you will be back with the lovely Raine."

Irritated with his analogy, I grumbled, "I don't wear panties, male."

"It's a saying, Kal." He laughed, walking away from Cassius and me.

Cassius was looking over at me and shaking his head, trying to stifle a laugh that he had attempted to hide behind his hand.

"Something amuse you, Cass?"

"Nope, nothing amusing here, Kal. Don't worry, friend, we will be back in AshFiera, and we will find Raine. There are only a few places Lazarus could hide her, and I know that Gezr would have kept track of her when he realized she was captured and that I wasn't coming back." His hand clamped down on my shoulder. Helping ground the anger that was beginning to flare.

"Thank you. I needed that." It was true. He helped me ground myself and refocus on what was truly important. Raine.

Theo had walked away a short distance from Cassius and me, right next to the falls in his family's estate garden. Looking at the ginormous natural structure, it was almost a replica of the falls in AshFiera. It would seem a nearly impossible coincidence; however, I had to remember that my mate was surrounded by so much magic that anything having to do with her had to have been in the designs of the Goddess.

While waiting for Theo to complete the last few tasks he had set for himself, my body vibrated with impatience. This was it. After months of waiting, I would have the female I love in my arms, and I would help take out her father.

He wasn't allowed to exist any further. The bastard posed a risk to my mate and her mother.

"Alright, just a few more things and the portal will open up. If I'm calculating everything correctly, you both will end up at another falls in AshFiera. The original falls are unobtainable, with Raine rendering them useless, of course."

I greatly appreciated Theo's willingness to help us. Even if I wanted to ring the male's neck, I was grateful nonetheless.

With his back to us, he didn't speak a word. His hands remained turned up toward the sky, and then his head tilted back. We could see his eyes were closed. For moments, all was still and silent. Then, the air shifted, and a familiar buzzing filled the space just before the black inkiness of a portal slowly grew in front of Theo.

Once it was fully formed, Theo took a step back and looked over at us. "Remember where you arrive when you get into AshFiera. That is the only spot where this portal will appear. It has been linked with you two and only the two of you. Even if someone were to try to follow you through, they would just fall over the ledge of whatever waterfalls this takes you to. Unless, of course, you are touching the person when you go through."

It took me a few moments to realize he never spoke a word. The portal was open, just waiting for us to enter.

"That's it?" I asked, remembering when Raine had opened the last gateway, and she had to speak a few words.

Theo looked at me with his eyebrow raised, "Ya, that's it.

Did you expect me to do more?" His stance turned defensive, ready to fight a verbal war against me if need be.

"You'll have to excuse me, but the last time I was around a portal was with Raine. In order for her to open the passage, she had to say an incantation. I thought that was standard for conjuring the magical gateways via witches and wizards, that's all. Apologies if I misspoke."

Dawning seemed to cross his face, and instead of the defensive stance he portrayed a few moments ago, his body relaxed, and a smirk spread across his face.

"I can see where it might be confusing. The portal that Raine opened was the one her mother created. And because her mother used an incantation spoken out loud, it had to be done the same way."

His hand waved around in the air as he spoke and stepped further away from the passage, "Alas, I think that is why your people's ability to shadow-jump from AshFiera to Earth was so readily accessible due to the verbal usage. In order to avoid such conundrums this go-around and, of course, after consulting with our coven, they thought it wise to do a non-verbal incantation and instead use the added powers from the falls themselves to fuel the opening of a new one."

It made sense. I hadn't a clue as to anything dealing with the magic of witches and wizards. But, in Theo's explanation, it clicked, and I found myself in awe of those who could think of those possibilities.

When I approached Theo, he flinched slightly—holding my hand out to him. His hesitation was warranted, but I needed him to understand that I was incredibly grateful for his help in getting me back with my Enayah.

"Thank you for the help, Theo. I appreciate it more than you know."

He nodded his head and finally took hold of my

outstretched hand briefly before letting go. It was the only thing left that needed to be said as I made my way toward the portal.

As I stood in front of the dark abyss, my mind reeled, and my heart thumped erratically. The excitement built. I would have my beautiful, fiery mate wrapped safely in my arms once again.

I didn't look back or wait to see if Cassius followed. I ran with a maniacal smile plastered on my face as I entered the inky darkness and let it swallow me whole.

Cassius and I entered his home shortly after arriving back in AshFiera. The portal had taken us, ironically, to a waterfall that wasn't far from his house, and we made it there without incident.

No one knew we were back, and we thanked the Goddess because the last thing we needed was to scuffle with any males we might have encountered who were helping Lazarus.

"Hey, you want a drink before we head out to find Raine?" Cassius asked, rounding the corner from the entrance into what I assumed was his kitchen.

Shattering and a curse came from the next room. When I entered, Cassius was cleaning up a broken glass with some amber liquid that was spread on his counter. He looked up, grinned, and shook his head.

"Sorry, Kal. Going through that portal was quite different from shadow-jumping, and I guess my motor skills were still a little jittery."

"No worries, friend. Just wanted to make sure everything was alright."

"Ya, all good. Hey, can you go into that cabinet next to you and grab a flask? I don't want to shatter any more of my glassware. Pandora doesn't want anything from the old home, and I don't want her to have to worry about replacing stuff when she gets here." He had a faraway smile as he finished cleaning up the mess he made.

"So, when all is said and done, you're going to convince Pandora to come back to AshFiera with you?"

"That's the plan, although if she told me she never wanted to leave Earth, I would give it all up just to be with her and never leave her side."

My friend was indeed a goner for the female. He would undoubtedly follow Raine's mother to the end of time, and I was happy for him. He deserved to have joy, and so did Pandora.

Turning, I reached into the cabinet to remove the black metal flask, but as I did so, a piece of paper fell to the floor at my feet.

Bending over, I picked the small paper up and turned back to Cassius. I handed him the flask and the piece of paper as well. "This fell out while I pulled the flask from its spot. Apologies if that was supposed to remain hidden."

He looked it over, and his eyes widened before he looked back up at me and said, "Kal." He paused, and it could have been only briefly, but my nerves were on fire, and anything little thing would set me off.

"Well, what is it?" I asked impatiently.

"Raine's no longer with her father."

Worry and anger started to swirl from deep within my chest. "What do you mean she's no longer with her father? Is my mate okay?"

He nodded, looking back down at the small piece of paper, "Yes, Gezr says she escaped from the mansion, and he has her and her Ashix, Beauty, hidden."

I didn't wait for Cassius to continue as I bounded out the

doors, looking around. I had no idea where Gezr holed up, but I would scour the world looking for him. He was the one who usually found me when we interacted, so it was anyone's guess as to exactly where he was.

Cassius came running out after me, gripping my shoulder before I could start panic shadow-jumping all over.

"Slow down, Kal. I know where he stays, and I can take you there. But you need to calm down. She's safe. That's all that matters at the moment. Before we go, we need to get ourselves ready for a fight." His gaze was concerned as he spoke.

"Why? Did something happen after she escaped?"

"Gezr's note is encrypted, so only I can read it, but he mentioned that Raine's father had already visited him shortly after she left. Lazarus is scouring for Raine and Beauty near waterfalls. He knows what they mean to your mate and her beast. We need to be prepared in case he comes back for another visit."

His reasoning was solid. My head was spinning, and I couldn't think straight. I was glad that I had Cassius by my side. He would be the logic I needed to pace myself so I didn't make any mistakes where it pertained to Raine. I could get myself out of most messes, but this was bigger than anything I had to deal with because it wasn't just me this time. It was both my little star and her Ashix she was so fond of that I had to think about.

Cassius knew it was pointless to ask for permission, so the next thing I knew, he was shadow-jumping me to an unknown building.

As he approached the doors, I scanned my surroundings—a habit I had picked up over the years as a Shadow Assassin—and found that there were just the two of us surrounded by a lush forest with no signs of footpaths in or out.

This told me that either Cassius used this building rarely or that it was his hidden safe house, and he only used shadow-jumping to get in and out.

Cassius swung the door wide open and nodded his head to let me know I was welcome to enter.

Once inside, he closed the door tightly, blanketing the room in darkness until a click and a soft golden light from a stone shone into the pitch-black room. Ever so slightly, the stone brightened enough to show the contents Cassius held here.

Rows upon rows of weaponry lined from wall to wall; each table was organized by the type and size of a specific piece of hardware. Everything that was in me was drawn to the bows and daggers. While the daggers were laid out perfectly spaced, the bows were hung next to them on a weapons rack.

Footsteps sounded from across the room, and when I looked up, I witnessed Cassius looking over his arsenal approvingly with a wide grin plastered to his excited expression.

He looked up and grinned even wider, if that was at all possible. "Choose whatever you like and as much as you like. Make sure to pick a few things out for Raine in case Gezr hasn't gotten around to grabbing anything for her."

"I'm assuming this isn't just your stash?"

Cassius hummed, "No, we share this with the other Shadow Assassins who are in line with taking out Lazarus and those who are, unfortunately, blindly following him."

"Cassius."

"Hmm."

"Thank you for helping me. And helping Raine."

He looked at me with shock, like I said something out of pocket.

"Of course, you are my comrade, and Raine is like a daughter to me. She didn't have the best start of an upbringing, with her father being Lazarus. But, when we imprisoned him, I stepped up to be a better father to her than her own had been. I like to think I had a hand in how she turned out today." He smiled wistfully. And a stray tear fell as he turned his back to me.

Growing up, Cassius was the pinnacle of Raine's upbringing. She became a fantastic female with a heart of gold. My Enayah was kind, caring, and fearless. Her choice to sacrifice herself to save those she loved didn't pass my notice.

She very well could have inherited that from her mother, but I felt a lot was contributed by Cassius staying consistent in her life and helping her channel the rage.

"Alright, I'm ready whenever you are," Cassius said.

Nodding, I quickly grabbed two bows, a plethora of arrows, and a handful of daggers. I made sure that a few of those daggers were smaller to accommodate Raine's hands. I had all the confidence of AshFiera and Earth that she would wield these beautifully.

"Now I'm ready."

Cassius strolled over to me from across the room and put his hand on my shoulder, "Perfect, let's go see that mate of yours."

We dissolved into the familiar darkness that engulfed us while shadow-jumping, and mere nano-seconds later, we were facing another home. Only this one was a large cabin with a wrap-around porch nearly the same as the one I had back on Earth.

A swing squeaked softly as my friend, Gezr, sat there rocking back and forth. He jumped up into a fighting stance. But, when he saw it was Cassius and I, he relaxed with a broad beaming smile.

"Cassius! Kalpheus! Finally, it's so good to see you males in the flesh." Gezr bounded down the stairs and embraced Cassius in a short hug before moving on to me. His squeeze was brief but welcomed.

It felt good to be back and in the presence of fellow males that I trusted.

"Where's my mate?" It was the only thing I had running through my mind. My body, heart, and soul were too impatient for small chit-chat when there was someone more significant I was itching to see.

"Hello to you too, old friend," Gezr laughed, shaking his head. "She's in the cave below, but–"

I didn't allow him to finish, and I was already jumping to the edge of the waterfalls. Looking over the ledge to get an idea of the layout, my ears perked up. Soft feminine grunts sounded from below, along with a hiss, before my mate's frustrated scream echoed outward.

Anger, rage, and fury boiled out, and then trickling fear gripped my heart within seconds. There was no question about it. My mate was down below fighting someone while Gezr was up here hanging out without a care in the world.

Did the male know what was happening? Was he betraying us to join forces with Lazarus?

There was no time to question him; I needed to get to Raine fast. Whoever was below with my female would regret the day he thought to lay his hands on my precious mate.

So, with a speed I couldn't comprehend, I shadow-jumped without a second's thought of the further danger that could be lurking below.

And what I saw next was the tipping point of my insanity. Standing in front of me was my mate, with a male's arm wrapped around her throat.

The male that held my beautiful star was Zynas.

Fury, as I had never felt before, raged out into the form of a roar that left my throat raw.

Both Raine and Zynas looked up, and while my mate's eyes

140

lit like a thousand shining stars, the male blanched, letting go of her neck immediately.

"Kal!" Raine's high, feminine voice screamed with excitement as she began to run toward me, but my eyes focused back on the male.

She stopped dead in her tracks when she saw I hadn't given her a warm greeting and was glaring at the male who stood across the cave. Oh, how I wished I could give her all of my attention at that moment, but all that was running through my mind was that this bastard had just been fighting my female. Although my brain was confused at that exact moment, it didn't catch up that he willingly let her run to me.

Because my brain didn't fully process the fact that she was further away from the male, I shadow-jumped and struck.

All I could focus on was the male in front of me and eliminating the threat to Raine.

I was in front of him in a flash and got a few good hits in before I could no longer move. My body was frozen, and I was further away from the male I had just been punching.

"STOP!" Raine was between Zynas and me, her hands spread and the barely visible purple hues extending out from her fingers, wrapping around not only my body but his as well.

It was good to see that my mate still had her powers, but the question remained: Why didn't she use them on Zynas just now?

And finally, what exactly in Goddess's name was going on?

Chapter Fifteen

Raine

Although a few days had passed since Zy's arrival, he left me alone most of the time. He still insisted that I continue to practice my combat skills and that he be the one to help me hone them.

Whatever the hell that meant.

Didn't he realize who taught me almost everything I knew? My father, of course, he may be a bastard whom I wanted gone because the Goddess knew if he wasn't taken out first, I feared he would take me out himself. His heart turned black, and there was no true love, only manipulation and control. But he truly gave me so many life lessons and skills that I would take advantage of now in my adult years.

So, without fail, every day for at least an hour, Zy was determined to train. We usually ended up in the large cavern at the bottom of the falls. There was a nice flat spot that allowed plenty of movement. I think he just wanted to get me alone and away from Gezr's assessing eyes.

When we were alone, his touches lingered, and his uncovered eye shone brightly with lust when he thought I wasn't looking. But I did. I looked. He was mesmerizing and knew my weaknesses even before I did. It was as if he was in tune with my body. It was a heady feeling that lent me strength where I least expected it.

Yesterday, Zy had me pinned beneath him yet again, and previously, I had conceded, only this time, I drew enough strength to buck him clear off me. The look on his face was priceless, and if I had my phone that Aunt Sam had given me on Earth, I would have snapped a picture to look at later on.

"Pay attention, little storm. You are leaving your left side vulnerable to any Shadow Assassin that could easily bury a dagger into your waist." Realization dawned on me as I blinked over my shoulder at Zy, who was close behind me.

His own body was rubbing ever so slightly against my backside. I had to close my eyes and breathe deeply to refocus myself on the task at hand. While daydreaming about the handsome jerk, he snuck up behind me. I should have known better.

"Where's your head at today, Raine?"

That was the big question, wasn't it? Where the hell my head was, well, of course, it was on him.

Even though Zy spent the last few days harping on me and being a downright hardass, I had to admit it felt good to be challenged. And he wasn't too hard on the eyes, either.

The air was electrified whenever we were alone, and our bodies collided. Mine responded and zinged with heat down in my core. If only it were easy to let go and embrace those feelings.

But I had to think of Kal and how much it might hurt him to know I was lusting after another male. Never in my life did I think I would be in this predicament. After years of being alone, no thanks to Zy, I was suddenly at a crossroads where my heart wanted not one but two males.

"Get out of your head, female," Zy growled in my ear.

"Fuck. You." I grated out as his hands slid sensually around my waist, fingers spreading across my belly as he pulled my body into his.

This was the part I despised the most because no matter how much I told myself to resist his touch, my body folded and sank into his involuntarily.

"Mmm, I do love when you give in and let your body do the talking." His whispers were like the lightest breeze brushing past the tiny hairs on my neck. Did he know what I had been thinking at that moment?

"In your dreams, Patches," I uttered breathlessly. He knew what he did to me, but I was determined to keep that little secret to myself for a while longer.

"What did I tell you, little storm? I don't like it when you call me that."

"You may not like it, *Patches*, but you do wear an eye patch, now don't you?"

"That's very true. However, I don't care for the nickname you gave me when you thought I was being an asshole." Zy's fingers flexed ever so slightly as his other hand wrapped around my arm.

"Thought? Ha, real funny, Zy. You were definitely being an asshole with all your brooding and growling outside of the shop. Where mind you, I accidentally ran into you because you were exiting it like a bat out of hell." Laughter quickly slipped through, and I realized I didn't mind it one bit—this version of Zy. I honestly enjoyed it, and it was growing on me.

"Apologies, my precious female. I was in a rush to make sure that your mother didn't see me. She would have immediately recognized me and knew something was going on. Although, she already had her suspicions long before she almost spotted me."

My cheeks heated as Zy continued to flex and loosened his fingers against me. I needed out of this and stat.

I found my opening when the hand that had been gripping my arm trailed up my shoulder and down the center of my back.

Flinging myself to the side, I tripped on a rock in the process and ended up doing a not-so-graceful somersault, landing hard on my knees. A hiss left my throat as the burning began. *Great, I scraped my knees.*

"You alright, little storm?" Zy's face contorted into concern as he watched me slowly rise from where I had been kneeling.

"Ya," I said, seething through my clenched jaw, "Just. Fucking. Fine."

"Use that." *What?* What in the world was he talking about?

"Use that anger and channel it through your fists. Now–" Zy positioned himself into a fighting stance. "I want you to advance on me and show me what you can do with that rage through the actions of your fists."

No problem, you don't have to ask me twice.

With a vicious smile spreading, I ran toward Zy, ducking out of his reach so I could get behind him. Only that's not how it went down as his arm wrapped around my throat. He pulled my back into his body.

A frustrated scream left my throat as I threw an elbow into his stomach. He slightly hunched over but didn't let up.

A roar echoed from across where Zy and I were training, and when we both looked up, Zy's body froze. While mine was itching to escape his hold even more now, and with enough struggling, he let me go.

"Kal!" My bright voice screamed as I ran towards my mate. I couldn't believe my eyes. He was here, in the flesh, and not just my body longing for him!

As I approached, my steps faltered as I took in the fury, lighting the eyes that were burning a hole in Zy.

And just when I was about to close that final distance, Kal disappeared, shadow-jumping to Zy and attacking him.

Shit, he walked in on our training and probably thought Zy was actually hurting me. I needed to stop them before they seriously injured each other.

Both of them were throwing punches, and although it looked as if Zy was making defensive moves instead of actually hitting Kal, he was still not trying to stop the fight from continuing.

The tingling began in the tips of my fingers. A grin covered my face at the familiar sensation, and I marched over to the two males with a purpose in mind. I would force them to stop this ridiculous fighting, and I would do so quickly. The power was coursing through my fingers readily, waiting to be free and wreck anything in its path of what I so chose.

Kal and Zy didn't notice how close I had gotten to them, so with a flick of my wrist, I let the power go. It wrapped around both males slowly at first, picking up speed as I willed it to work faster.

When I knew I had a grip on them and no one would get hurt, my magic separated them quickly.

"STOP!"

The only sound was the lingering echo of the word. Both males had frozen in their motions and looked at me in shock. Was there a little bit of awe on Zy's face?

"Now that I have your attention, do you two promise to behave if I let you go so we can talk like adults instead of children throwing hands?"

Silent nods.

"Good, because I don't think I can hang onto either of you for much longer." It was a good thing, too, because my powers faltered and snuffed out altogether, leaving me breathless.

Luckily, Kal was closest to me, catching my body as I

wobbled on my feet. "Thank you," I said, enjoying his hands finally touching me.

His hand gripped the side of my face as he stared into my eyes, "My Enayah, even if moments ago I didn't seem happy to see you. I want you to know today truly is a gift from the Goddess."

Then, his lips were on mine, and the whole world fell away. Nothing else mattered but this moment, being back in Kal's arms, his lips gracing mine. Those hands, oh how I missed them, with one gripping my face while the other dug his fingers into my waist. The sensations were exquisite, and I couldn't wait to rip his clothes off.

A throat cleared behind us. Zy. I had forgotten he was still in the cave.

Kal pulled back and glanced over at the male, who was interrupting our embrace. Kal glared, and a giggle escaped my throat at the seriousness he suddenly had across his—huh, shaved face.

My fingers stroked along his jaw to garner his attention. "I love this."

"You do?" He asked, bringing his focus back to me.

"Yes, however, don't get me wrong, I do love you with your stubble as well."

He grunted, "Would you prefer I grew it back?"

I shrugged. To me, it didn't matter. As long as he was happy and we were together.

"The only thing that matters is that you are back with me. I missed you."

He pulled me closer to his body, trying to melt us together as much as possible, "I have missed you as well, little star."

My face heated, and a snicker escaped. Being away from Kal for months hadn't changed anything between us. In fact, I felt more in tune with him than I had before. It was like pure oxygen shooting into my lungs, letting me breathe better than I have in months.

"So, now that you guys have been reunited, can we get on with our lesson, Raine?" Zy, the ever-present pesky fly buzzing around, piped up.

Rolling my eyes, I turned in Kal's arms to face Zy, who was now closer.

Kal then leaned over to look around me, "Is that what the two of you were doing? It looked to me like you were choking her when I jumped down here."

"Our female has her strengths, no doubt, but currently, she is defenseless until those bracelets are removed. They mute the strength of her Shadow Assassin background along with the powers from her witch lineage as well."

"Our female?" Kal asked as he examined the bangles that were still, unfortunately, attached to me—an ever-present, magic and soul-sucking prison.

Zy crossed his arms over each other, and his stance turned warrior, ready for anything to go down. "Yes, our female. While she may have already mated with you, she is and has been betrothed to me for years."

"Aw, yes, that's right. The betrothal she didn't ask for from your father or hers."

"That's true, but I don't think this is entirely one-sided though. Is it Raine?" Zy and his big mouth. He just couldn't let anything slide. The infuriating male had been determined, and when Kal was back, he decided I wouldn't and shouldn't hide my feelings for him. He knew what he did to me and somehow knew the feelings I had developed over the past few short weeks.

I cleared my throat. It was now or never, and I had to be true to Kal. So, I turned back in his arms to face him and face whatever hell he wanted to give me.

"Kal, you know that I love you with everything. Our souls are bound in ways I can't understand. But my soul is also beginning to bind with Zy's, or it has been binding with his since we were kids. I'm not sure, and I can't explain it. There is just this immense pull that I have for you both." I closed my eyes for this next part. I didn't want to see the hatred and disgust when I admitted what had transpired between Zy and me. "And while we have been apart, Zy and I kissed a few times, and I didn't necessarily pull away until you popped into my mind, but I yearned for his touch again and again so many times."

There I said it, and all the guilt I had been feeling build was no longer so heavy.

"Raine, look at me." Kal's voice was soft and understanding. Slowly, I peeled my eyes open to look at him, and what I saw wasn't disgust or hatred but love and kindness. "Does your heart truly lead you that way?"

All I could do was nod, the emotions clogging my throat, and a lump formed in the middle.

"Then who am I to stand in the way of my mate's happiness?"

Wait, what?

"So, is it safe to say you are not angry at me?"

"No, my love. You are incredible and deserve to be protected and cherished. Having another partner to help look after you doesn't hurt. Plus, he's a good fighter, even with missing one eye." Kal chuckled.

The tension that had seemingly built in my body was released, and I molded it into Kal's arms. Another body shadowed behind us, and Zy was at my back.

He and Kal exchanged looks, and Zy pulled my body into him, separating us slightly. But Kal was quick to squash that gap as if his body demanded to be attached to mine.

"I told you we would figure this out, little storm. I had a

good feeling once Kal was back, things would right themselves, and you could see there was nothing wrong with how you felt." Zy whispered against my neck, scattering goosebumps along my body.

Oh, thank Goddess, because it was tiring to dodge my feelings and Zy's advances constantly. However, since we left the mansion, he had been oddly less handsy. Minus today, of course, something had been brewing between us, and I think it was because the universe was telling us things would be okay and Kal would be back. Something along those lines, I suppose.

I wouldn't question it any longer. And, so, I let myself enjoy the embrace from both males with me sandwiched between them. But it didn't last long.

With one last kiss to the side of my neck, Zy pulled back, and I turned around to face him. He was stepping away with a dazed and happy expression.

"Where are you going?" I asked, confused. Wasn't this what Zy had been working towards? Getting me to not feel guilty for my feelings? And now he was stopping.

"I'm just going up top, my beautiful hurricane. You and Kal have some making up to do, and I think that should be best done with only the two of you. We have plenty of time to explore things further between the three of us. But, this—this you both need." He reached his hand forward and pinched my chin with two fingers, directing my gaze to his. "Don't worry, I'm not going anywhere else."

And then he shadow-jumped, leaving Kal and me alone.

Kal's hands grazed along my arms, and his chest was at my back. His face angled down, pressing his nose into my hair and taking a deep breath.

"Goddess, you smell divine. Want to go for a swim?"

"Is that what you want to do now that you have me alone?"

"Do you trust me?" Kal held out his hand, waiting for me to take it and express that I did trust him.

So, I took it and looked deep into those honey-speckled eyes I had been missing, "Of course I do, my mate."

"Mmm," He hummed, "I do love to hear you call me your mate. Come on, let's strip our clothes and enter the water."

The mischievous glint in his eyes shone brightly, leaving me breathless and needy as I knew now what he was planning to do and where.

Chapter Sixteen

Raine

Kal's grip around my hand tightened as he led me to the edge of the lake, perfectly nestled underground and out of view from prying eyes above.

My stomach flipped as Kal turned back to face me. A smile spread across his face as he looked deep into my soul. Being back with Kal felt like I was home, but something still felt missing in the back of my mind.

Instead of diving further into my feelings, I stripped from my clothes and underwear.

I was completely naked, and while I watched Kal dispose of his clothes next, a shiver ran down the entirety of my body, leaving goosebumps behind.

"Cold, Enayah?" Kal asked softly.

"No," I whispered back.

Kal finished undressing, and he stepped back into my space, taking me into his arms. I sank into his embrace, soaking in his warmth and touch. I had missed this so much these last few months. It had felt like an eternity without Kal by my side.

He leaned back slightly and took in my face. "I have missed you, my beautiful star. I nearly drove myself mad thinking about what was going on while you were here."

"I'm okay, Kal. It wasn't anything I couldn't handle. Plus, I had Zy there to help me." I let a small smile slip. It was hard to gauge what was going through Kal's mind with the perspective that I had feelings for Zy as well. He had told me it was okay to feel the depths of my attraction toward the male whom I had spent the last few months with, but my eyes turned downward, and the guilt was still at the surface.

"Hey, look at me, Raine." Kal's voice was soft yet commanding. "It's okay to love more than one person. I'm glad you had Zynas there to help you. One less thing I have to do on my own. Now we can move forward together."

"So if we are going to move forward together, why didn't you insist on Zy staying, then?" I asked, smirking.

"Can you blame a male for wanting to get his female alone? While I have no issues with Zy, I am thankful for his retreat. He knew I needed you without his presence. It makes me like him just tiny a bit."

His smirk widened as his arms tightened around my body, lifting me into the air.

Wrapping my thighs around his waist, Kal turned and walked us into the water, deep enough that the surface reached our chests.

Playing with his hair, I gripped a handful while placing my lips on his. The kiss started soft and sweet with tender touches, but Kal soon took over.

His hands were demanding. While one gripped my ass cheek, the other trailed fingers up my back leaving electricity coursing through my veins anywhere he touched. They found their way into my hair, grasping the strands lightly, sending a slight pinch of pain that turned my core into a molten puddle.

Even though we were in the water, I knew I was wet and ready for him. It didn't take much of his touching, and I wanted more. So, I pushed my tongue into his mouth, which he greedily accepted and took what I had been missing these last few months.

A moan escaped my lips, which fueled Kal to abandon gripping my hair, trailing his fingers down my back, over my hip, and making their way between our bodies.

When his finger touched my clit, I tore my mouth from his and tilted my head back, gasping for air. His finger began circling the bud that was aching for touch. The electricity that had trailed down my back moments ago moved to where his finger currently lay.

Even though his touch was gentle, the sensations were anything but, and they slammed into me like a tidal wave. I had been so deprived of touch that Kal's circling burst through me, leaving me quickly rising to my release.

"Yes, Kal!"

"Such a good girl taking what you needed. Don't think that's the only one you get. The next one will be with your cunt soaking my cock." He panted, "Goddess, you shine so bright when you shatter for me."

He removed his finger from my body but only to reach further between us to his hard cock. Gripping the base, he aimed instinctively for my entrance. The water made it hard to see anything, but I felt the moment he was there as he sunk into me slowly.

The breath hissed between his teeth when I was fully seated, and before he began to move, his grip tightened on my hips.

"I want you to look at me when I take you, my Enayah. I want to see those beautiful eyes when I bring you to ecstasy again." The words sounded like they were an effort to push out in the midst of our entanglement as so many sensations gathered between us.

His emotions were clouded over my own, but eventually, they mingled perfectly together when Kal began to move in and out of me.

It was an effort to keep my eyes on him when all I wanted to do was close them and sink into the rhythm of our pleasure. But I kept them open, and my gaze bore into Kal's. His love and devotion poured into every slam of our bodies meeting.

Kal's breathing picked up along with his pace, and he gently laid his forehead against mine, but his pounding became jerky and uneven. I knew he was close as I was. His moans mingled with mine, and our lips crashed together briefly before I ripped away to scream his name, "Kal!" I was sent flying into an oblivion of perfection as my release pounded through my core to the motions of his hips.

My mate wasn't far behind as he reached his release, moaning my name over and over as his hot cum filled my pussy, leaving me feeling even fuller than before.

"You are my heart, my Enayah. I never want to be separated again. Promise me we'll always fight to stay together no matter the consequences." Kal's words both filled me with joy but also gutted me because I wouldn't promise to stay together, damned the consequences. Because those repercussions could potentially lead to death, and I would forever protect and save him from that fate for as long as I walked this world. Even if it meant being separated again, I would do it.

"I will always strive for us to stay together, but I wouldn't change what I had to do months ago, and I would do it all over again if I had to. I couldn't bear living in this life without knowing I would one day see you again. You can't fault me for saving your life."

Kal wiped the tear that had escaped and rolled down my

cheek and gently pulled himself out of me before responding, "Don't worry my sweet star, we won't be put in that position again. We have Zy to throw at them." His chuckle echoed in the cave, and I couldn't help the smile that escaped.

"We are not throwing Zy at anyone. Behave, my mate."

"Mmm, say that again." He demanded.

"What that you need to behave?" I asked, knowing full well that's not what he wanted.

"No, my sweet star, the very last part." He said, staring at my lips, waiting for those last few words to be uttered while his touch roamed, igniting the embers of a fire beneath my skin.

"My. Mate."

A squeal left my throat and echoed around the cave as Kal twirled me around in the water. Spreading kisses along the column of my neck and shoulder.

Thank the Goddess, we were already naked because those kisses led to Kal retaking me, fast and hard. Our pleasure rippled out through the cavern. We didn't care if anyone heard from above. All we cared about was being consumed by each other.

A while later, Kal and I emerged from below and found Zy sitting on the front porch, staring out into the forest.

Zy's attention turned toward us, and he grinned. Oh, and did that smirk do something profound inside. I just had several mind-blowing orgasms moments ago, but my body was roaring to go again. This time, it wanted Zy. But we had things to discuss—unpleasant things such as what to do with my father and how to do it.

"Took you two long enough." Zy chuckled deeply.

"Was someone getting impatient?" I asked, raising an eyebrow at the appealing male in front of us. There wasn't a hint of jealousy from him, but I was still wary of the new situation we were granted. Would it stay that way, or would someone inevitably make me choose?

This also needed to be discussed because I don't think my heart could take it if I had to choose between the two males. They both clearly wiggled their way into my heart and soul. I would do anything to keep the beginning of our happiness from falling apart.

Zy's glinting eyes roved over my body in appreciation. Like he was a starved male staring at a big juicy steak and potato dinner, his perusal made my cheeks heat, and I had to look away.

"I may have been slightly impatient. After all, those sounds you were making down below left so much to my imagination. I hope soon that I'm allowed to have a front-row seat to those delicious moans." My eyes snapped back to Zy as he slowly curled the side of his lip up seductively. Showing off his fangs. When he saw where I was looking, he licked the tip with his tongue.

An involuntary moan left my throat, and his smile widened.

Kal leaned into my side, bringing his face to my neck. "Mmm, keep that up, Zy. Our mate smells amazing when you talk to her like that."

"What?" I squeaked. "Kal, you can't just go around and smell my neck. And then encourage Zy to talk to me like that again."

My face pounded with embarrassment while my body began to heat, leaving my core to pulse. Goddess, these males were dangerous for my sanity. If they continued, I was afraid I would jump one or both of them. We had things to do, but that wasn't one of them.

Yet.

With my face still beating red, I looked around for Gezr to make sure he wasn't in earshot. I didn't see him anywhere. If he had been around, it would have been too late, and he would have heard the males talking dirty to me, leaving me more embarrassed than before.

Then, my eyes lingered around the skies, looking for Beauty. It was eerily quiet, and she wasn't flying around. I couldn't feel her either.

The fire opal around my neck started to pound, but I ignored it. I was back to looking in the skies for Beauty. She was always seen flying around, especially with the male Ashix, who was always stuck to her side like glue. But then the necklace started to pound harder.

Panic settled in my bones when I realized I hadn't seen Beauty all day.

"Zy, have you seen Beauty at all?"

He shook his head, "No, I haven't seen her since yesterday. Everything okay, little storm?"

"I don't know yet." And I didn't. I was more on edge these last few days with the lingering threat from my father and his loyal Shadow Assassins scouring AshFiera for Beauty and me.

"Kal, can you take me back down to the caves? I want to see if she's maybe hiding out down there." He turned to me and nodded his head.

"Ya, of course, Raine. We can go check it out. But, we were just down there, and I didn't hear any noise or see her." Kal's face was a mirror of my worry. He knew how much the Ashix meant to me, and if I lost her, I would lose a piece of myself.

He tightened his hold on my body and shadow-jumped us below the falls. Zy was right behind, showing up a moment later from his jump. At this moment, I was thankful I had both of them by my side.

My eyes traveled the entirety of the cave, but I knew I

wouldn't find her out in the open. Kal and I were just down here after all.

"BEAUTY!" Her name ricocheted around us, and once all was quiet, the slight chuff of her breath sounded from the entry of the enclave, which had been magically altered to protect those who needed it.

I approached the entrance and glanced in. It was empty to the naked eye. The fire opal that dangled down my chest began pounding harder, and I gripped it in my fist as I walked through.

It had been empty before, but now I was watching Beauty curled up in a newly formed nest. My body moved forward on its own, and when I was close enough, her head tilted up, her eyes lazily taking me in.

Through our bond, her love and contentment shone brightly. Her feelings were more assertive and radiated more loudly than before, leaving me breathless.

I closed the rest of the distance and knelt next to her nest. My desire to touch her grew. She seemed okay, but something was different about her, and it left me with questions that I knew she couldn't answer.

"You scared me, girl. You have been quiet today and not flying around like usual. Where's that naughty male Kovidar at?" Love burst through my veins, leaving my body shivering. "Calm, Beauty, you are a beacon of feelings today." She perked up and nudged her head into my body. A giggle left my throat at her affection. She sure was in a good mood.

"Well, I'm glad you are safe. Make sure it stays that way, my beautiful girl." Leaning my head in, I placed it softly on hers.

"My mate, you still in there?" Kal's voice interrupted our connection.

"Ya, still here. I will be out in a moment."

Turning back to Beauty, I hugged her around the neck

before standing. "I love you, Beauty. I will come check on you later."

As I reached the entrance to this portion of the cave, Kal stood with his arms crossed, glaring at me. Although I was pretty sure he still couldn't see me, when I exited enough for the magic to be left behind, his glare softened, and his eyes brightened as he took me in.

"Everything okay, my Enayah?" Kal's stance relaxed, and he waited for me to approach, so I willed my body to move itself right in front of him.

"All good. Beauty's inside making herself comfortable. She built a nest past the magical borders. I'm assuming she knows it's safer to sleep down here than the stables." I wrapped my arms around Kal, hugging his body close to mine. There was still an inkling of worry regarding Beauty's behavior, but I would brush it off for now. She was safe, and that's what mattered.

"I couldn't agree with her more. Safer for her, of course, not you, my mate. You stick to my side or Zy's." Speaking of Zy, he was walking over to us from across the lake.

"What were you doing way over there?" I asked. He looked bulkier and more armed than before.

"Just grabbing a few weapons I stashed down here earlier. Are you ready to go back up top? We should grab something to eat."

"Yes, I'm starving. My stomach is on the verge of making its existence known." I laughed.

"Perfect, Kal, if you don't mind?"

"Not at all. See you up top." Kal stepped back and let go of my waist, shadow-jumping out of the cave.

That left me alone with Zy for the first time since earlier in the day. Only this time, it felt so much more different. I knew all along his feelings for me, but I had fought them. Now, I could let myself explore this connection I had with the male.

He stepped up close without touching an inch of my body, and it took all of me not to demand that his hands roam.

"May I jump with you to the top?" He had never asked before. Why would he start now?

"That's new coming from you, Zy. No demands? No taking what isn't freely given to you?"

"No, my little storm. This time, I let you take control. So what will it be? Will you let me touch you willingly, or should I get Kal back?"

My breathing increased, and I stepped into Zy's body, making contact. His breath hitched as I slid my hands up his hard abs and over his pecs, letting them roam around his neck and tangling my fingers into the hair at the nape of his neck.

It didn't take much pulling for him to obey as his head descended, our lips meeting in a slow, sensual kiss. It was blissful and heady, letting his lips caress mine without the feeling of guilt nagging at the back of my mind.

Zy groaned into my mouth. His hands found their way to my waist, and he gripped hard on the edge of pain. Our tongues tangled in an exotic dance as the heat between us became scorching. Once again, the pulsing in my center returned, and I wouldn't have minded stripping my clothes, but this time with Zy.

Before that could happen, though, Kal yelled down from above. "Come on, you two, Gezr's back, and he wants to talk with the three of us."

Zy's pained groan left me giggling. "I know he's your first mate, Raine, but I swear by the Goddess I will pummel him into the ground if he interrupts us the next time."

"Hey, I heard that dickhead." Kal's shout rained down on us. I couldn't hold it in any longer, bursting into laughter so hard my stomach began to ache, and tears dripped down my cheeks.

"Whatever. The male can keep his hide, but next time we

are alone, there will be no laughter leaving those lips. The only sound coming from you, my love, will be you screaming your mates' names over and over as we give you so much pleasure. Nothing else will matter."

My eyes widened, and the laughter died down, "You sure have a dirty mouth on you, Zy."

"Only for you, my storm."

"We should get up top. Kal and Gezr are waiting."

Zy's hand cupped my cheek as he stared deep into my eyes, "We should, but we have time for one more kiss." His lips were on mine again. Only this time, it was short and sweet. Nothing like before, when all thought left my mind while his touches consumed me.

Just as our lips parted from each other, Zy shadow-jumped us back to Gezr's home.

The two males were waiting for us on the porch. Kal gave a smug look while Gezr shook his head.

"Come on, you three. Let's go inside and wait for Cassius to return. He has something important he's bringing here," Gezr announced, walking into his home without looking back to see if we had followed.

Of course, we did because at least while I was out of the cave, I had always stayed inside Gezr's home, safe, in case my father or one of his loyal dogs stopped by. They never had, not since that first day I escaped, which was a genuine relief but also put me on edge some days.

While inside, I lounged on the couch, waiting for the tea Kal insisted on making me. I watched the two males who had my heart. They spoke lowly to each other but stopped when footsteps sounded outside.

Cassius entered Gezr's home. His eyes lit up when he saw me, and mine filled with tears. I rushed over to him, wrapping my arms around his torso and sniffling into his chest. "I missed you, you big lug."

"Missed you too, little Ashix." I didn't hate it when Cassius used the nickname my father had given me. Instead, it brought up so many memories of him helping my mother raise me, especially when I turned to anger to cope with my not-so-missing father.

He pulled away and looked down at me. "I'm sorry I wasn't here earlier. Before I came to see you, I had someone I needed to meet and bring back with me."

I pulled back, looking past Cassius' shoulder. There in the doorway stood the female I had saved from my father's wrath back in the city, "Andromeda?"

Chapter Seventeen

Raine

"Raine, it's good to see you again." Andromeda moved further into the room. As she walked toward where Zy, Kal, and I stood, her steps were graceful, like that of an ethereal goddess who could bend males to their knees with her magnetism alone.

Her eyes were intent on mine. She was there for a purpose. My body shivered, knowing that the intentions involved were that of my males and myself.

She stopped a few inches from me, holding out her hands. She gestured for me to place my palms within hers, which I did. Unsure of what else to do, I waited patiently and watched as she examined my wrists where the bangles still lay.

"Your father made sure to recruit a powerful witch in our world for these." She nodded to herself as if she was answering her statement. I didn't speak, though, because I had no idea where she was going with this.

"Nevertheless, he didn't have someone as powerful as myself in his little band of misfits. This should be a cakewalk to take off. It also looks like the power has diminished significantly already." Her eyes traveled from the bangles to my face, examining me and nodding when she found what she was looking for. "They were close to breaking, metaphorically speaking. Whomever your father had employed to do these were either careless or they purposely made it so the powers would drain slowly."

"Okay, so what do we do now?" I asked impatiently.

"Now, you let me work my magic. Afterward, we have a lot to discuss with your males." Andromeda went to work, although it didn't take much effort. Her hands clenched around both of my wrists and the magical cuffs. She twisted the jewelry one way and then the other. The metal began to heat. It was almost on the edge of too much sweltering warmth until suddenly, cool air brushed against my wrists. The heavy weight of those bangles disappeared, and everything rushed back, leaving me heaving for air.

"Holy shit." It was all I could manage as everything in my body tingled and buzzed delightfully.

Kal and Zy were behind me, gently touching my back. Their fingers' stroking lit a fire under the skin of my entire body, and my heaving turned to gasps as I tried to orient myself with the full strength of my powers and their presence, which seemed to fuel it even further.

It was like I was feeling renewed, that all was beginning to fall into place as it should.

I looked up at Andromeda, mouth slightly open in awe of this young female. "Thank you. You have no idea how incredible I feel without those weighing me down."

She laughed, "Of course, I wouldn't have been able to stay sane as long as you have without my powers. But then again, you grew up not knowing exactly what was inside you all along, didn't you?"

I nodded my agreement, understanding that I had not known who or what I was for all those years. My powers were starting to settle, but the intense wave that rippled through my body kept pulsating to my heartbeat, distracting me in wonder.

Andromeda smiled, and then her eyes cast downward onto my neck, narrowing. "Where did you get this?" She asked as she reached for the fire opal, which was still safely nestled around my neck.

Her thumb brushed over the stone, and it began to vibrate lightly, making her eyes widen.

She waited for my response, and when I didn't answer right away, she cleared her throat, leaving me scrambling to say, "Sorry. With my powers back, I'm having a hard time concentrating."

"Don't worry, that will lessen soon. Tell me, Raine, where did you find the fire opal?" She asked again.

"It was after we left your father's shop. Zy and I walked down the street to another establishment called The Serenity Crystals. It called to me while we were inside browsing." I shook my head. I hadn't said a word to Zy, but I couldn't shake the voice that had spoken to me twice. The first time was in the shop, and it was gravelly, almost distant. The second instance was just before my father showed up at Gezr's home when we stood outside of the falls.

"I was drawn to the necklace, and at the time, I didn't think anything of it, but it spoke to me." Andromeda lightly dropped the necklace back to my chest and took my hand into hers. Her eyes were intense, and she was looking deep into mine.

While she stared at me, her eyes turned pale before words left her throat, "The fire opal drew you in. It was meant for you to find. It will help balance what has been cast into a spin on our world. Don't ever take it off, and don't let your father get to it. For his hands were the ones to taint the balance, and in its wake, it has caused chaos and unrest amongst those otherwise peaceful and good."

She held tightly to my hand as her daze lessened and her pale eyes returned to a purple hue. I hadn't noticed them before, but they were beautifully unique.

"I won't take it off, ever," I vowed. The two males at my back shifted closer.

Zy's deep voice softened as he asked Andromeda, "If her father gets his hands on this, what will happen?"

Andromeda scoffed. "What do you think would happen? He would use it against Raine." She looked back at me and said, "Do you know what this necklace can do?"

I shook my head. All I knew was that I could hear a voice calling to me from within. Where that voice came from, I still didn't know.

"It lets you communicate with those you normally wouldn't. You said it called to you. What did the voice sound like the first time?"

I thought back to that first time in the shop, "It was like monotone, not quite feminine and not quite masculine."

"Okay, and what about the second time?" Kal asked this time, surprising me. The heat from his body was so close to mine that it seeped into me, giving me the strength to keep going.

"It was more feminine and bright, happy, more spirited. It gave me comfort, and I wasn't scared of whomever that voice belonged to."

Andromeda perked up, "You know whose voice that was, Raine. Think about what and who was around you at the time."

And so I did. The only two beings near me were Gezr, who certainly didn't have any kind of femininity. That left only one creature. "My Ashix, Beauty?" It came out as a question, but I knew the answer to that already.

Her eyes lit up, and excitement filled the room. I fidgeted

from one foot to the other as the emotion filling the space was so overwhelming I didn't know how to block it out. Andromeda noticed my shift and toned down, "Sorry. But—yes, I believe the feminine voice you heard was from your beast. The fire opal has begun its job of helping you communicate with her."

I frowned, "Okay, that explains a lot, but what does that have to do with my father and him getting it?"

Andromeda gripped my hand tighter, "He seeks to destroy anything that would help others. The fire opal is only called to those who wouldn't abuse its power or use it for wrongdoings."

"And he would absolutely destroy it. He knows of my bond with Beauty." I said.

She nodded, "That he does."

Panic gripped me. If he got ahold of the necklace, he would absolutely use it against Beauty and me.

If he got ahold of Beauty, for that matter, it would end me, crush my soul, and possibly kill me. Was that his end goal? If so, what kind of father would do that to his own flesh and blood?

But that answer was right in front of my face. I just didn't want to acknowledge the fact that a parent would be so cruel to their child. Yet, he showed me numerous times how brutal and manipulative he could be.

Unshed tears formed in my eyes as I thought of the little girl I used to be, pining for her father's approval.

As I stood there staring at the ground, contemplating what would and could happen, two warm bodies pushed their way onto either side.

Looking from one male to the other, my unshed tears started rolling down my cheeks. Silence had descended into the house as the emotions rolled through the room. Solemn and grim.

They each reached a hand forward to catch those tears, wiping them as if they had never appeared. Having both males beside me lessened the ache that built up in my heart and throat.

Andromeda, observing the three of us, stepped back and folded her hands together in front of her stomach. "I have something important to tell you three. And I want you to pay attention because this isn't a story spun from fairy tales. This is what the fates of the Goddess bestowed long ago."

We didn't speak, holding our breaths as we waited for the untold truths to be revealed.

"Years ago, tragedy struck a family. Not just any family, mind you, but a family that produced strong, powerful males." She turned, gliding over to the window looking out into the woods.

"There was a mother, father, and two sons. One day, while the father and eldest son were out hunting, the mother and the youngest, an infant son, were left peacefully resting until dangerous males showed up at the home. She was at the mercy of the treacherous males and begged for them to spare her infant. She pleaded with them and offered her life in exchange for his."

Tears rolled down Andromeda's face as they formed in my own eyes. I couldn't help the emotions take over as hers filled the room with sorrow.

Kal gripped my hand while Zy wrapped his arm around my waist, pulling me to his side. The room was somber, and it was starting to dawn on me where this story was going. But I had to wait for her to finish. Something was gnawing in the back of my mind, and anxious energy was beginning to form in the pit of my stomach.

Andromeda continued, "They took the life of the female and stole the young male away. Bringing him to people who would raise him but never truly love him. As the males grew older, they both became fierce Shadow Assassins, never crossing paths until one female brought them back together. Their souls entwining with hers, their tethered hearts forming into one and completing what the Goddess decreed."

She fully turned and walked back to where the three of us stood, taking each of our hands into hers. Turning Kal's palm, she placed mine in his, interlocking our fingers together and then placing Zy's over the top. Her eyes met ours, and it was then that I knew she was speaking of us.

Zy and Kal were brothers, and *I* was the female who brought them back together.

"Years ago, there was a prophecy floating around the Shadow Assassin community. It was told that the Goddess presented herself to one of the very few Seers in AshFiera. She spoke to the Seer about a male who would be a false leader—bringing chaos and disorder to the very loyal males of AshFiera. The only way for this leader to be overthrown in his growing power was if three Shadow Assassins bonded together, creating something unstoppable. The Goddess spoke of the female being the only one of her kind. Not only would she be a shadow-jumper, but she would also descend from a witch. The males would be brothers and powerful shadow-jumpers on their own."

This new revelation left me with so much to unpack. I was still reeling from the fact that Zy and Kal are brothers. Did they know?

It made sense, though, and was clear as day. Kal had spoken of his parents, who barely showed interest or love for him but were clearly in love with each other. He had told me about it all those months ago, and I had always thought it was weird that parents treated their child that way, pawning him off to others to take care of until their untimely death.

Then there was Zy and him telling me about the death of his mother and brother. But that they had never found his brother's body. It was all coming together, like missing pieces to a puzzle, making the picture whole.

Zy was the first to speak several moments later, "And you believe we are the ones the Goddess spoke of?"

"I know you are the ones she spoke of because it was my mother who the Goddess spoke to. And when I was older, she shared her visions with me, the ones with the three of you." Andromeda's hands still gripped ours together tightly. She smiled, let go, and walked toward the door. Her hand was ready to open it before she stopped.

"I have to go, but before I do. I must tell you, you three are meant to bond as one. For three bonds is better than two, and your mate is going to need your strength soon." Without another word, Andromeda was out the door and walked toward the tree-line where another male was in the shadows, waiting for her before they disappeared altogether.

"The fuck?" Kal's question was a reflection of my own. "Why do Seers have to be so damn cryptic sometimes?"

I laughed. It was true that sometimes having a Seer tell you something important was more of a headache than anything. It was best just to live and let shit happen when it was supposed to. It made flutters burst inside, thinking of what came next and what the hell we were supposed to do.

"Well, looks like that's our cue to, uh, see ourselves out." Cassius piped up, pointing his finger toward the door. "Gezr, you coming, bud?" He elbowed Gezr in the stomach, grabbed a bottle out of one of the cabinets near the door, and walked out without another glance back.

"Oh, um—ya. See you guys later. Uh—make yourselves at home. I suppose?" Gezr's face was bright red as he backed up with Cassius, heading for the opening outside. Once they were out and the door shut, I turned to Kal and Zy.

"So, do we want to talk about what Andromeda just threw at us?" I wanted to make sure my males were comfortable and understood what I had figured out before Andromeda was finished with her story.

Kal spoke up first, "I, for one, think that's a great idea. However, I'm starving, and I think we should talk about this over dinner. Don't you agree, Zy?" Kal was including his now-discovered brother in our conversation. Zy wore a frown and had since Andromeda started speaking.

"Yeah," he nodded. "I'll make dinner. Raine, why don't you and Kal get comfortable on the couch while I take care of it?" He walked away into the kitchen without another word, like he was on autopilot.

That made me worried. Zy needed me now more than ever. Kal seemed to be taking this discovery in stride and didn't seem bothered by it.

I leaned in, kissing Kal deeply, our tongues tangling, our breathing combining as one before I pulled back. "I'm going to help Zy. I know he said we should get comfortable, but I think he needs me by his side. Are you okay with that?"

Kal's smile brightened, "Of course, my Enayah. I agree. He seems out of sorts. I don't remember those days like he does, so I never knew I had a brother or that my parents who raised me weren't the people who birthed me." He shrugged, hugging me tightly, placing a light kiss on my temple before he strode into the living room.

I readied myself to face whatever I would find in the kitchen. Would Zy be stoned-faced? Would he be angry? Or would he be happy he finally knew what had happened with his brother? Who turned out to be not only alive but someone he would share a life with from now on if the prophecy is to be trusted.

Shaking my head clear, I walked toward the kitchen to the clinking and scrapping of utensils on pans and plates, toward the male who I had yet to bond with in the same way that I had united with Kal.

Chapter Eighteen

Raine

When I entered the kitchen, Zy's back was toward me. He was in front of the stove, stirring something in one of the many pans lined up on the counters.

"What the hell happened here? Did you do all of this in the few short minutes you have been in the kitchen?" My mouth gaped as I kept eyeing the counters and the island that sat in the middle.

Zy's body froze. He glanced over his shoulder briefly and went back to stirring. "I couldn't decide what to make for us, so I started one dish and then thought a different one would be better. And then ultimately decided on something easy."

I hummed, "Hmm, I see. Well, what did you decide to make for dinner?"

He kept stirring and didn't turn around or answer. I made my way to the stove and stood behind him. Placing my hands on his waist, I bent to glance around him and saw there was a smaller pan with a red sauce steaming. The bigger pot he was focusing on was boiling with water and what looked like curly noodles.

Even though the aroma of food made my stomach begin to speak of its hunger, I pressed my face into Zy's back. Breathing in his masculine fragrance that put me at ease. My hands left his waist as I let them slide up from the chiseled abs to his chest. Hugging him from behind.

He sank into my embrace but kept stirring the noodles.

"Do you want to talk to me about it without Kal?" I asked. He was so silent. It wasn't unusual, but my heart hurt for them both, especially Zy, who remembered his mother and brother all those years ago. Thinking they were both dead and gone, and then poof, suddenly, here was his brother. Alive and well.

"No, little storm. It's alright, we can talk about everything together. I don't want to leave my brother out." He said, sounding somber but at least slightly elated.

"Okay. Why don't I at least help clean up what you didn't use while you finish cooking."

He turned abruptly, grasping my body. Sinking his fingers into my hair as he laid his head atop mine.

"Thank you, Raine. You are everything to me. My heart. My soul. You seem to know just what I needed even without me speaking it."

Leaning back, I looked up at him, "But all I did was hug you. It wasn't anything special."

He shook his head, "Anything you do is special. You are my comfort, my home. And that hug was exactly what I needed to shake me out of my never-ending spiraling inner dialogues."

His riveting stare took me in before his head descended, placing his lips against mine. His kiss was tender, soft, and sweet. It was not the all-consuming thing that I desperately desired now that I had let myself freely love Zy along with Kal. But at this moment, he needed tenderness more than passion.

Sizzling spattered behind Zy, and he wrenched himself from me. "Shit!"

Boiling water flowed over the pan's edge onto the stove. Zy hissed as he moved the pan off the heat to a cold burner.

"Fuck!" He swore, shaking his hand out. I stood there watching him as he frantically shut off the burner, causing a giggle to bubble out. He turned and stared bewildered at me.

This caused me to burst into more laughter. He looked annoyed, and I raised my hands in a placating gesture.

"Oops, guess I was too good and distracted you from cooking."

"It's a welcome distraction, my little hurricane. Don't worry, dinner isn't ruined. It's actually ready. Why don't you go get Kal." He gripped my chin with his hand and tilted my face up for another kiss before moving to the sink and draining the noodles.

I hurried out of the kitchen and found Kal already up off the couch and headed my way with a vast, seductive grin.

"What?" Was all I could muster. The glint in his eyes sparkled as he stalked his way toward me.

"Nothing, my sweet female. I just love hearing your laughter. Did you make Zynas feel better?"

"I think so. Or at least I hope so. But only time will tell, especially after we talk about what Andromeda said. Dinner's ready, by the way." Kal reached for me, wrapping his arms around my back and breathing in at the crook of my neck.

"I heard. Let's eat then, shall we?"

Dinner was delicious and filling, but it was silent. No one wanted to start the conversation, and the air was thick with—

well, I couldn't quite tell if it was regular tension or something sexual. Both Kal and Zy kept giving me seductive glances as I forked piles of saucy noodles and shoved them into my mouth.

Toward the end of dinner, on my last bite, I finally couldn't handle it anymore. "Oh, for Goddess's sake, what?"

They looked at each other before Zy answered, "It's nothing, sweet storm. You just have a way of eating that is so exotic, and I think I can speak on Kal's behalf, but I am itching to strip you bare."

Kal happily nodded with a widened smile that made the skin at the corners of his eyes crinkle.

I looked at both of them like they were crazy, "I'm just eating. You two are weird if that turns you on. You both are stifling the air with your sex emotions, and it's clouding my head."

"Good, then we can just get straight to business," Zy said, wiping his mouth with a napkin and pushing his plate away.

"Uh—no. I don't think so. We need to talk about the fact that you two are brothers and how we are meant to bond as one." I said, exasperated.

"Fine, you want to talk about it? Here we go," Zy blew out a breath. "There aren't enough words to tell the both of you how grateful I am that we were brought together. While I know nothing can change the past. I don't think much needs to be said to move forward. As long as you, Raine, are comfortable with two males vying for your attention and love, we can take this one day at a time. Nothing needs to be set in stone right now."

He stood from his chair, his movements lithe as he made his way to kneel in front of me. Zy took my hand in his and pressed kisses to the palm, sending flickers of electricity up my arms and making my nipples harden under my bra.

"I know we aren't nearly close to what you and Kal have, but I want to hear from you. Are you okay with having two males love you for the rest of your life? To have *me* love you for the rest of our lives?"

A tear slipped down my cheek as I looked at the male kneeling at my feet. "Are you getting sappy on me, Zy?" I asked, wiping my tears and trying to hold it together. This was a first, seeing him completely baring himself.

He was usually full of jokes and snark. Don't get me wrong; I didn't mind that part of him, but this part—the part where he laid his feelings on the table—I could get used to and fall deeply, madly, more in love than I already was.

His sly grin said everything, even though he spoke them out loud, "Only for you, my hurricane."

Kal left his chair as well, joining Zy at my feet. He gripped my other hand, "I know that most people live a life as a couple, but I think the three of us can make a change in AshFiera. You know, just like Andromeda said." He kissed the palm he held. "Like I said before, I am okay with sharing. We were meant to be. After all, the Goddess decreed it. I harbor no jealousy when it comes to Zy. And now that I know he is my brother, it makes complete sense why I don't mind him touching you the way I do." He paused briefly before continuing, "Now, if it were any other male, I would have to rip out his throat. With Zy, it feels right to have him with us."

I blew out the breath I had been holding and nodded my head. "Okay. I mean, I was already on board before Andromeda told us about the prophecy. So I'm unsure of what the hell we are waiting for?"

The two males looked at each other and shook their heads. "Just needed to be sure, little storm," Zy said.

They both stood and held out their hands, waiting for me to finalize the decision that I knew I'd already made.

So, I took their hands, and they led me to the room that I had called mine since leaving the mansion.

One of them closed the bedroom door behind us, and I went directly to the bed. Sitting down, I stared at the two males who had taken up most of the room. They stood side by side, watching me with growing desire swirling in their eyes.

Kal was the first to move, his hands pulling my shirt over my head and quickly unclasping my bra, leaving the top half of me naked. He groaned as he marveled at my hard nipples that were desperately waiting for him to take them into his mouth.

I didn't have to wait long as he began devouring one nipple while pinching the other and then alternating as if the other one was being left out.

Zy watched from across the room, not moving, waiting to be invited. So, I crooked my finger in a come hither movement. And that's all it took for him to uproot himself. He kneeled at the edge of the bed, gripping onto my pants, and pulled them down along with my underwear. His movements were swift as both items were flung across the room at lightning speed.

His hands gripped my thighs, spreading them apart. He growled, staring at my already glistening center. I was already so wet just thinking about being with both of them that I didn't know I needed anything other than to be filled. But Zy had other plans.

"Fuck, you smell so divine." He groaned before moving into my center. His tongue began lapping at my core, circling my entrance before dipping the tip of his tongue inside, leaving me a whimpering mess.

With one male at my center and the other lapping at my breasts, the sensations took over and were so overwhelming that when Zy finally reached my clit, it was like fireworks exploding. He gave my sensitive bud a few flicks, circling his tongue before gently sucking, sending me over the edge. My release crashed like tidal waves, drowning me in so much pleasure I almost lost consciousness.

With my eyes closed, my breathing began to even out. I could hear rustling in the room. Lifting my lids, I watched as both males kept their eyes on me as they slowly slipped their clothes off—one by one.

Even though my body just had the most amazing orgasm, I felt myself stirring again as I watched skin being exposed by both of my males. And soon, they were both gloriously naked, making their way back to me.

The bed dipped as Zy lay down. "Come here, my beautiful mate." His deep voice growled as he held out his hand for me to take.

Crawling his way up the bed behind me, Kal hissed in appreciation. And when I looked back, he was staring directly at my ass, stroking his already hard cock. His eyes found mine, and he cocked an eyebrow, waiting for me to keep going. *So impatient.*

But I was close enough for Zy to grip his hands around my upper arms and pull me up the rest of the way. Situating me to straddle his waist. His hardness pressed against my entrance. He gripped the side of my face, making sure I was paying attention before he spoke, "Are you sure this is what you want? We can stop anytime if it's too much."

"No," I said, shaking my head. "I'm ready to be wholly yours and Kal's."

"We will go slow, my Enayah," Kal said huskily. The bed dipped as he climbed on, positioning himself behind me. "Zy will take your sweet cunt, and I will take you here."

His finger circled my backside, and for a moment, panic settled in. He hushed, "I will prepare you first. Do you trust me?"

Nodding, "Yes, I trust both of you."

"That's what I like to hear. Now be a good girl and ride Zy's cock while I work your backside to take me." Kal slipped from the bed, checking the drawers before returning with a container. "I brought this and placed it in here before dinner." He said, noticing my frown as I watched him open it and dip his fingers inside, coming out slick with what I assumed was some kind of oil.

I turned back to Zy, who was watching me with so much love and desire it left me breathless. Leaning forward, my lips crashed into his, a moan leaving his throat. His hands were lightly gripping my thighs but soon gripped harder to help move my body up. His cock was now better poised to enter my core. I was ready for him. I was prepared for both of them.

Slowly, Zy's thick member filled me so full. He pulsed as he bottomed out inside my aching core. Hissing as we waited for Kal behind me, "Sweet storm, you are perfect. Your cunt is gripping me so tight with your wet warmth. You feel divine."

"That's the second time you have used the word divine regarding me." I lightly laughed before a deep moan left my throat as Kal's slick finger began pushing into my ass. One at first, as he pumped the single digit in and out slowly before adding a second one and then a third.

I had trouble staying still as I began to rock to the rhythm of Kal's pumping. In front of me, Zy's forehead began beading sweat, and he seemed to be trying to concentrate on the sensations he was also feeling.

Kal's fingers left only to be replaced by his throbbing, slicked cock. "Breathe," Kal instructed as he pushed in past the barrier of my backside.

"Full, so fucking full." I panted.

I thought I was full before with Zy in my pussy and Kal's fingers in my ass, but that was nothing compared to two cocks filling me to the brim.

"Just relax, Enayah. Let go, and let us make you feel good." Kal whispered into my neck.

And so I did. I let my body relax, and when both males felt my body become pliant, they began moving in tandem. One plunging in, and the other pulling out in sync.

It was exquisite and so overwhelming all at once. My moans filled the room as each male began frantically slipping in and out of each part of me. Soon, their groans followed, and it spurred on the teetering pleasure that built, second by second, until my body exploded. Shattering me into pieces, only to be put back together as each male followed me over the edge, finding their release.

The warmth of their cum filled each part of me and left me whimpering.

Their emotions flooded within me. We were connecting on a deeper level than I could have imagined. Their love, devotion, and admiration spiraled beautifully together.

"Do you feel that?" I asked, breathing heavily and wondering if I was the only one sensing them deep inside.

"Yes." They both answered at the same time.

"Enayah." Kal breathed against my neck.

"Little storm," Zy whispered as his hands found their way onto either side of my face.

I couldn't see Kal's expression, but if it was anything like Zy's, absolute wonder and love was shining through.

Kal kissed my shoulder before slowly sliding out of my backside and laying on the bed next to Zy, who still had his now softening cock inside me.

He soon pulled out and nestled me to the side closest to Kal so I was cradled in between the two males, perfectly protected and loved. Smiling to myself, I nudged my face into the crook of Zy's arm. Kal turned to his side and lined his body with mine as he flung an arm around my waist, nuzzling his face into my neck.

Zy's low voice whispered against my hair, "Sleep, Raine.

We will bathe in the lake when you wake. Then, we will discuss the future."

"Mmm." It was all I could manage before warm darkness took hold, and I was fast asleep in the safety of both my mate's arms.

Chapter Nineteen

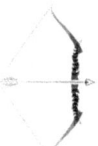

Kal

I awoke with a smile on my face, and my mate nestled into my side. At some point in the night, Raine had turned, seeking out the comfort of my body. Her leg was thrown over my hips, and I couldn't help my cock was already beginning to harden at the mere brush of her silky leg against the unruly appendage.

It honestly had a mind of its own. I didn't want to disturb her, so I ignored the throbbing and closed my eyes again, soaking in her warmth.

A throat cleared before my body could be pulled under, and I snapped my eyes open, looking over at the male on the other side of my sweet Enayah.

Zy was glaring at me with his one eye as he glanced down to the blankets, where my cock showed itself, tenting the material upward.

"What? I can't help my body wanting our mate again. She's so irresistible and alluring. I'm sure you're not immune to her charms." I pointed out.

"That may be true. However, I want to give her a break. We can't be pawing at her all hours of the day and night. She will get worn out quickly, and eventually, she may not want to touch us at all if that happens. Let's just take this at her pace and let her initiate." Zy's logic was sound, but I didn't think I would follow it. She was too tempting.

"We need to wake our mate and get washed. I'm sure that Gezr and Cassius will be coming back soon."

I waved my hand at him, "Eh, I wouldn't count on that. I snuck out of the room while you both were drooling on each other and found a note in the kitchen. Cassius cleaned up our mess and then proceeded to scold us in the note like children. He also mentioned that he and Gezr would be waiting for the three of us at The Hollow Falls Tavern."

"Alright, well, I will leave you to wake our sleeping beauty. She may have snapped at me a few times when she was at the mansion, so I don't want to be at the end of *that* after the bonding we just had." Zy said, untangling himself from the sheets, walking around, and scouring for his clothing that was scattered around the room.

"No problem," I said gleefully. Moving my hands, I roved them over Raine's body until they found her perfect ass and squeezed, smacking it lightly.

She began to rouse, oh so beautifully, and hummed, nestling further into my body.

"Beautiful Enayah, it's time to rise and shine. We must get ourselves clean and then meet Cassius and Gezr for some drinks." I squeezed her ass again and smacked it slightly rougher when her eyes remained closed.

"No–don't wanna." she slurred. "Sleepy and comfy. Don't want to move." She turned her back to me, shoving her delicious ass into my already stiffened cock.

I groaned, "If you keep that up, little star, I'm afraid we

won't get anything done the rest of the evening." Gripping her hips, I squeezed, nuzzling into her neck, "Cassius and Gezr are waiting for us at the tavern. I'm guessing that's where we are meeting a few fellow assassins. So, my beautiful mate, you need to get that tempting ass up and dressed. At least until we go wash off in the lake below."

This seemed to have the effect I was hoping for. She jumped out of bed and ran around the room in a hurry, looking for her scattered clothing. My brother did a fantastic job of tossing her clothes. *Huh, it's still weird to call him that,* I thought.

Raine was ready, and I realized I had been sitting here watching her all along without getting my clothes on.

She cocked her hip to one side and raised an eyebrow, "Kal, didn't you just chide me into getting my clothes on? Get up, lazy bones. I'm ready for a dip and to check on Beauty before we go to the tavern. Come on!" Her laughter filled the room until she walked out the door, likely to find Zynas.

Shortly after getting Raine out of bed, she grabbed a snack and then shadow-jumped to the lake below the falls.

Now that she had complete freedom of her powers, neither Zy nor I had to jump with her. I already missed the sensation of pressing her body up against mine whenever we needed to jump.

When I reached the shore, Raine was already stripped naked and swimming leisurely around, seemingly waiting for Zy and I to join her.

My eyes scanned the cave surroundings, but Zy wasn't there yet. *Perfect, a little alone time with our mate.*

"You joining, or are you just going to stare all day?" Raine's question floated across the water, startling me into motion. I stripped my clothes so fast that I could have sworn I heard a few stitches rip.

Oops, oh well.

"Coming, my mate. You don't have to ask me twice!" I said anything to get near her again, especially when she was oh so naked, unprotected from my wandering hands.

Splash!

Shadow-jumping in the air near Raine was reasonably straightforward. Getting my mate more drenched than she already was and listening to her sputter was priceless.

"Kal! What the hell!" She yelled, wiping water from her face.

My laughter echoed as I scooped her into my arms, twirling our bodies around in the lake. She glared at me as I stopped spinning.

"Not funny. What if you had landed on me?"

"Don't worry, little star, I knew where you were," I said. Trailing kisses along her neck, stopping whatever she was about to yell.

Everything around us seemed to sizzle. Every touch, every caress, every moment our skin connected was like lightning striking through the rain.

She pulled away, breathing heavily. "You're a terrible male." She said, with no bite to the words, only longing.

"Hey, you two finished?" Zy said, standing on the shore with his arms folded, glaring at us with his remaining eye.

"Zy, join us!" Raine pouted.

He shook his head, "No, sorry. You two need to hurry up. Cassius stopped by. It sounds like a few Shadow Assassins are waiting to meet you, Raine. With more on the way."

Raine's frustrated sigh reflected how I currently felt. Things were just starting to get heated. Of course, I knew we needed to leave shortly, but I was hoping to get handsy once again with my delectable little mate. I guess that will have to wait. I was a patient male. I could delay having her beneath me again a little longer.

My eyes followed Raine as she left the water, drying and dressing quickly. I followed shortly after. There was no point in staying in if no one was joining me further.

"I'm going to go check on Beauty before we go." She said, and before she moved toward the magic-laced cave, she turned to Zy and me. "I need one of you two to jump me to this tavern since I don't know where it is. So talk amongst yourselves and decide who gets to jump with me."

Eyeing Zy, I gestured to him, "You can jump with her, brother. I got to have extra time with her just now. Only fair I share our mate with you."

"Gee, thanks." He deadpanned.

As we waited for our mate to leave the magic cave, my ears picked up a one-sided conversation she was having with her beast.

"Hey Beauty, how are you doing, girl?" She paused briefly. "Goddess, I didn't think it was true, but I can hear you clearly now. And yes, my males are taking care of me." Another pause, "Well, you don't need to worry about me. I have those two doofs out there to protect me if something happens. Plus, I have my powers back, you know. I can also take care of myself if need be."

Yeah, we knew she could handle herself. We felt deep down how much power she had. When we bonded earlier, it was like the instant snap of a rubber band. She was there, in my heart and soul, singing loudly without using words, only the tug of her emotions.

"Okay, lovely girl. I have two males patiently, or maybe not so patiently, waiting for me. I will see you tomorrow morning. Love you, sweet Beauty." Raine said, finishing her check on the beast.

She left the cave and headed our way. Stopping further down the slope when she heard the beat of wings getting closer. All three of us looked up and saw the male Ashix, Kovidar, descending from above.

He swooped down and entered the magic-laced cave, instantly disappearing behind the cloaking of Gezr's deceased mother's magic.

Raine returned her gaze to us and smiled brightly. She skipped the rest of the way before standing in front of us.

"Well? Did you two decide who's going to jump with me?" She asked, batting her eyelashes.

"Of course, Enayah. Zynas is going to take you. I know where the tavern is. I will meet you both inside." I said, stepping into her and giving her a quick kiss before I jumped just outside the tavern.

When I reached for the door, it swung open, and Cassius stood there.

"What took so long? I was just about to come to retrieve the three of you." Cassius asked.

"Apologies, friend. We ended up taking a dip in the lake to get clean, and then Raine had a lovely conversation with her Ashix." I snorted at the expression across Cassius' face as his mouth gaped open.

"She actually spoke with the beast?"

"Of course, she usually does, from my understanding, but this time, she was able to hear her back. Thanks to the fire opal necklace and, of course, Andromeda freeing her from those cuffs her father put on her." Seething through my teeth at the mention of Raine's father. Whether I brought him up myself or someone else, it always left me wanting to pummel the male into the ground.

"What do they–" Cassius was interrupted by Zy jumping in with Raine.

When she spotted us near the entrance, her smile lit up. "And what are you two males talking about?" she asked.

I gave her a lazy smile, "Just telling Cassius why it took us so long." A blush crept up her neck to her cheeks as her eyes widened.

"You did, huh?" The redness in her cheeks deepened as she glanced back and forth.

"Ya, that we went for a swim, and then you decided to have a little chit-chat with your beast," I smirked, knowing full well she thought we were discussing other things. I wouldn't dream of speaking about our private doings unless it were with Zy.

Evident relief fell over her face, and her grin followed.

"Alright, who is taking me inside and dancing with me?" She asked as the band began to play an upbeat tune, muffled by the door of the tavern.

I grinned, holding out my hand for her to take. I was itching to get my hands on her again, as always, and show her who was the 'fun' mate. Zy shook his head, placing his hands in his pocket. He shrugged and walked past us inside as Cassius held the door open. We followed and watched as he went to the bar, ordering a few drinks.

Raine squeezed my hand, giggling as she dragged me over to the dance floor. There were a few couples there already, laughing and twirling around to the beat of the music.

This fueled Raine, and her desire amplified as she moved closer to me. My hand automatically went around her waist while the other took her palm into mine.

As I twirled her around, feminine laughter rang out over the band's symphony, which included the strings of a violin, the beating of the drums, and the strumming of a guitar. The fast rhythm charged our energy to the max, and when they strung into another song, Zy stepped in behind.

With my body moving in front and Zy gripping Raine's hips we closed the distance and swayed with our mate seductively sandwiched between us. Her laughter peeled out as her head leaned back against Zy's chest. A flush spread from her cheeks down her neck and chest, dipping below the hemline of her tank. Raine's happiness radiated around us in our very own bubble.

It was glorious watching her let go and enjoy herself in the midst of turmoil.

When the song started to slow down further, I nodded to Zy, silently telling him to take over and continue spreading the happiness radiating from our mate.

"Drinks are at the table with Cassius." He yelled over the music. I nodded and made my way to where our friend had been babysitting several drinks.

As I approached the table, Cassius lifted his glass in a toast to himself before downing the liquid in several gulps.

"You itching to get drunk tonight, Cass?" I asked, eyeing two glasses that were already empty next to him.

"Eh, I figured tonight I could let go. Tomorrow will be the start of possibly many days without reprieve." Cassius' eyes were already beginning to get glassy as his face turned into a dreamy state, with the latest drink already making their effects present.

I slowly sipped the amber ale, watching Zy and Raine's bodies meld together in a more sensual dance now that the band had slowed the songs down.

Their lust trickled down through our new bond, leaving me shivering at the intensity. My cock started to harden as I watched them gaze lovingly at each other as they swayed closely.

Taking another sip, I decided I would join in their sensual dance again.

Before I could reach them, Raine's shrill scream echoed over the band playing. Her voice ricocheted around the room, filling the space with her agony as sparks of purple lightning shot outward, sizzling wherever the bolts landed.

My body had frozen in place as I helplessly watched her collapse in Zy's arms. He slunk them both to the floor as he held tight to her convulsing body. Her panic had struck down through our bond, leaving me to catch my breath.

As soon as I came to my senses, I was instantly by their side. I cradled Raine's head in my hands, tilting her face gently toward mine. Once my hands were on her skin, the convulsions stopped, and her breathing evened out. Little whimpers left her throat as she nuzzled into Zy's body.

"Raine, little star? You need to open your eyes and tell us what's going on." I said, but the look on Zy's face filled with dread as his eyes found mine.

"Beauty." She whimpered. Zy immediately hauled her up off the floor, and a scowl formed as he headed to the table.

All was silent in the tavern now as onlookers watched us with trepidation, waiting for more of her powers to wildly fly around. I knew none would now that she was a little more coherent.

"You need to get Cassius and Gezr. Head immediately to Gezr's home and find out what's going on." Zy said hurriedly.

"What happened to our mate?" I asked. Confused about why she reacted in such a way without anyone touching her aside from my brother.

"She's linked with Beauty, and I think something might have happened to the beast. When we were younger, she unknowingly bonded with a deer that we were hunting, and when she was forced to shoot it by her father, she instantly felt its pain. She barely bonded with that animal, so she wasn't nearly as consumed with agony as she just was moments ago. When that all happened, there was no lightning shooting out of her. But, now her intense bond with Beauty and that happening, I'm afraid of what we will find." The shaky panic in his voice was brought out as Zy gazed down at Raine, who was now limp in his arms.

I didn't wait much longer before I called out to my two friends, who were already gathering other males in the tavern. Some of the males had already been there, with more arriving only moments ago. Relief twisted inside at the show of males who were ready to defend us.

Looking at those who stood before me, I commanded them with a vengeance on my tongue, "Let's go."

While several males shadow-jumped before me, I turned back to my brother and our mate. Stroking my fingers through her sweat-soaked hair.

I kissed her temple, whispering, "Don't worry, Enayah, we'll get to Beauty and ensure she's safe. You are my soul. We will protect you and your beast." Reaching, I squeezed Zy's shoulder before moving back and shadow-jumping to Gezr's home, where I wasn't prepared enough for what came next.

Chapter Twenty

Raine

I was being torn apart. It was all I could comprehend as I lay limp in Zy's arms on the floor of the tavern. One moment, I was slow dancing with one of my mates, and the next, I was barely able to think clearly aside from all the pain radiating through the entirety of my body.

Breathing was becoming more complicated by the second. While my heart beat wildly in my chest, I thought for mere moments: *this is it; I'm going to die.*

I wasn't in control of my body or my powers as lightning flew wildly out the tips of my fingers. The once boisterous tavern was now silent apart from distant sizzling as my lightning hit everywhere all at once.

Distantly, I worried for those around or in the path of my zinging bolts. I hoped none of them hit any innocent bystanders.

Another jolt of shooting pain squeezed around my heart, leaving me breathless and losing consciousness.

Slowly, I emerged from the depths of darkness as a pair of

hands caressed my face while another pair held me close to the warmth of a muscular body. *My mates.*

What was happening? Why was I in so much pain, and why was it still lingering?

Just then, trickling anger and fear invaded my bond with Beauty. Something was incredibly wrong, and I needed my males to get to her quickly. "Beauty," I managed to breathe out.

The sensation of being lifted followed as I was cradled in one of my mate's arms. My eyelids were so heavy I couldn't pull enough strength in myself to open them and see who was holding me. At least for now, I was still conscious, but everything around me was muffled as if I were submerged underwater.

My mates were speaking, and shuffled footsteps clattered around as several bodies gathered near us.

Fingers caressed through my drenched hair as more muffled words were spoken. Those fingers left my scalp, and lips brushed against my temple briefly.

I tried to reciprocate, but my body wasn't listening to my mind. I willed it to open my damn eyes and grasp onto whoever was leaving me. Something was incredibly wrong. I was so weak and only getting weaker as the seconds ticked by.

Darkness took hold again until the woosh of water trickled into my wakefulness. Along with shouts from several males. At the same time, intense heat followed against the entirety of my left side. *Something was on fire–did they have a campfire going?*

We were back at Gezr's. I knew that much. The flow of magic filled me, lessening the ache that was still pounding through my heart and out of my veins to the rest of my body.

My eyelids were finally light enough for me to open them. When I did, I shut them quickly. There was a large blaze, lighting the darkened sky brightly. The fire! Reopening them, I squinted against the onslaught of light, blinking enough for them to adjust.

What I saw froze my body, which was still cradled in one of my mate's arms. Gezr's home was engulfed in flames that reached toward the heavens.

Sitting up with the help of my mate, who I now realized was Zy, I looked around for Kal. He was spotted with a large bucket throwing water on the house and jumping out of sight, only to reappear with more water.

There was a lump beginning to form in my throat when I didn't spot my Ashix. Where was she?

Sensing the first signs of my panic, Zy helped me get stable on my feet as my strength started trickling back. Pain still radiated through my body. I needed to find her. I needed to get her healed.

"Where is she, Zy?" I croaked, still searching the area.

His booming voice hollered into the darkness, "Has anyone seen the beast?"

An unknown male answered, "We'll go search for her now, Zy." As time passed, my impatience wore out my sense of reality.

"Zy, please help me look for her. She's injured badly. I can still feel her, but it's getting faint. She's slipping." I pleaded, my throat clogged with emotions as I barely got the words out.

"OVER HERE! SHE'S OVER HERE!" Another male shouted it was coming from one of the edges by the falls.

Zy shadow-jumped to the male in an instant. What I saw nearly brought me to my knees as I wailed in horror.

"NO, NO, NO!" I screamed, mustering up enough strength to wretch myself from Zy's hold. I clambered over to the nearly still body.

Beauty was splayed out. Her wings bent wrong in several

places. The slow rise and fall of her chest told me she was barely alive. It didn't matter, I would save her. I had to.

My heart lurched as I felt her tug on our bond. It was so faint I barely caught it. A choked cry left my throat as I threw myself to her side. My hands hovered over her body. I didn't know where I could touch her as there was so much blood covering her once bright, pearlescent scales. The shocking red coated so much of her that it was flowing freely in several places.

Turning my head, I yelled at Zy, who was standing close but far enough to give me space. "Get me something to help stop the bleeding."

He didn't move, though. He stared at me with sorrow in his tear-filled eyes. "My mate, she's not long for this world. There are too many wounds and too much blood lost. You just need to sit with her and comfort her over to the next world. Where she will be free to fly with the Goddess."

"NO!" I shouted. "I'm not giving up on you, Beauty. There has to be something."

Raine.

A feminine voice whispered.

It's okay, female. Your male is right. Not much longer, and the Goddess will call me.

Panic rippled through my heart, "No, Beauty, you have to let me help you. Please, I can't lose you. I will lose a part of myself if you leave me. Please don't leave me! PLEASE!" I continued to plead. Hoping that with enough begging it would help heal my companion.

I will always be with you, little Storm Surge. I leave a part of myself with you. Hidden where no one else can go but you. Make sure when I am gone, you take good care of her for me.

Confusion sliced through my mind, "Take care of who

Beauty? What are you talking about? Please, I'm begging, don't leave."

Below. Below. Below.

She chanted, her words on the cusp of whispers, as I began to realize she was slipping and there was absolutely nothing I could do. I was too late. I had failed my bond and vow to protect her with everything I had.

"I'm so sorry, girl." I choked, the lump in my throat clogging all reason, making it hard to speak without a sob leaving me. "I'm so sorry I couldn't save you. I'm so sorry I wasn't here to protect you. I love you so much."

Hush, none of that. You gave me purpose when I was lonely all those years ago. It was a blessing watching you grow into the female you are today. Protecting you when I could. Now.

She paused, taking a deep breath, and for a moment, I thought this was her final breath. But she continued.

I bestow upon you my legacy. Please protect her while she can't protect herself. You. Are. My. Flame.

I watched as her eyes closed. She took one final breath, her body releasing it slowly as the life inside diminished. An excruciating stab of pain seized my heart, and an aching scream left my throat, filling the silence until all that was left of me were sobs.

My cries filled the space around us. When I looked behind me toward my mates, I realized several males were lined up. Kal and Zy stood closest as they held a silent vigil for my Ashix.

They both approached, kneeling beside me, sharing their grief for me. With me.

Crunching steps approached, and a familiar hand gripped my shoulder. Cassius. "We are here for you, Raine. I'm so sorry." He said.

I nodded. It was the only thing I could manage to do as my throat bobbed, trying to swallow the lump. Grief settled deep in the pit of my stomach as Beauty's body turned cold to the touch where I kept my hand.

Time slipped by as we sat in stillness.

A light tugging began to pull the cords once taut from my bond with Beauty. I wouldn't let myself hope that it was my beast coming back. She was long gone, her limp body unmoving. But, that tug. It grew and became insistent.

I stood abruptly, my limbs almost tangling within themselves.

My mates stood with me. "What's the matter?" Kal asked, high on alert for any lurking danger that was hidden from our eyes.

This was far from danger, though, something eerily familiar.

"I don't know yet. I'm being pulled, summoned by something." The mere light tugging was fierce and pounding, aiming my gaze in the direction of the cave Beauty made a nest in.

It couldn't be.

"Where are you going?" Zy asked.

"Below," I uttered, echoing what Beauty had been chanting in my mind. Then, I shadow-jumped to the entrance of the cave without waiting for their reply.

My heart hammered rapidly as the tug lessened the closer I got to an invisible destination. A low, trilling vibration called out to me. The summoning of someone waiting for me. Waiting. What was it Beauty said? *Protect her while she can't protect herself.*

I moved on autopilot through the zing of magic, allowing me to see beyond its hidden barrier.

What I saw in front of me left me speechless. Tears sprung to my eyes as I inched little by little to the edge of Beauty's nest. Nestled safely inside, untouched, was a light pink scaled egg that shook lightly as I moved closer.

That tugging spiked and beckoned me to reach out.

Closer.

Its whisper trailed around me like wind blowing through leaves.

"RAINE!" Both my mates' voices boomed into the cave, causing me to flinch.

I ignored them and took hold of the Ashix egg, cradling it closely to my chest. I was afraid I would drop it, but I was not able to let it go either. Relief overpowered everything else as I held the last piece of Beauty.

"Damn it, Raine, answer us!" Zy's low growl was menacing and threatening. I rolled my eyes at their impatience. They knew where I was at. They just couldn't see me, was all.

"So help us, little star, if you don't answer in the next few seconds, I'm going to spank that delectable ass of yours," Kal said. Did he think that was actually a threat? I would like to see him try catching me and doing as he promised.

"Goddess, will you two shut up for a moment." Annoyance vibrated outward as I tried focusing on the small trundle of a bond that began forming.

There! Ah—yes, there it was. Grabbing hold of the mental cord and tying it to the other severed cords, which had left me empty with the absence of Beauty. I finally felt more than a sliver of relief come into view as those new cords began taking hold.

A small claw scraped the inside of the egg, and a tiny sound squeaked through, amplified by the fire opal around my neck.

I am your flame.

I sucked in a breath at the sweet little voice that spoke softly, reflecting her mother's last words. I was only imagining what this could mean for our future—a future without Beauty but with a new bond forming.

Sitting near the nest, I sobbed, rocking back and forth with the egg nestled next to my aching heart. Until roaring blasted outside of the cave past the flowing waters of the falls.

"Shit, it's the male Ashix, Beauty's mate." Zy hissed.

Still holding onto the egg, I left the nest behind as I entered the main cavern. Kovidar stood poised to lunge at my males, who held their hands up, trying to placate the angry male.

This was the first time since my magic was restored that I was able to be near the male Ashix. Well, it was now or never to see if this necklace amplified to beings not bonded with me.

"Kovidar," I called out. He turned, hissing in my direction, and when his eyes landed on the egg I now held, he advanced. "Kovidar, stop! Beauty meant for me to find your daughter."

He still advanced, but the closer he got, the more his words trickled down.

How dare you handle my young, you insolent female. Regardless of whether you were Beauty's companion, I will end you.

His viciousness should have startled me, but they only showed me how much he was hurting himself, losing the female he bonded with.

Before he could get any closer, I took a step in his direction.

Foolish female. Do you wish for a faster death? Then so be it.

"I may be foolish, Kovidar, but your mate entrusted your young with me before she took her last breath."

He skidded to a stop as he glared, or at least I was pretty sure he was glaring. He was pretty fucking scary compared to Beauty. I had known her like the back of my hand, but with him, I hadn't spent enough time around him to tell entirely what his demeanor was like. But I was guessing he was a more growly male than my joyful female, which was a contradictory contrast considering the female Ashix were more known to be vicious.

You heard me, female?

I rolled my eyes, "Of course, I heard you, *male*. Now, are you still going to try to eat me?"

His head swung back and forth. *That is a good enough answer for me. If I get eaten, well, I guess that's it for me.* I thought, ambling to where he stopped.

"Raine, stop. Don't move any further. He's a furious male; he just lost his mate, and you are currently holding his offspring. We don't know what he's going to do." Kal urged.

"It's alright, Kal. He may be angry, but I have his daughter, and I don't think he would dare put her in harm's way."

Kovidar continued to watch me as I moved closer.

How do you know that my little one is a female?

His question startled me; didn't he know? "Your mate told me before she died. How do you not know if she knew?" His huff and smoke billowing out gave me pause before I finished closing the distance between us.

Female Ashix always know what their young will be. She hadn't told me yet. She wanted you to be the first to know. And now that her wish has been granted, you granted me the gift of learning as well. I thank you, female.

"Raine." I smiled, pushing my hand outward, hesitating before placing my palm against his side. "My name is Raine, not female."

Apologies, Raine.

"It's okay, Kovidar. Can my mates come to me? They look like they are going to pass out if I don't get them near me." I said, looking over at both Kal and Zy, who were ghostly white and clenching their hands into fists.

This is agreed.

I gestured to Kal and Zy so they could approach. Their eyes never left the male Ashix as they reached me and stood close to my back. Hands reaching for my waist on either side.

As we stood near Kovidar, more scratches came from within the egg. I giggled as I felt her love encompass us.

My mate chose her companion wisely. She would rip me to shreds if I separated our young from you. While I will not be able to bond with her until she sheds her shell, I must entrust you to keep her safe, for I must gather more males to take vengeance on the shadow males who I chased from here.

"One of the males you seek is my father." I paused, looking back to my mates and turning to the Ashix, who was already planning destruction. "Maybe we can help each other. I don't want homes and cities to be burned down because my father can't control his need for power. What if I helped lure him and his loyal males out?"

I waited for Kovidar's answer. He had to agree. Otherwise, I was afraid both AshFieran and Ashix would suffer significant losses.

This is agreeable, Raine. I shall gather males and seek you out. We are now bonded as well, so it won't be hard to find you. May you soar and be successful in drawing these males out. Keep my little one safe.

He launched off the ground abruptly, and the males behind me let out loud, dramatic sighs. Leaving me to return their sentiments on the emotionally eventful evening. "You two are so dramatic."

"Dramatic? You would be too if you were afraid your mate was about to be Ashix chow." Kal quipped.

"See, dramatic. I had it handled. You forget I have this." Tapping on the opal to remind them what helped communication between those unable to speak out loud.

This beautiful gem was beneficial. No wonder Andromeda panicked and urged that I keep it out of my father's hands. Because right now, I think I just recruited wild beasts that would otherwise be uncontrollable.

Recruiting the Ashix to help take down the male who slaughtered one of their own. My father was slowly turning AshFiera into a chaotic, dangerous place to live, and I would be the one to stop his reigning havoc.

Chapter Twenty-One

Zy

"**D**o you know what you are doing there, little storm?" I asked. Watching as the female who completely encompassed my heart with her dainty little hands handled her little Ashix egg carefully.

"I'm just holding the egg, Zy." She gave me a look like I was an idiot male for even daring to question her. "I do need to get her somewhere safe. She's heavy. My arms are going to be jelly soon."

I stepped up, gently placing my hands under the egg to help ease the weight from my mate. "I can take her. I promise not to drop the egg so we get her to safety."

She shook her head, "No, I need to do this. It's really sweet of you to want to help, but she's under my protection now. Beauty entrusted this to me."

"And you are under our protection, little storm. Please let one of us help you." Raine's swollen eyes looked up into the one I had left. Turmoil swirled in hers as she contemplated if she would let us help.

"If you're worried about Zy's missing eye and him possibly dropping the little one, I can take her," Kal said. My head turned to my newfound brother, glaring at the male who dared point out the obvious, making our mate more nervous, indicating that I was incapable of an easy task.

"Watch it, *brother*. Just because we didn't grow up together doesn't mean I don't have free range to beat the shit out of you." I growled, still holding my hands under the Ashix egg to help keep the weight minimal for Raine.

Kal snorted, "Please, *brother*. Like you could beat me. I'm the master at getting out of tight situations."

"Ha!" Raine's loud laughter echoed along the walls of the cavern, "I could beat both of you. After all, Kal, did you forget I won the fighting competition back on Earth?"

She gave him a flirty grin, reminiscing about her past with him before everything happened. Kal's grin widened, his eyes sparkling in mischief. Before he could pounce on our little mate, Cassius shadow-jumped in the cavern, interrupting us.

"Everything okay down here?" He asked hesitantly. Cassius looked around at us, doing a double take, when his eyes landed on the egg. Soon enough, they widened, and he looked at Raine. "Is that?" He started.

Raine had been holding it together pretty well until Cassius spoke. I was so close to driving my dagger into his hand. However, I knew if I inflicted pain on the male, Raine would hang me by my balls.

She sniffled before answering, "Ya, it's Beauty's daughter. She told me that I'm meant to keep her safe." She swiped her cheek against her shoulder, resuming her hold on the blasted heavy egg. "We should probably get her somewhere secure. I can't stand here forever holding her."

Cassius cleared his throat, "Good idea. We have another

safe house we can take you guys to. It's not near any waterfalls, unfortunately."

"I don't think it's a good idea to be near any falls at the moment, anyway." I turned to Raine, still holding onto the egg with her. "You'll be safer away from them for now. Your father is going to increase his search near any that are in AshFiera."

Her throat bobbed before she nodded, "Okay. I will follow your lead, Zy."

My heart soared, nearly escaping from my chest, at her trust in me. Elation tingled through my body, leaving an unexpected warmth deep within my core. I wanted to wrap her up in my arms and kiss her until all the pain that surrounded her heart and soul dissipated.

Being careful not to crush the Ashix egg in between the two of us, I stepped closer to Raine. Taking her into my embrace, my back facing Cassius, I glanced over my shoulder at the older male. "Which safehouse is it?"

"It's Kojax's," Cassius answered.

I snorted, "Do you think that's a good idea to bring all of us there, considering Gezr is his brother?"

"Do you think I would lead my mate's daughter into danger?" He asked incredulously. "Besides, Lazarus has no idea that Gezr and Kojax are brothers."

Raine's head popped up. She tried looking around my large body at Cassius but could only manage a sliver of her eyes to glare at him. "What's this about a mate, Cassius? Who are you talking about?"

When he didn't answer, her eyes narrowed further. Kal laughed, only for it to turn into a cough to cover the chuckle from our mate when she turned those narrowed eyes to him.

"It's nothing, little star. We can talk about it later. Come on." Kal said, approaching the backside of Raine, laying his hands against her waist, attempting to distract her. His face descended into her hair, inhaling before glancing back up, giving me a shrug as if to say, '*What? I can't help myself*'.

I couldn't say I blamed him. Her scent was intoxicating. An aphrodisiac. Something only she could drive us wild with.

When we reached the safehouse belonging to Kojax, several males were stationed outside the home on high alert. Many of the males I recognized, but only a few I didn't.

Raine shifted closer to me, clutching the egg in her arms. She observed the visible males as they curiously examined her and the egg she held.

"Can we trust these males?" She asked, her voice wobbled with anxiety. It crushed me to think she didn't know who else to trust aside from the small circle of males she knew.

"Yes, I know most of them. I don't think that Cassius or Kojax would allow anybody here without knowing they could be trusted. You are safe here, little storm." I said, tucking a loose strand behind one of her ears. She blushed, placing the side of her head against my shoulder, allowing me to wrap my arms behind her back. "Let's get the young one inside and somewhere safe. We can rest afterward. I'm sure there will be more Shadow Assassins, male and female alike, showing up tomorrow and wanting to meet you officially. Plus, we have to plan how to lure your father out somewhere on our playing field."

She gave a single nod, and we found ourselves taking one of the bedrooms toward the back of the safe house. Here, we would be far from almost anyone staying at Kojax's but still close enough that, with the added protection, there was little to worry about.

Kal and I watched as our mate placed the Ashix egg on the

bed. Placing two pillows down, one on either side, likely to prevent it from rolling as the little Ashix wiggled around inside.

Raine opened the closet and found several blankets stashed on one of the shelves. She walked to one corner of the room and began to make a nest with them.

It was amusing watching her rummage around the room in a mothering way, finding other soft items to place around the nest she had created. Something deep inside caused an ache, and all I wanted was to make her the mother of my children. *Some day, when she is ready, you moron,* I chided to myself.

Now was not the time to begin that chapter in our lives when we hadn't explored each other fully and selfishly.

She was finished putting the final touches to the softest nest I had ever seen when a yawn took hold. She grabbed the egg and placed it down gently, patting the top as lightly as she could.

"Let's get you to bed. You can check on the little Ashix in the morning." Kal said, swooping in and lifting Raine off her feet. He placed her gently in the middle, taking her shoes and tossing them haphazardly on the floor. He laid his body next to hers, brushing his boots off the edge before snuggling into her backside.

Raine patted the side of the bed that had remained empty. "Zy, there's a spot just for you. Kal is keeping me warm from behind. I need you for the front." She rubbed one hand along her arm, mockingly shivering. "Brr, see, I'm so cold. I need warmth. Now."

The last of her words were punctuated with the force of a demanding female. Any male who could resist such an invitation was lost to the black void of death. And I wasn't that male.

Joining my mate and Kal, I laid on my back facing the ceiling. Raine's arm slung over my lower waist while her leg wrapped itself around mine. Her thigh, so close to my cock, it began throbbing.

No, I was a patient male who would let her lead. She didn't need me clawing at her clothes when she had been put through so much this evening. I would hone in on the temptations tonight. Tomorrow would be a different story if we found time to be alone.

There were already so many males around. I knew tomorrow there would be more, and even a few female assassins would join. They wanted to meet Raine and help in any way they could to free the people of AshFiera from Lazarus' growing need for power.

Synchronized breathing filled the silent room. Both Kal and Raine had fallen fast asleep while I lay here, still painfully awake. But not for long. Their rhythmic breaths lulled me into the darkness of my dreams. Once Lazarus was taken care of permanently, all I could think of was that AshFiera would be a safer place for Raine, Kal, and any children we might have with her in the future.

Chapter Twenty-Two

Raine

I was hot. Scorching where I lay as an arm wrapped around my waist, making the heat that much worse. That arm tightened when I tried moving away. A moment later, a light groan sounded directly next to my ear.

"Where are you going, my pretty little mate?" Kal's soft, groggy voice spoke when I tried to move again.

"I'm too hot, Kal. You are like a fucking sauna, I'm sweating." I said, still trying to pry his fingers that had further gripped, digging into my hip.

"That's okay. You can be sweaty. It's perfect." He grumbled.

"You're such a weirdo. Let me up, you leech." If we were going to continue sleeping so closely together, we would need some kind of fan or something because this was stifling. It was beginning to sour my mood. I wanted to lash out, but I refrained when I remembered that this shouldn't be taken for granted. I just got Kal back after months of being apart. And now I felt like an asshole.

The door to the bedroom swung open, and Zy stood in the

middle, glaring at Kal and me, who were still entangled in the sheets. "Get up. There's already a horde of people here waiting for you both." Zy said grumpily. *Who the hell stuck a stick up his ass?*

"What's your problem, mister grumpy pants?" The question flew out before I could stop it. Zy's eye narrowed, and he took a few steps toward the bed, gripping the bottom of the sheet that still covered us. With one hard tug, he stripped it. I shivered from the sudden cold that swept over me, even though I was sweaty and Kal's heat was seeping into my back.

"Up, or I will get cold water to splash on you both." Zy threatened, walking out of the bedroom without another glance.

At that moment, he reminded me so much of the time Aunt Samara threatened to do the same thing when I wouldn't leave my bed. That felt like so long ago, and I missed her and Gigi so much. I wondered if I would ever see them or my mom again.

Kal loosened his grip on my hip and stood from the bed, "I don't know about you, my little star, but I do not feel like getting cold or wet this morning."

"Same, but might I remind you, Kal, that you were the one preventing me from leaving the bed?" I said, quirking an eyebrow as I watched him put his boots on.

"Touché." He said, reaching the door and waiting for me to get up as well.

Zy never returned to the bedroom; Kal and I left to head to the main living room. When we entered, several assassins were sitting and standing in various places, their eyes tracking every movement I made as I walked over to Zy, who was sitting in a large seat.

When I was close enough, he took hold of my wrist and tugged me down to sit on his lap, rubbing his hand along my thigh while the other lightly traced circles around my wrist.

Cassius cleared his throat, commanding attention as the room quieted down.

"We all know why we have gathered here today." He paused, looking around the room at all the AshFierans. "To stop Lazarus once and for all. His destruction of our society has increased. The collaboration with Darrem has left even more people without sustainable nourishment. AshFierans have now taken to murdering others for their food stores. There aren't enough Shadow Assassins who are on our side to counteract the violence happening among the villages and cities."

"So what do you suggest we do? The males responsible for this mayhem are untouchable. Lazarus has a large group of loyal males surrounding him at all times. No one has seen Darrem in days, either. He's not at his home nor his large warehouse." One of the males in the back of the room spoke up.

Several feet shifted as the tensions went taut. I waited for anyone to answer, but all was quiet until I decided to speak up. An idea had been brewing ever since my conversation with Kovidar in the cavern yesterday. The male Ashix wanted revenge against those who killed Beauty, and I agreed with him. It was time to lay out what I thought was best.

"I have an idea." All eyes turned to me. And the extra attention caused heat to pool into my cheeks.

"Go on, little storm. Tell us what you are thinking," Zy whispered, shifting me so I stood. His body, standing with mine, gave me the strength to keep going.

"We need to lure my father out, correct?" I asked no one in particular, keeping my thoughts going. "So, let's lure him out to my home. He's trying to find me any way he can, and what better way than to plant a seed inside his loyal group."

"How do you expect to do that, Princess?" Kojax stepped into the room. The title my father demanded the males call me by grated on my nerves. He knew it, too, when a small smile graced his lips.

I rolled my eyes, "Nice to see you too, Kojax. Now shut up while I finish." Snickers filled the room while Kojax's smile widened. He gestured for me to continue. "My father is obsessed with having control over not only me but my mother. Her powers are what drew him to her in the first place before I was even born. So let's use my mother's presence as a distraction."

Cassius interrupted, protesting, "I don't think so, Raine. No way in hell will I allow your mother to come back to AshFiera only to get kidnapped and potentially killed again."

This startled me as I didn't understand what he was saying. "What do you mean, Cass? My mother is alive and well and back on Earth. She wasn't killed?" It was more a question than a statement as I was trying to process the possibility she actually did die in front of me.

The room went quiet, and dread filled me. Did she really die? But how is she alive now?

Cass must have seen the questions written plainly across my face when he answered them, "She did die, little Ashix. She got lucky because whatever witch brought her back knew what they were doing. She had barely slipped from this world when they revived her." He said, his eyes filled with sorrow as if he remembered a conversation they must have had. A conversation I wasn't privy to because I had shoved my mother and Kal through the portal, closing it off from anyone coming or leaving AshFiera.

"Okay–Okay. That's a lot to process." I took an unsteady breath, lifting my head to glance at everyone in the room. "I still think we should use the ruse that she's here, only obviously not bringing her into it. We can use the Ashix to surprise the males who travel with my father as they are itching for revenge against them for what they did to Beauty, and–"

"Use the Ashix? How in the world do you plan to do that?" The same male from earlier questioned. He stood with his arms crossed and a scowl on his face.

I smiled sweetly, "By talking with them when Kovidar returns."

"No one can talk to those beasts, ridiculous female." He chuckled.

Kal stood beside me, gripping my hand tightly. "Don't speak to our female that way, Neftus. Not unless you wish for me to rip out your tongue and make you choke on it."

My eyes grew wide, and I smacked Kal on the stomach, "Behave, mister. That's not very nice."

"I don't care, my little star. He's not being very nice to you." Kal tilted my chin up to meet his gaze, giving me a quick kiss before turning back to the male, glaring daggers at him. The male at least had the sense to shrink back and stay quiet.

"I can communicate with Ashix using this." Holding up the fire opal necklace to show the arrogant male, I heard gasps around the room.

A female Shadow Assassin slowly approached, reaching for the necklace. Her finger rubbed against it, her eyes softened as she gazed at it and then me. "You are Goddess blessed, Raine. She willed it for you to find because she knew you would need it."

"Andromeda said the same thing," I whispered. "And my mother, as well, a long time ago." The female assassin dropped the necklace, stepped back, and kneeled in front of me. "What are you doing?" I asked in a panic.

"It has been years since the Goddess has blessed anyone with the knowledge to speak to the beasts of our world. Especially with the Ashix, as they are her vessels here. I will follow your lead and your command." She bowed her head slightly.

Several of the males followed her actions and knelt in front of us. I shifted, uncomfortable at the turn of events. I wasn't meant to lead. I just put my two cents in on a plan. This became so much bigger than I had anticipated.

Looking across the room at the kneeling assassins, I took a steady breath. It was a little disorienting, but I knew that if I had my mates behind me, they would help guide me along the way.

"Then, it's settled. We need someone to go back and tell my father they have spotted my mother returning to our home, and then we wait for his males and him to show up. We'll use the Ashix as a last resort. My father will be left for me, so if you come across him, only injure him. I want to have a few words before I leave him for Kovidar to do with as he pleases." I said, watching as heads nodded. Now, I need to figure out who the male would be to go.

I didn't have to decide, though, as Kojax stepped up. "*Princess,* I will make sure he receives the news of your mother's return. You can trust he won't believe anyone else in this room but me. I have done things to prove to him I was loyal so that we would have the upper hand if we needed it. And now we do."

"Kojax, how many times do I have to tell you not to call me Princess?" I asked, narrowing my eyes as a grin spread on his face.

"Apologies, old habits." He said nonchalantly.

"Once I have spoken with Kovidar and given him instructions on what we are doing, then you will go tell my father. Until then, check in every day if you can do so safely."

Kojax bowed before shadow-jumping instantaneously from the house. Soon, the other males and females left as well. Leaving the dwelling empty aside from my two males, who still stood near me.

Kal let go of my hand and wrapped his arm around my waist, pulling me into his front. He grinned down at me with a glint of lust shining through his eyes. Behind me, Zy snorted, causing me to look over at him. "What?" I asked.

"Nothing, just Kal can't seem to keep his hands to himself. I told him we needed to let you lead things." Zy said, glaring at Kal in the process.

I laughed, turning back around to wrap my arms around Kal's neck as he lifted me, pulling my legs around his waist. Looking back at Zy, I winked, "Don't be silly, Zy. I will always want you both. You don't need my permission to touch me, you know."

"Well, in that case," Kal said, spinning me and heading for the room we're sharing. A high-pitched squeal with laughter left my throat at Kal's antics. He knew what he wanted. And what he wanted right now was me.

When we reached the bedroom, Kal crawled on the bed with me still clinging to him, gently placing my back on the mattress. He began trailing kisses all over my face, making his way to my throat. When his lips reached the apex of my neck and shoulder, a moan escaped, and my fingers dug into the hair at the nape of his neck.

A door quietly shut in the distance. We had forgotten about closing it in Kal's haste to get me into the bedroom and on the bed. It seemed that Zy had followed and taken care of that for us.

The bed dipped as Zy joined. And a moment later, his lips descended on the other side of my neck, following what Kal had just been doing.

Kal unhooked my feet from behind his back, continuing his trailing kisses over my shirt until he reached my leggings. Lifting the hem of my shirt, his warm lips swept over my lower stomach.

His hands pulled my pants and underwear down over my feet, letting them drop to the floor.

He lowered himself further, gripping my thighs in his hands, spreading them apart. His face descended to the inside of my thighs, licking and kissing, taking his sweet time, avoiding the place I wanted him most, as my body heated and tingled. My center was begging for his lips and tongue to play, but he kept teasing me until I couldn't take it anymore. "Kal, so help me if you don't–ahh!"

He was there, his tongue circling my clit and sucking it gently in between his lips. I bowed my back off the bed at the intense, sudden sensations giving Zy the opportunity to lift my shirt higher over my breasts before his lips sucked on one of my nipples.

The dual sensations sent me soaring, nearing my release, but Kal sensed I was getting close, and he backed off, lifting his head to look up at Zy. "Get her shirt off." He growled out.

Zy didn't waste time. He lifted the shirt the rest of the way off me and went back to lapping and worshipping each breast, not leaving either one out for too long.

Satisfied, Kal grinned and began his ministrations again. Licking and sucking my clit into his mouth as a finger found my center and entered agonizingly slow. I needed more. I needed them both. Before I could voice my demands, Kal added another finger into my core and pumped.

A moan escaped, and I tilted my head back in ecstasy. That second finger was what I needed as my orgasm crashed into me, leaving me panting and screaming both Kal and Zy's names into the room.

Before I could come down from my release, hands gripped my thighs, flipping me to my stomach, lifting my ass in the air. Kal groaned, ripping his clothing off before moving behind me. His hips lined up with my ass, his hard cock nudging my entrance before he slowly slid in, letting me get used to his hardness.

Then Zy's cock came into view in front of me. I hadn't realized he had also taken his clothes off until he was there. Laying down beneath me, he gave me the perfect position to bend down and take his throbbing member into my mouth while Kal started pounding from behind.

With Kal in my pussy and Zy in my mouth, I couldn't contain my moans as they both took their pleasure from my body. Zy's fingers laced themselves into my hair, navigating my mouth to go faster, taking him deeper. When I gagged slightly on his hardness, he backed off, but not before he tightened his hold. "Come for us, little hurricane." Zy panted, looking down at me.

"Yes, good girl, look at you taking Zy in your mouth and me in this tight cunt. Now, do as Zy says and come for us." Kal gritted out.

My eyes watered. I wildly pushed back toward Kal, making his hips slap harder against my ass. Only a few more hard thrusts and I was tumbling over, moaning and swallowing around Zy's cock as the pleasure rippled through me. Zy's loud groan followed, along with swearing, as he let go, giving me his cum, shooting into my mouth. I swallowed greedily and then popped off his tip when I couldn't devour anymore of his pleasure, breathing heavily as Kal kept pounding harder and faster behind me.

His thrusts became erratic before he let his release take over. Thrusting more shallow and slower as he came down from our shared pleasure.

Removing himself entirely from me, I crawled up the bed and snuggled into Zy, who was lying on his back with his eyes closed. When I laid my head into the crook of his arm, his hand reached my hair, and he began fingering the strands.

Kal joined us, spooning my ass from behind again. "Mmm," He moaned, "I think I enjoy being the big spoon very much." His fingers trailed lazy circles lightly along my hip as all three of us relaxed into each other.

Zap. "Kal, what the fuck?" I said, startled, looking behind me at my mate. Where in the world did that come from, and why the hell did it feel like my lightning?

"Shit, I'm so sorry, Raine. I have no idea what the hell that was! I felt a slight buzz leave my fingers before you yelled." Kal said, surprised himself by the fact that he had just given me a little shock on my hip.

Zy cracked his eye open and looked at both of us. "Quiet, I'm trying to sleep. Our mate drained my energy with her smart mouth."

"Hey! Aren't we a little concerned about what just happened?" I asked.

"No? Go to sleep, my mate. We will figure it out in the morning." Zy said, unbothered while sleep already consuming him.

"Fine, but we need to bring Andromeda here and ask her if she knows anything about this. Do you think our bonding has anything to do with you zapping me with my powers?" I said. So many different possibilities ran through my mind as I considered how this could be feasible.

"I'm not sure, but I agree with Zy. Let's get some rest. It's been a stressful last few days, and it's growing late. I love you, Raine. All will be well, and we will get some answers tomorrow." Kal said, gracing me with a kiss on the back of my head.

He dozed off quickly, but my mind still wandered for a while longer. Did both Kal and Zy inherit my abilities when we bonded together? Did they possess anything else of mine? Only time would tell, and maybe even Andromeda knew something.

She was a seer, after all, and obtained knowledge about the prophecy and the significance of the fire opal.

Kal is correct. We will figure it out tomorrow. I would ensure one of my mates had Cassius retrieve her as soon as possible. We had some time, or at least I hoped we did before Kovidar came to find me. I hadn't felt any tugging on our bond, so I knew he was still far away. Once he finished what he needed, I was sure he would find me.

That was tomorrow's problem, though.

My eyes were beginning to get heavy now that the males on either side of me were fast asleep, their breathing even, and their bodies melded to mine. We didn't need a blanket tonight. Our heat kept each other warm enough, and if we did have one, I'm sure I would wake up drenched in sweat again.

Sleep pulled me under, and while all that swirled in my dreams were my two mates and the purple lightning they wielded. They took down as many Shadow Assassins as they could before any of them could reach me.

Chapter Twenty-Three

Raine

Morning came too quickly as I groggily felt around for my mates. Neither were in the bed or room, for that matter.

My eyes struggled to stay open as I saw the sun barely peeking through the curtains of our room.

Clanging and a loud bang reverberated in the direction of the kitchen. A second later, two male voices started bickering back and forth in hushed tones. *How sweet, they were trying to be quiet,* I thought, leaving the bed to see what the commotion was about.

When I reached the kitchen, Zy and Kal were covered in a white powder, and the counters were filthy.

"What are you two up to?" I asked, startling them both as Kal held a wooden spatula, ready to whack Zy with it. When he saw me, he quickly lowered the utensil he was going to substitute for a weapon.

"Nothing, our lovely mate. Just making some breakfast in bed for you." Kal said sheepishly.

"Can't do breakfast in bed when your mate is woken up by loud noises and bickering in a different room." I smiled, letting them both know it was in jest. Their bickering was entertaining, to say the least, and I loved how they stopped what they were doing when I walked into the room. *A girl could get used to that.*

"Hungry?" Zy asked. He was holding a plate that was filled with pancakes, eggs, and bacon. Seeing the loaded plate made my mouth fill with saliva that I had to swallow, making sure I didn't drool out the side of my mouth when the aroma reached my nose.

I hummed, taking the plate from Zy's outstretched hands, and headed for the table, which happened to be the only surface in the room clean.

"Thank you. You both know how to spoil me."

"Of course, Raine. We know a great way to please our female is by filling her stomach in more than one way." Kal said, wiggling his eyebrows suggestively, popping a piece of bacon in his mouth before filling up his plate.

We sat in silence while I devoured the breakfast they had so thoughtfully made for me. While it was quiet in the room, my thoughts turned to Beauty. How much I missed her already and the emptiness that surrounded the piece in my heart she had carved out for herself.

I hadn't really thought about her all day yesterday, and I didn't even know what they had done with her. As soon as it came to mind, I needed to know. "What did you do with Beauty?" I asked, breaking the stillness in the room.

Zy cleared his throat, "A few of the males shadow-jumped her down to the cavern below the falls near your home and dug a big enough hole to bury her in. It's far enough away from the lake that if it ever floods, it shouldn't reach her resting place."

My throat bobbed. I knew they would have buried her, and I was thankful someone else took care of it because I was unsure if I had enough strength in me to do it myself. At the very least, I knew where she was located. I could visit anytime I felt down or just needed to be near her again.

"Can I go see her?" I asked.

"I think we should wait until we have dealt with your father." Zy's authoritative voice told me this wasn't negotiable, but I had to try.

"Please, Zy. I just—need to be near her." I whispered, staring at my now empty plate.

"Enayah, I agree with Zy. It's not a good idea right now." Kal chimed in.

"Two against one, huh?" I said, anger sizzling just beneath the surface.

Both of my males felt the shift between our bonds, and they were out of their seats so fast I barely blinked. Two sets of hands roved over my face, arms, and thighs as they tried to calm my growing anger.

"They're right, you know. It's not smart to be anywhere near waterfalls right now. Not with your father, who is still actively looking for you." Andromeda's voice broke through the red haze that had begun to cloud over my vision.

"Fine," I said. Giving in immediately, knowing that Andromeda knew something I didn't and I wouldn't argue with a seer. "I won't go to the falls right now, but when this is all over, that is the first thing we are doing." I looked at both my mates with unshed tears. "I need to say goodbye and let her know I found her daughter, and she's safe." I shifted in my seat, aiming my body in Andromeda's direction and trying to ignore both males seated next to me.

"So, when the Seer comes and says not to go, you relent, just like that?" Kal said, tapping the tip of my nose.

I batted his hand away from my face, scowling, "Well, she can see stuff you and Zy can't. So, ya, of course, I'm going to listen to her." I rolled my eyes at them in annoyance, letting out an exasperated sigh.

Andromeda, sitting in the opposite seat, proved my point when she folded her hands and laid them on the table before speaking.

"Which is why I am here. You want to know what happened last night?" It was incredibly eerie to know that someone could see into the intimate details of someone's night. She didn't say anything else. She was waiting for us.

"Yes, Kal zapped me on my hip. Which is one of my powers, and I'm curious; do they both have something of mine? Can they stop someone in their tracks using wind like I can? Do you think it will give us an advantage over my father?" The rapid questions spilled out of my mouth like word vomit. I had such hope inside anything would help because three with powers were better than one.

"Slow down, Raine." She chuckled. "I can't answer the last question, but I can tell you that yes, when you three bonded, your essence entwined with theirs, giving over a piece of yourself."

Zy shifted next to me and said, "So, if I wanted to, I could summon Raine's lightning?"

"Yes and no. You need to practice wielding the magic before you can successfully use it. I suspect you will have a few weeks to work on it before the male Ashix comes calling." Andromeda stood, leaving the table, and headed for the door. Cassius suddenly appeared and smiled at us.

"Ready to head back to your father's shop?" He asked her, extending out his arm for her to grab a hold of him.

"Yes," She glanced back, smiled and waved. "See you guys in a few weeks." Then, she and Cassius left, shadow-jumping to her destination.

It had been a few days since Andromeda had visited us, instructing the males to 'practice' their newfound magic.

They both decided it was a good idea to use it on each other. *I swear males will be males anywhere I go.* I thought, remembering all the times the guys at Gage's gym would challenge each other on who could lift more or who could hit the hardest.

My smile widened remembering those days, even though, at the time, I was grieving for my mom, who I thought had died. I still enjoyed making new friends and learning new things in a world that wasn't mine.

Zzh. The swirl of a purple flash whizzed past as Kal threw another lightning bolt toward Zy, nearly hitting him.

"Zy, you're meant to stop the lightning with your wind, not pull it to you," I said, standing up from the lounge chair. Someone had conveniently pulled it out onto the back patio. I'm assuming it was Cassius. He knew I would enjoy sitting back, watching my two mates go at it.

It was hot watching them work up a sweat. Which eventually graced me with some bare-chested action when they got too warm and needed to discard their shirts. Which usually resulted in an intense sex-induced session with one or both males before they went back to it.

"I do know that, little storm." Zy bit at me while dodging another bolt.

"Touchy." I teased, moving toward the males. "Let me show you." Moving to one end of the lawn, I steadied myself. "I want both of you to shoot your lightning."

They gaped at me like fish. Zy went to speak, but I held my hand up to hush them.

"Not another word, I have been doing my own practicing. I want to show you what you can do with enough concentration."

Glancing at each other briefly, they looked back at me and hesitantly let go of a bolt each.

Before the two purple hues could reach me, I had already gripped them with my wind, slowing down the trajectory. Controlling the shifting and movement of where I wanted that line of buzzing electricity to go.

I sucked them in toward me at a faster pace, and before either one could hit me, I aimed them up into the sky. Twisting, turning, and rolling them into a ball. When they were high enough, I bunched the ball so tightly that my hands shook.

What I was about to do, I hadn't tried it yet, but I had pictured it so many times in my mind that I wanted to do it.

Whipping my hands apart, the ball of light burst into shards, lighting the sky brightly.

They shone, still in the sky like stars, until they started to fall slowly, and then they reminded me of lightning bugs in the summer.

When a few of the shards touched my skin, a light tingling crawled over my arms before disappearing.

Both Kal and Zy shadow-jumped to me, smiling and shining with awe.

"You are exquisite, Enayah." Kal breathed out, taking me into his embrace, pecking gentle kisses along my lips and cheeks.

Zy swept me into his arms away from Kal a moment later, taking over and kissing me harder than my other mate had.

I pulled away and looked up at Zy. "You'll get it; you both will. I'm already proud of how far you have come in the last few days."

The scowl Zy usually wore on a daily basis, as of late, softened. He leaned down, barely grazing my lips, tantalizing me with a secret, desperate wish for him to devour me again. When he showed his softness, only for me, my burning needs ramped up, leaving my core throbbing.

"Should we continue our efforts? Or should we take this inside?" He breathed against my lips.

Gazing into his face, my lips pouted, "You would make your female wait? I think you both need a break, don't you?"

Zy's growl left him as he lifted my body up and over his shoulder. A squeal left my throat at the sudden shift in my equilibrium as Zy strode to the house on a mission.

We spent the rest of the afternoon together in several different positions, with Kal joining in after Zy spent some time alone with me.

This went on for another week. They practiced their magic on each other and then worshiped my body. Every day, I grew restless, waiting for Kovidar to show up.

Kojax also started to get restless as activity ramped up at the mansion my father occupied.

Where was Kovidar?

Every day, the question popped into my head, and every day, all was silent aside from Kal and Zy's grunts. Their magical efforts improved drastically, but they still made mistakes, and some people ended up burned.

It was a bright, sunny morning when I felt a tug on my heart. At first, I thought it was Beauty's daughter. So, I ran to the bedroom where she was kept safe, nestled in piles of blankets. There were more added recently, which was the result of my thoughtful mates who knew I fussed over making sure she was kept warm and from harm.

The tug was more insistent now that I was near the egg, but it was tugging me in a different direction. Outside.

"All will be well, little one. Your daddy is here." The slight movement made me pause. I waited for her to move more, but when she didn't, I knew I was needed outside when Kovidar's tugging became more severe.

Kovidar sat in the clearing at the back of the house, where Kal and Zy usually practiced shooting each other with their new magic.

He looked regal with his bright purple and blue-hued chest puffing out. His nostrils flared before his purple eyes zeroed in on me.

"Hello, Kovidar. It's been a while. I was expecting you to come find me sooner," I said as I made my way over to him. Hesitantly, I placed my hand on his chest. A low rumble vibrated beneath my hand as he lowered his head to mine.

Tears threatened to build, and with the bulge, I swallowed down. Beauty used to do the same to me when she would greet me, making me miss her all the more. After a few weeks, my heart still ached intensely for that missing piece of her.

Hello, little female. I have been busy gathering several males to help me take revenge against those who killed my mate. They eagerly await your instructions. But first. How is my little one fairing?

"She's still in the egg if that's what you are asking. I'm unsure how long an Ashix stays in their enclosure, but she's barely moved the last few days." I said, smiling thinking about how Kovidar's first inquiry was about the young he created with Beauty.

Ahh, she will be ready when she is ready. Do not fret, little female. She can sense it's not safe yet through you. As can I.

My smile faded. I hoped I wasn't causing the little one distress. It had been tough to control some of my emotions the last few days. Waiting wasn't really a strong suit of mine. Impatience was like a second skin. It overruled my most common sense and made me edgy.

A pinch of awareness tingled in the back of my mind. A

blossoming warmth filled the space surrounding Kovidar and me.

My little one is already showing you how much she loves you. You worry too much. We can take the high emotions you AshFierans are too afraid to let run wild. It is not in our nature to keep those in or hide them.

Now, forget your troubles. We are here to end this struggle plaguing our home. What do you have planned, and where should my males and I be?

I spent the next half hour reviewing what I thought was a good plan: where we were going and when. When I was finished, Kovidar took off to discuss our plans with the other wild Ashix.

It was still unbelievable that I could speak with him. All because this necklace decided to call upon me.

Kal stood in the doorway, watching Kovidar fly off in the distance before turning to look back at me. His feelings trickled through our bond, and his adoration flowed, heating my cheeks as I bit my lower lip.

"Everything alright, my beautiful little star?" He purred, holding one hand on the doorway, cocking his hip to one side, looking as delicious as ever.

"Absolutely," I said desirously.

My body was on autopilot as I sashayed to Kal, titling my head in a silent request for his lips to surrender to mine.

My wish was granted instantly. His lips moved over mine, hands roaming greedily as they gripped my ass, lifting me into the air. He took me into the bedroom, passing up Zy, who was in the kitchen making breakfast.

I wouldn't surpass any time spent alone with either one or if we happened to land in bed all together. The need to be constantly around my mates grew. The closer it got to the final day, the closer it got to where I would unhappily be reunited with my father.

Would I have to be the one to end him, or would it be one of my mates? It didn't matter to me. Just that he needed to be stopped. I just didn't know if I would be able to kill my father. Deep down, the little girl in me still hoped he would change just for her.

Chapter Twenty-Four

Raine

I t had been two days since Kovidar left the safe house where my mates and I were staying.

Today, we would travel to my home. The place I hadn't been back to in several months. Not since I had closed off all portals in AshFiera. It felt like an eternity ago.

A sigh left me as I impatiently waited for my mates to finish strapping every weapon they possibly could to their bodies. Kal glanced over to me and smirked while Zy continued his checks with a scowl on his face.

"Almost done, little star. No need to huff your annoyance at your males." Kal laughed. He finished hiding three vials of the concoction they had made to impair anyone with jumping abilities.

He didn't want me to 'huff' at them? Well, too bad, I was just enough of a brat to do it again. This time, I made my sigh more dramatic, rolling my eyes and standing near the entrance of the house with my hands on my hips.

Both my mates glanced at each other before Zy suddenly

appeared in front of me, wrapping his strong arms around my waist. He leaned his face into the side of mine, whispering in my ear, "Keep up the attitude, little tempest, and I will fuck it right out of you."

My knees buckled slightly, and a whimper left my throat at the low growled warning Zy uttered. He held onto me tightly and chuckled, knowing damn well what his dirty mouth did to me.

"Go on, then. Do it." I breathed out, testing to see if he would keep his word and playing with the proverbial fire I loved to stoke.

Kal being a fun sucker this morning when he usually wasn't, interrupted, "Sorry to burst this bubble, but we have to get going. The others are waiting on us."

He was right. We had people relying on us, especially Kojax, who risked his life to tell my father and his loyal males that my mother was supposedly in AshFiera.

I stood on my tiptoes, brushing my lips against Zy's, "You better follow up on your threat later, my mate." Before he could speak, I silenced him, pressing my lips harder against his, backing away to give Kal a kiss of his own before we set off.

Something caught my eye by the front door. There was a neatly wrapped present lying on the floor with a note attached.

"What's this?" I asked, picking up the wrapped box that was oddly light.

"No idea, love. Check the letter before you open it." Kal said. Annoyance flared as I glared at my mate. What did he think I was five? Eager to open a gift before knowing who gave it?

That led me to think of the time I found a present on my bedside table when I was younger. I had ripped open the package along with the note on top of it. Inside were black bag gloves that Uncle Cass had gifted. I didn't know at first who they were from, so when I ran into Mom, I hugged her tight and thanked her for the gift. She laughed and told me they weren't from her. When Cass found out I hadn't read the note, he teased me for weeks.

Okay, he had a point.

When I opened the letter, I glanced over its contents. It was from Andromeda. She explained that inside was a pair of magic-laced manacles specifically made for my father. Not only would they further nullify his shadow-jumping and diminish his strength, but they would also make the person who wore them mute, unable to speak and use their voice.

It was perfect. He wouldn't be able to conjure up an escape this time.

I had decided that keeping my father alive and with the inability to escape again was more of a punishment than his death. Would there be a chance he could find a way to escape? Of course, that possibility was brought up more than once with my mates. But I was adamant that we needed to take this route and not the other.

Opening the box, I presented the manacles to my mates and grinned. "From Andromeda, she sent her regards and said she would see us later. Here." I shoved the letter at Kal for him to look over while attaching the magical cuffs to my belt.

Now, we were ready to go. My confidence soared thinking about how this would turn out as I skipped over to Zy while waiting for Kal to join us, which wasn't too long after.

Holding onto both Kal and Zy's hands, I shadow-jumped, taking them with me. I had decided to reappear at the falls in the woods near my home. The magic of the water flowing beckoned me like a tantalizing lover, letting the push and pull seep into me before closing my eyes. I let the magic regenerate any aches I had been feeling the last few days from all of our training. It was refreshing. Opening my eyes, I noticed both males were intently watching me.

"What?" I asked, cheeks turning pink with embarrassment. I still wasn't used to so much attention from not one but two males.

"You're so beautiful, Enayah."

"You're exquisite, little storm."

As they spoke over each other, I knew that they both loved me. The air was heavy around us, and they were gently amplifying their devotion through our bond.

Smiling, I retook their hands. "I love you both so much." Taking a deep breath, I steadied myself and glanced in the direction of the home where I had grown up. "I'm ready. Let's get this over with."

We stopped at the edge of the forest and looked over the place I had called home. Several of the Shadow Assassins we had been conversing with over the last few weeks stood around the yard.

Viewing everything, my gaze found my mother's once lush garden. It was nothing but rotten, crippled vegetables and black dirt. It hurt to see that the love she had once poured into the earth was now dead, sick without her magic nurturing it along.

Then, as if expecting to see her, I followed the worn path to the giant moss-covered boulder where Beauty used to sit and watch me for hours on end most days.

Choking back a sob, I turned, making my way up the steps of the deck and into the house. I didn't want to think about those memories right now. All I wanted to think about was what today would bring.

The foyer was devoid of the tables we once had. They were broken when Kal and I had charged in at the males who were occupying my home at the time.

When I walked toward the living room, I stopped. The

room looked as it had before. The couches moved back along with the small coffee table in between. Someone had been here and cleaned the place up before we arrived.

My eyes found Zy leaning against the doorway. He must have seen the question on my face as he smiled. "I had several males take care of the place while we were at the mansion in Ozryn. I didn't want you to come back to a home in disrepair."

So he was the one. My thoughtful mate, even when I had been so angry and hated him for helping my father. He took care of my home. "Thank you."

Wiping a tear from my cheek, I finished looking around, leaving the house to speak with the assassins who were anxiously waiting.

Kojax stood on the ground in front of the group, waiting for the go-ahead to tell my father, Lazarus, that my mother was here.

"You all know what to do. If you can take any fellow assassin prisoner using this," I held up one of the vials I had stashed on myself. "This will render their jumping useless and weaken them. We have brought enough for everyone to have several. Uncle Cass?" The male, who was more a father to me than my own, stepped forward with a bag. He handed out several vials for each assassin before the bag was empty.

My voice strengthened, and my confidence soared as I looked over those who graciously volunteered to help end this madness. "The Ashix should be here soon. The male Kovidar is my newly bonded companion, and he wants revenge as much as I do for the death of Beauty, his mate and my first bonded friend. You will not interfere with what they want. They are our allies and will guard the woods for any unexpected visitors."

"How will they differentiate us from the ones they seek?" Asked the female assassin who had been at the safe house a few weeks ago.

Holding up my hand, I wiggled my fingers, letting out tiny sparks of power flow over the small group. Several grunts and gasps were let out as my magic took hold.

"What the hell was that?" Grunted one of the males.

"I gave you all a temporary bond to my powers. The Ashix will recognize it from Kovidar. Since he's bonded to me, he carries the same signature. They won't touch you." I said.

"Any other questions?" Heads shook, and everyone dispersed, hiding in several places around the property.

Kojax was the last one to leave, but before he did, he turned to the three of us and said, "I will have to be among the males who come searching. Your father would suspect something if I didn't join. Do not be surprised to see me among them."

"So, does that mean I get to punch that face of yours for all the times you called me princess?" I asked. Zy growled beside me. "Hush, you grumpy male." Turning to Zy, I raised an eyebrow, daring him to continue.

"Perhaps, princess." Then, Kojax jumped before I could say anything further. Oh, I was definitely going to have fun finally laying my fist on his face when he returned.

Kal, Zy, and I made our way to the edge of the woods to hide ourselves among the brush. We knew it wouldn't be long before males would show.

Behind us, rustling leaves and twigs snapping made us turn. We didn't see anything in plain sight. Then, I felt him, Kovidar.

Hello, female. Do not worry. It is only me and the other Ashix males. We sensed the others already in the woods. They carry a piece of you.

Whispering, I responded, "I needed you to know who was on our side. It would have been hard for you to know otherwise. Can't have you kill off good Shadow Assassins who only want to help our world instead of hindering it."

You are an intelligent female. Beauty knew it as well.

Before I could open my mouth to respond, the forest's harmony silenced moments before a group of assassins appeared in front of my home. My eyes wandered around, looking for a familiar male. My father. He wasn't among the group. A hiss left my throat. "He's not with them," I whispered as low as I could to my mates.

They shifted closer to me, Kal gripped my arm. "What do you want to do?" he asked, keeping his voice hushed.

"We need to take care of these males quickly. Maybe one of them will tell us where my father is."

Before anything else could happen, the Ashix were on the move. Several hisses and growls passed above our heads, making their way to the group of males. Several assassins were taken in the grips of claws and flown away from the area. Echoes of screaming distanced themselves the further the Ashix flew.

"NOW!" I screamed, leaving my hiding place next to my mates and shadow-jumping into the fray of the scattered males. The others joined when they saw I was in the middle.

I jumped onto the back of one male, wrapping my arms around his throat and jabbing him in the neck with a vial before he could jump with me on his back. He slumped to the ground quickly. Several other assassins surrounded me now, closing in rapidly.

"Come princess, we will take you back to your father. We promise not to hurt you. Too much." Sneered one of the males closest to me.

I chuckled before leaping onto the male who had spoken with another vial ready in my fingers. While on him, I pushed out my lightning at the other two, who tried prying my body off the first. They stumbled back onto their asses before my two mates were on them, stabbing them with the concoction as well.

The other male I clung to gripped a fist full of my hair and pulled hard backward. I almost lost my grip on him when suddenly, I felt his strength leave him. He tumbled to the ground with my body landing on top.

When I looked at him, his eyes were open, and he was blankly staring into the sky, lifeless. My eyes scanned my surroundings and found Zy breathing heavily with his hand stretched out toward me.

When he saw me staring, this set him in motion, and he was immediately on me, wrapping his arms around my body and shoving his face into my hair.

"Don't you ever do that again!" He was still trying to catch his breath after exerting so much power, more magic than I'm sure he was used to into the male.

"Did you stop his heart?" I couldn't help but be proud of Zy for doing it. That was one thing we hadn't practiced because if we did, it would have meant taking a life uselessly.

"Ya, I didn't think it would work. I had no idea what I was doing. All I knew was that male had a hold of my mate's beautiful dark hair, and I saw red." He clutched onto me harder before Kal came up and pried me away from Zy.

"You know, I was having fun out there." I tried reassuring him. "It reminded me of when I met Kal at the charity boxing event." Smiling, I looked up at Kal and saw his eyes turned dreamy. Likely remembering our time in the ring. The memories were as vivid as if it happened yesterday. Even though we had been 'fighting,' Kal was more handsy than anything during the whole round. It gave me a better edge than if he was genuinely trying to fight me.

Zy turned to Kal, and there was an even bigger scowl on his face, if that was even possible. "The fuck? Did you lay hands on our mate?"

"Woah, it was nothing like that. She kicked my ass anyway and won the fight." Kal said proudly.

I raised an eyebrow, gaping at Zy, "Don't worry. He didn't

hurt me. If anything, he was grabby. Couldn't help himself."
Laughing, I left the safety of Kal's arms to join the others who
were gathered around the surviving assassins who had been
struck with weakness due to the concoction.

Kojax spotted us and smirked, "Looks like you didn't get a
chance this time, princess."

My teeth gritted before I lifted a smile to the male, "Ya, too
bad for me. But lucky for you, *male*."

Chuckles rang out in the group. Uncle Cass stepped in,
"Alright, that's enough, you two. If we want to make it believ-
able that your mother is here, we need to have one of those
males–" He said, pointing to the bound group. "Guarding. If he
sees no one outside, he'll get suspicious. We have several males
who are certainly uncooperative." He turned to the group to
address them. I crossed my fingers, hoping there was at least one
who was here against his will, "Is there any male among you
that would like to have the chance to redeem himself?"

Before anyone could respond, excitement flowed through
the bond with Kovidar. A moment later, he flew over us, causing
everyone to freeze.

*I will leave you to the rest of the males, little female. You have
honored us on this day. I will find you again when it is time for
my little one to take flight.*

Before I could respond to him, he turned and was gone,
leaving the bond silent.

No one spoke up for several more minutes as the tension
started to ease until a male shifted on his knees. "I will help."
Several of the others gave disapproving grunts and groans. A
few of the silent ones glared at the male.

It looks like we have a winner. I approached the one who
had spoken and asked, "What's your name?"

He was startled when he realized how close I had gotten,
"Tyar."

"Why do you wish to help us, Tyar? After all, you are here helping my father 'capture' my mother once again." I stared down at the male. My fists clenched to control the seeping anger that was slowly spreading through my veins.

"I—" He paused to look around at the others who were captured with him. But, he squared his shoulders and straightened himself, regaining some semblance of confidence. "I didn't want to help your father. He has my mate and child under constant guard. I haven't seen them in weeks. I'm not even sure if they're still alive."

My heart twisted. My father was cruel enough to separate a male from his child and mate. I should have known some of these assassins might not have been so willing, but how many exactly were here against their will?

"Zy?" I called out. He knew enough about my father's workings. I wanted to know if this male spoke truthfully or if he was trying to play with my emotions, knowing how much I craved having a father who actually loved me.

"Yes, little storm?"

"Is this true? I know you have seen things others haven't, considering your old position with my father. Has he threatened others using their families as leverage before?"

He held my hand, bringing it up to his lips, softly kissing the backside before nodding.

"There are not a lot of males he has done this to as he wished to keep as many willingly on his side as possible. But, there are a few I know who have had their families stripped from them." Zy answered solemnly. He glanced at Tyar, who was still kneeling in front of us. "I remember when your mate was brought in. She fought and caused several males to have bleeding and broken noses." Smiling, his eyes found mine again, "I believe we can trust this male. The others, however, are here of their own accord."

Nodding my head, I looked back at Tyar. "If you help convince my father that my mother is indeed here, we will help rescue your family." I stood, looking at the males and females who were helping on our side. "If we can help it, take any male or female assassin prisoner to weed out the unwilling from those who chose to help my father. If what Tyar says is true, we can't harm those who my father is using. It would only show we are just like him, which we are not."

Kojax approached, lifting Tyar to his feet and untying his bound hands. "I will go tell Lazarus we have captured Pandora. You will stay here and stand outside acting as a 'guard' to the house. If you betray us, I will take you out myself, " he warned. The male nodded in agreement.

The rest of the group dispersed with the bound assassins, and we were left waiting for them to come back. We knew my father hadn't sent everyone he had at his disposal. Those assassins were just the ones he knew would be expendable. Zy mentioned that the more robust males weren't here, and he suspected my father kept them at his side for protection—*the coward*.

We had devised a plan: Kojax would leave and tell my father the news, and Tyar would stand outside the house, 'guarding' the door and signaling to the others once we had made contact with Lazarus, my father. The others would then go into the surrounding woods to take out any males who joined in the fray, while Kal, Zy, and I would wait in the house.

It had been several hours since Kojax left. I couldn't sit still as the anxiety crippled my limbs numb. If I stopped moving for a moment, they would likely stop working altogether. So, I kept pushing until I felt the shift.

Clutching onto my mate's hands, I whispered, "He's here."

It was all that I managed before footsteps clomped up the stairs toward the front door—stopping just before the entrance. Some words were exchanged between Tyar and who I thought was likely my father before the door creaked open.

"You are a good male, Tyar. I will ensure your family is released when we return. You have proven yourself to–" My father didn't finish his sentence when he turned and found me standing in the doorway to the living room. Kal and Zy were just out of sight on either side of me.

My father smiled. "This is much better than I was anticipating. They didn't tell me they had you as well." His smile faltered when both of my mates stepped into view. Anger grew in his eyes as they blazed red with the realization that this was a set-up.

Before he could jump out of sight, I gripped him with my wind, holding him in place. Grunts and screaming followed outside as Tyar signaled the rest of the group.

Immediately, I could feel the strain of my powers as my father struggled in my hold. He was strong for a male. I would have to hold him as long as I could for one of my mates to administer the concoction.

"Someone better have a vial and inject my father already. I can't hold him for long." I gritted out between the strain of holding him in place.

Zy was quick and jumped over to us, stabbing my father in the neck forcefully. He shouted his displeasure at the sudden pain I had known all too well.

I held him still, keeping my distance as I waited for the concoction to take hold.

"Raine–please." My father pleaded, looking up with tears

forming in his eyes. Seeing him vulnerable tugged on something deep inside.

"You gave me no choice, father. You're destroying AshFiera and the people in it. Starving families and creating monsters who murder so they don't die themselves from the lack of food." I had to stop a moment, taking a deep breath to control the lump forming in my throat. I hardened my gaze and spat, "And you killed Beauty. By doing so, you killed a piece of me when you did it. Are you happy with yourself?"

He shrunk on himself, showing signs that he was weakening further, "No, my little Ashix. I'm sorry. I didn't mean for her to be harmed."

"Bullshit! You were scouring the waterfalls, knowing what they meant to me. And when you found her, you didn't think twice, ordering your males to injure her so far that she DIED IN FRONT OF ME." I screamed, then with just a whisper, I stared into his soul, "You nearly killed me."

I waited to see some kind of remorse, but there was no genuine sorrow in his swirling emotions. He acted like he cared and pretended to be sorry, but his feelings couldn't be contained by my gifts as they swirled from anger to hatred and determination.

"Raine–" He started pathetically.

"No!" I cut him off. "You gave yourself away already, *Lazarus*." He no longer deserved to be called father. He wasn't one, and I realized then that I would never have the love I craved from him.

His anger seethed deeper, leaving a black haze crowding into the emotions. He straightened, resolving something within him. Showing his true self, "What will you do to me then, daughter?"

I sneered, "I am no longer your daughter, Lazarus. You don't get to call me that anymore. I am but a stranger to you. And as for what we will be doing with you. Well, we have a special place to put you where you will no longer have contact with anyone. And these," I held up the manacles that were attached at my side for him to see. They were the ones Andromeda had dropped off with a note earlier that morning. "These will prevent you from using your shadow-jumping. Oh, and also from speaking as well. Andromeda added that little touch. Should keep you from trying to rally anyone to your side this time."

While I held my father still, I walked over to him, stopping just before. He craned his neck to look up at me, and then I smiled sweetly and squatted to bring myself to his level.

"You'll have enough time to reflect on the poor choices you have made until your body gives out from old age. Maybe in that time, you can choose to learn from your mistakes, but you will never be able to prove them. Not as long as you continue to breathe." I said.

Just before straightening, my father grunted, and suddenly I was on my ass. Stunned. *How the fuck did he get free from my hold?*

Just then, he was on me, and sudden pain exploded around my lower stomach.

He whispered in my ear, "Tell Beauty I said hello. It shouldn't be too long. The poison will work faster than the blade."

His booming laughter filled the house as one of my mates gripped his neck, pulling him off me.

Grunts and what sounded like fists pounding into flesh were in the distance until gurgling and gasps followed until it was silent. I couldn't see anything. The pain was too much for me to look around, but I knew one of my mates had ended him.

When I was able to look down, I hesitantly touched the handle of the dagger that was sticking out of my stomach. No, not just any dagger. It was the black-handled one that my mom bought for me the day I ran into Zy in the village. The same one I had to leave behind the day I escaped to Earth. He had taken it from my bedroom and used it on me. To kill me.

Oh, Goddess.

Zy was next to me, cradling my head in his lap. I looked up into his eyes, tears filling mine, causing him to blur in my vision.

"Poison—he poisoned the blade." I choked out.

"Fuck. KAL!" Zy shouted. A moment later, Kal was on my other side. Zy glanced at him, panic sliced through our bond, "The bastard poisoned the blade. What do we do? There's not enough time to get her to a healer."

Kal's hands were touching my face, beckoning me to close my eyes at his touch. Everything was fading fast. Black etching at the edges of my vision as I grew more tired by the second. "No, stay awake, Enayah. Keep those eyes on me." Kal began scooping my body into his arms.

The movements jostled the blade, and a pained cry left my throat. It was agony. I wanted it to be over. "I'm sorry." I sobbed. "I love you both." Consciousness slipped further, and it was the last thing I could muster. I needed those words to be heard so that when I left this world to join the Goddess and reunite with Beauty, they would have those to hold onto and carry with them for the rest of their lives.

"No, don't you dare think you get to leave so easily, Raine. We have a whole life left to explore together. You, me, and Zy." Kal uttered. Before darkness consumed me, the last thing my consciousness registered was his body turning toward Zy. "We need to get her to the falls and into the water both of us need to be with her."

Chapter Twenty-Five

Kal

No. *This wasn't happening.*

We watched helplessly in slow motion as Raine's father lunged at her.

Fury erupted from my throat as I reached Lazarus first. My fists flew into the smirk he so proudly wore. My body's fury allowed me to land more punches without thought before wrapping one hand around the insolent male's throat while the other reached for the dagger attached at my hip. My mind went blank as I shoved the blade violently into his throat.

He was no longer allowed to live. He wouldn't stop hurting our mate, so his life was forfeit. He would cease to exist in a world where Raine was thriving.

I watched the life slip from his eyes. My anger was so clouded I barely heard Zy yell my name.

He was a mess as I approached his hunched form while he frantically told me the dagger had been poisoned. The bastard actually stabbed his own flesh and blood.

"We need to get her to the falls and into the water," I said after scooping up our mate, cradling her into my arms, being as delicate as I could without jostling the blade sticking out of her stomach. But my efforts weren't graceful as Raine let a hiss slip between her lips. I turned myself toward the falls and shadow-jumped.

This had to work. Theo told me about the significance of waterfalls for their people. And how the magic flowing down could heal someone on the brink of death enough to get them to a healer.

When we arrived hours earlier before the fights began, Raine had tilted her head, closing those green orbs, soaking in the magic all three of us felt. It didn't affect Zynas or me as much as Raine, but we could tell how much she basked in the power.

As I appeared at the top of the ledge beside the falls, I looked down, making sure I could find a flat spot to jump to. I hadn't been to the bottom of this one like the falls outside of Gezr's burned-down home. No, all I remember of this waterfall was jumping toward the portal Raine had conjured in her panic. I wasn't exactly paying attention to anything else but getting to her.

Rocks crunched underneath Zy's boots as he looked over the edge with me. Silently nodding, I shadow-jumped to the water below, with Raine lying limply now in my arms.

Her breathing was shallow and strained. But as we stood in the presence of the mist, she was already growing more substantial, and being so near to the flowing water, her heart started pounding harder. It wouldn't be enough to seep the poison from her blood. I needed to submerge her entirely in the waters of the lake.

Walking into the crystal-clear wetness, I let it lap up and over our bodies until the edges of the surface were chest-deep. I gently lowered Raine, looking around for Zynas. He needed to be here with us. The closeness of our bodies and our bond would strengthen her. I didn't know how I knew this, but my mind was screaming, *closer, closer.*

He was already making his way through the water toward us when I spoke.

"The dagger is still lodged in her stomach. You need to pull it out and let the water help heal her." Cradling Raine closer, my hands were like vice grips, holding on, clinging her to my front as if my life could seep into her skin and save her.

Zy's hands trembled as he looked down at our mate, whose face was the only thing visible on the surface.

He gently pulled the dagger from her stomach, tossing the weapon to the shore. Blood ran in rivets from her wound. We held our breath, waiting for the flow to stop. Seconds later, the red tendrils disappeared, and color returned to her once-blue lips. Her pale cheeks reddened while her heart pounded fiercely under my hand that lay against her chest.

Zy noticed the changes as well while we watched her slowly come back to us.

"How did you know to bring Raine to the falls?" He asked, staring intently at our mate. His eyes had yet to leave her.

"Eh, something a pesky friend of hers mentioned while I spent time on Earth away from her." The annoyance returned, remembering the dreamy looks Theo held while talking about Raine.

"I will have to thank this friend for their gallant advice."

"No–no, you don't want to do that. You wouldn't like the male anyway." I couldn't hold the chuckle in that I was desperately trying to hide. Zy was a more possessive male than I was, and I knew that if he met Theo, he would undoubtedly lose his hand or tongue. Maybe even both.

"This friend is a male?" He growled.

I knew I shouldn't goat my brother, but it was just too

tempting. "Ya, and he has the hots for our mate. So keeping him away would be best, or maybe not just to see the look on your face while he shamelessly flirts with her in front of us. So, let's keep the contact between the two at a minimum. Unless, of course, you want to kill him? But then you would receive the wrath of our mate for ending the life of her friend. And I would gladly let you take that downfall."

Zy grunted. Running his fingers through Raine's hair under the surface, gazing lovingly down at our still-unconscious female.

His voice was hoarse as he spoke, coaxing our mate to wake. "Come on, little storm, you have to wake up. You're not allowed to leave us. You have to grow old with us, fight with us, go back to Earth, and eat–" He paused, looking up at me. "What was it she loved so much?" He asked.

"Burgers, fries, and ketchup, so much ketchup," I answered, smirking down at her.

"Yes, we will go back there and get you burgers, fries, and this ketchup Kal has indicated you have so much of. Then you'll give us lots of babies to keep us busy while we watch them grow."

"Zy," I said, raising an eyebrow at the blubbering male. I glanced back to our mate, trailing the back of my fingers against her cheeks. "You don't have to give us babies if you don't want them. Don't let Zy's unusually sappy display bully you into doing something you don't want." Leaning forward like I was whispering a secret to her but keeping my voice loud, Zy heard, "Don't worry, little star. I'll slice his balls off before he even thinks about implanting his seed inside you."

Raine's lips twitched. She responded groggily, "Please don't cut his balls off. I might need those later." Her eyes remained closed as she took a few deep breaths.

We huddled closer to her, lifting her head entirely above the water.

"How much of that did you hear?" I asked excitedly. She was coming back to us. Even if her eyes weren't open yet, she was responding.

"Everything after Zy asked me to wake up." She opened her eyes slowly and glanced at Zy. "I would love to have your babies. But maybe let's hold off for now? I'm extremely sore."

He actually smiled, gripping her head in his hands, bringing their foreheads together. "Deal. Your healing takes priority."

She turned her head slightly, gazing into my eyes, when she noticed I had stayed quiet. "Kal, what is it? Where's Lazarus?"

She must have sensed my growing unease. How could I tell her I killed her father after he attacked her? Would she forgive me? There was no other choice but to send him to the depths of hell. He wouldn't stop coming for her, which was proven when he nearly killed her. We were fortunate enough that I remembered what Theo had told me. And even more so with these falls being so near her home. Even with shadow-jumping to the other falls, it could have taken too long. I wasn't exactly in my right mind thinking my mate was about to die.

Mustering up the courage, I looked into her eyes and confessed what I had done. "Your father is dead. I–I killed him after he attacked you with that dagger. I didn't give him a chance to defend himself or do anything further."

Her shaky hand reached for my cheek, caressing lovingly against the beard I had let grow back. "Kal, it's okay. It had to be done. He would have found a way out of our prison." Raine shook her head, "He somehow gained the strength to overpower me, even with the concoction running through him. I don't know how he did it or if he found something to counteract the drug, but it was as if we never even administered it to him."

Taking Raine's hand in mine, I kissed the palm, closing my

eyes, taking in her scent that would forever be ingrained into my soul. I was thankful that I would continue to bask in her aroma after what happened. "All I could think about was how he so easily slid that dagger into you. His daughter. Then, the anger took over, and I lost control."

Zy brushed a piece of wet hair away from her forehead. His touches lingered on her, as did mine. We almost lost her today, and I was sure it would take both of us a long time to let her out of our sight.

"How are you feeling, little storm? Do you think you are strong enough for us to leave and go back to the house we've been staying at?" Zy asked, water dripping down his forehead as the residual mist covered us from the falls we were near.

Raine nodded, attempting to sit up in my arms. Then, she fell backward in a hiss. "I'm still incredibly sore, but I think we can get out. I don't like feeling weighed down in my wet clothes. And I don't think the falls are going to heal me any more than they already have."

I nodded, turning toward Zy, "Do you want to bring her back, or should I?"

His throat bobbed, and he stepped closer, "I will bring our mate back. Can you check on the others to make sure everyone made it out okay?"

"Absolutely." Placing Raine in Zy's arms, my touch lingered on her. "If you need anything, my stunning mate, make sure to order Zy around. He's your servant until I rejoin you both."

Her laughter peeled out of her, and a second later, she gripped her stomach, "Ow, ow, Kal, you can't make me laugh like that. But, I promise to make Zy my little slave." She wiggled her eyebrows while Zy grunted.

He started walking toward the shore, cradling our mate protectively in his arms before they disappeared out of the cave.

I decided to jump from where I stood. There were zero fucks given for how soaked my clothing was.

When I arrived at Raine's home, I was greeted by Cassius and Gezr, who had just finished moving a few dead assassins in one spot. My eyes trailed over the fallen comrades. A few I recognized and remember sparring with years ago when we were all young males. It was jarring to see some of the males I had once thought honorable turned by Lazarus's cruel ruling. Sadness and anger at their loss of life stormed into my heart.

Gezr's hand clamped down on my shoulder, shaking me out of my ire, "Where's Raine and Zy?" Before I could answer, two males exited the house carrying Lazarus' dead body. They brought him over to the already growing pile of deceased.

"Kalpheus, what happened inside, and why in Goddess's name are you wet?" Cassius' curious glance looked between Lazarus and me.

"Raine and Zy are back at the safe house. I killed the bastard after he stabbed Raine with a poison-dipped dagger." I said, their stares turned shocked. "She's okay. Zy and I brought her to the lake below the falls. I remembered what Theo said about them. For witches and warlocks, it helped heal those on the brink of death. It was a close call, though. We almost lost her."

Cassius's eyes widened, "Shit."

"Mhm, but I just came back to see if you guys needed help. If not, I would like to join my mate at the house."

"We got this, Kal," Gezr said. "Go on, join your mate and brother. We are going to take the assassins we have captured to Ozryn and lock them up. They will have to be interrogated. There are still some unaccounted for that Kojax mentioned weren't here. They are trying to find Darrem as well. We think he might have a few Shadow Assassins protecting him."

Cassius stepped forward and abruptly hugged me. "We'll come see you three when we have more information. Stay at the house until you hear from one of us. And give Raine a big hug for me."

I stepped back, leaving the males to take care of the aftermath we had left behind.

When I reached the house, my clothes were still soaked. I removed my shirt, left it on the porch railing, and removed my shoes before entering the home.

With my body on autopilot, I found Raine snuggled into Zy on the bed we shared. Her eyes were closed. And I stood in the doorway, staring at her body, ensuring she was still breathing. When I saw the gentle rise and fall of her chest, my heart soared. She was still okay, or as adequate as someone could be, with a wound to their stomach.

Zy shifted on the bed, and my attention was drawn to him. His once-closed eyes were focused on me. He silently placed his finger on his lips, indicating to keep quiet. I moved into the room, gathering dry clothes before leaving and heading for the bathroom.

A chill was beginning to set into my bones from the heavy, wet clothing, so I stripped out of the remaining items quickly. Warming myself in the shower before changing and joining Zy and Raine in bed.

I shifted as gently as I could, lining myself up behind our sleeping mate. My hand roamed over her thighs and settled on her hip. I wanted to wrap her body into mine but resisted the urge since that would have required my hand on her stomach to pull her toward me. She was incredibly fragile at the moment, and I would just have to endure being tender until she healed more.

Her head shifted to the side, eyes still closed, and a hint of a smile graced her lips. "Kal." She whispered.

"I'm here, we both are. I have something I have been meaning to give you." I rustled around behind my back, blindly looking for the box I placed on the bedside table. "Here, I hope that you will wear it always."

She took the box, opened it, gasping, "Oh Kal. It's stunning." Raine lifted the bracelet I found the day I went shopping with Samara. It inadvertently matched her fire opal necklace that she never took off. With rounded beads of topaz and pearls that reflected the same color of Beauty, it wasn't magical like her necklace, but it complimented the jewelry nicely.

"You can look at it more tomorrow. You need to get your rest. Sleep, my beautiful mate." Kissing her shoulder, I took the bracelet, hanging it over one of the bedpost corners.

"Mhm, promise to be here when I wake up?" She asked sleepily.

"Of course, little star. We'll always be where you are." Her head turned back into Zy, nuzzling into his chest.

Moments later, her breathing evened out. I released the deep breath I had been holding in and nuzzled my face into her hair, drifting off while thanking the Goddess for keeping our mate from the brink of joining her.

Chapter Twenty-Six

Raine

Wake.

The whispers of a small voice startled me. Was it the little Ashix? The sun hadn't risen yet, my mind was racing, and the little voice inside my head had woken me.

The little youngling had been silent in her egg for so long that I wondered if she was alright. But every day, when I touched the outside of her egg, I felt a pounding warmth surrounding my heart. Relief would flood through me at the connection that slowly continued to grow each day.

Gingerly leaving the comfort and warmth of my mates who were still lazily sleeping. I crept over to the makeshift nest where Beauty's young was still housed in her shell, safely lying in bundles of blankets, untouched and unmoving.

As I placed my hand upon the outer shell, I felt her eagerness to enter the world shift. She was ready, and I believed she would make an appearance sometime today.

A booming knock woke my mates, making me snatch my hand away from the egg so I wouldn't knock it over.

"What–what, who the hell is knocking so loud this early?" Kal groggily flung the blankets from his body, leaving both males without the warmth they had snuggled into before I left. "Raine?" He asked, looking around for me in the darkness.

"Down here, Kal, I was just visiting the little one," I said, waving a hand so he could see where I was in the dimly lit room.

"Goddess, get back in bed."

"Someone's at the door, my love," I said, already attempting to rise from the floor. It had been a few days since my father so kindly stabbed a dagger into the middle of my body. The twinge of soreness was still present, but every day, it was better. My strength improved little by little.

Zy grunted, heaving his body from his side of the bed. "Don't get up so quickly on my account, Kal." He grumped. "I got the door. Get some clothes on, I don't want to look at your dick this early."

I racked my gaze over my less grumpy mate, who stood from the bed, giving me an eye full of his hardening cock.

His throat cleared, "Like what you see, my little mate?"

"Maybe," I answered, still working to remove myself from the floor. Kal came over, reached down, and helped me to my feet when he realized I was struggling.

At least now my face wasn't in the direct line of his tempting dick. "Thanks, Kal."

His dazzling smile broadened, "My pleasure."

Zy opened the door without waiting any longer for Kal to dress. "Goddess, Kal. Put some fucking pants on. No one wants to see that." Cass grumbled. His complaint drifted into the room from the hall.

"My mate always wants to see it. Don't you, Raine?" I didn't say a word, giggling at the horrified look on Uncle Cass' face as he backed up further into the hallway to avoid the scene.

I gave Kal a quick peck on the lips before joining Zy in the doorway of our room. When I looked out, Cass' face was grim. My smile faded, "What's wrong?"

"There's been some unrest in Ozryn the last few days since Kal killed your father. Darrem has finally shown his face. He's taken over the mansion with the missing assassins that were unaccounted for."

"What do you need us to do?" I asked.

Cassius shook his head, "You aren't going anywhere, Raine, but I do need your mates."

"Bullshit, I'm coming. I have healed enough. Plus, what can Darrem do anyway? He doesn't have abilities like the rest of us." Crossing my arms, I glared at him.

"You're still healing. I–"

"I don't care. We have been waiting for Darrem to show his face, and now that he finally has, you're just going to ask me to sit this out? No. I'm coming." Turning to face Zy and Kal, who finally strolled over to the doorway fully clothed, I dared them to tell me what to do.

Kal raised his hands, "If our female wants to come, I'm not stopping her. She's just going to shadow-jump there by herself anyway."

"Kal's right. I would rather have her by our side, where we can protect her, than have her out there on her own." For once, Zy didn't fight me over something I wanted to do. I smiled and leaned into him.

"Alright, well, so be it. Everyone is already here waiting for your lead, Zy." Uncle Cass said.

It had already been determined that Zy would take over leading the Shadow Assassins once things had settled. He was already primed to take over before his father was murdered by mine. So, he was the obvious and logical choice.

At first, he protested, wishing for the three of us to lead, but Kal and I refused. We only agreed to help navigate any decisions he couldn't conclude on his own. Reluctantly, he accepted the position.

And now here we were, standing in front of a crowd of loyal and reformed assassins. The ones who initially fought for my father relinquished themselves quickly during the chaos at the home I grew up in. Many had families held hostage as leverage to help carry out the nefarious plans my father had devised.

"This will be quick. Darrem has no abilities. The only thing he has power in is the control he has over the food supply. But today, that ends. Take as many comrades as you can prisoner, but if your life is in danger, do what you must." Zy's booming voice echoed around the group, out into the treeline.

He was their commander and leader, and I was proud to stand next to him as he led the large group into what I hoped would be our final fight.

Something deep inside insisted this would lead us to finally bringing peace back to the people in AshFiera.

I just hoped it wouldn't take long. My bond with the unborn Ashix kept pulling me toward her, but my bond with my mates was so much stronger. I hoped she would wait until we came back before making her way into the world. She had to know it was still unsafe.

Zy had jumped with me to the gardens in the back of the mansion. We crouched low in the flowers while waiting for Kal and the others to join us. Shifting feet sounded from behind, and we knew that everyone had followed quickly.

Zy whispered, "My guess is Darrem will be in the large ballroom. He's likely already been alerted to our arrival, so be fast."

We no longer crouched, instead running rapidly through the garden as we made our way to the back of the mansion without incident.

Kal opened the door and peered inside. Nodding, he entered through the doorway, and we followed closely behind. The assassins with us spread out quietly and quickly, making their way in different directions to subdue anyone on guard.

Kal, Zy, and I made our way to the ballroom with no one in sight. When we reached the door, Kal kicked it in, alerting anyone inside that we were there.

When we entered the room, Darrem sat in the chair my father had deemed his 'throne,' with several assassins shielding him in a semicircle.

"Ah, there she is. The elusive Raine." Darrem taunted. His fingers curled over the armrests' edges, squeezing slightly. "I have been waiting days for you to show that ravishing face of yours after your father was killed by none other than your mate, Kal, is it?" His tone was mocking, almost smug.

"Are you assuming I had no idea that one of my mates killed my father?" I asked, unsure where this was going.

"Oh. Well, I am glad they disclosed something so vile." He sneered.

"What's vile is what my father was doing to AshFiera, with your help, I might add. You are just at fault for his demise as he was."

The anger on his face turned to amusement. "Well, it was needed regardless. With him out of the way, I have taken over. I do control the food supply, after all. It's only fitting that I rule AshFiera politically as well."

Ya, buddy, I don't think so.

Several males surrounding Darrem shifted on their feet. Attracting my attention.

I quickly glanced around and tracked eight males, all waiting for the word of someone who undoubtedly held no power.

I took one step forward, my mates closely following, until I signaled with my hand for them to wait.

"I'm only going to offer this one time, Darrem." Making sure to meet each male's gaze, I spoke directly to them as well. "This goes for you all as well. Surrender now, and no one else has to die."

Darrem's laughter rang out, echoing in the ballroom.

"You think I'm just going to lay down like a dog and do as you say?" He stood from the 'throne,' placing his hands behind his back. "No, my dear. You're going to do as you're told. Or I'll have your mates killed, slowly, in front of your face. Then, I will take you as mine, and you'll give me children who possess whatever power your father insisted you held. Though, I have yet to see anything for myself." He snickered. The males surrounding him chuckled in unison.

"Fine," I seethed through clenched teeth, "Have it your way, then."

Lifting my hands, I let the wind take hold, gripping two males who stood next to each other. Manipulating their bodies, I slammed them together, knocking them unconscious.

Kal and Zy saw what I was trying to achieve and immediately took action, mimicking what I had just done. Two by two, the males surrounding Darrem were knocked out and left on the floor motionless.

He stood alone, stunned. His mouth opened and closed as he glanced around at the males lying at his feet. His eyes found mine, leaving me to smile menacingly.

"What was that?" I ridiculed, cupping my hand to my left ear. "I don't think I heard that correctly."

Darrem looked around at the males lying limply on the ground. He was the only one standing, and since he didn't have the power or strength of a Shadow Assassin, he had little choice but to surrender himself.

He sneered, "You think you can just take over everything I have amassed? You know nothing of what I have done for AshFiera."

I glanced over at the male who helped my father starve innocent families and turned those desperate enough into criminals. "I think we can manage, I'm sure there are other males and females who have been working for you that would gladly take over and not let others starve for their gains."

Anger flashed through his eyes, and his fists clenched together as his jaw tensed. Hatred was written plainly across his face, and when he stepped toward me, my reflexes flinched. Without realizing it, my hand shot forward, and I let out the slightest wisps of my lightning.

When it reached Darrem, he fell to his knees and convulsed until I let go of that tiny power I had inflicted on him.

He peered up at me, pleading, "Please, have mercy. I will do anything! I-I promise not to let families starve."

Tsking, I slowly walked up to the male with my mates closely in tow. "Oh, I will give mercy alright. I won't kill you. No, instead, you're going someplace more fitting for you and all the other males who decided to help my father."

His eyes widened, and then he shrank in on himself. He was sobbing like a coward. He had no actual power. He was just like my father, using those with more strength and skills to do his bidding.

We would take over his food supply and dole it out to

worthy males and females in AshFiera who only wanted to do good.

The shuffling feet of two males entered the ballroom behind us. When I turned, ready to zap whoever came through, I quickly lowered my hands. Relief flowed through my ragged, fried nerves as I spotted Kojax and Gezr striding toward us.

"I see you took care of everything here," Gezr said, glancing at the limp males and a kneeling Darrem.

"Our mate handled most of it. Her instincts guided us to the correct path." Kal smiled, wrapping his hand around my back. Zy's hand found mine, squeezing tenderly as we watched more assassins find their way into the ballroom.

No one spoke as they immediately set in motion, gathering males and jumping with them to wherever they were housing the other prisoners.

Their fates would be reviewed after a time spent in solitary alone. Most would likely get a second chance, but those who didn't learn a lesson would be kept locked away for the remainder of their lives.

A sudden insistent tugging began. My heart raced as it grew. My lungs worked overtime as I sucked in air that seemed to be blocked.

"The Ashix." I gasped out before shadow-jumping to our safe house without my mates.

Stumbling, I made my way to the bedroom. Collapsing in front of the rocking egg. Placing my hand against her shell, the Ashix inside calmed, letting up on whatever power she held over me as I gasped fresh lungfuls of air.

Keeping my hand against her egg, I dragged myself into a kneel.

"I'm here, little one." I wheezed out.

Crashing and clattering reverberated outside of the bedroom, then came Zy's roaring, "RAINE!"

"Here—I'm here, Zy." Rushed, clambering footsteps found their way into the bedroom.

"What is it? Why on Goddess' mercy did you disappear like that?" He asked worriedly.

"It's the youngling. She called me. It was so intense I couldn't ignore it." Kal appeared in the doorway next, huffing, out of breath, his eyes wild as he took me in.

"Don't ever do that again, Enayah. You made us worried sick!" His movements jerked as he kneeled next to me. He noticed my hand touching the Ashix egg. "She's coming, isn't she?"

I nodded, still holding my hand against the hardened shell. Slow slithering moved inside beneath where I touched when a small crack formed.

More cracks appeared horizontally as she began turning and pushing against the inside of the egg. The images penetrated my mind as if I were inside with her.

She gave a big jerk, the crack widening until I could spot her movements below my hand. Instinctually, I lifted it away, and when I did, the egg broke open entirely. The top half tumbled to the side, leaving me to view the youngling who slowly uncurled herself from her cramped ball.

Scales shimmered under the sunlight that beamed in through the open window. She was grimy coated from the stuff inside her egg. I couldn't see her colors come through yet, and I was desperate to know if she looked like her mother, Beauty, or if she held her own colors.

Zy was entering the room with a towel in hand, heading back toward us. *When had he left?* I had been so engrossed in the young Ashix hatching that I didn't realize he had exited the room. "Thanks," I said, and then I turned back to the Ashix, wiping her little scaled face.

She emitted a trill and bumped into my hand. Tears filled

my eyes as I kept cleaning her until she was strong enough to roll out of the bottom half of the egg and into my lap. I was suddenly a mess as her still dirty body curled into the cradle of my thighs.

Kal had another towel and helped work on cleaning her. Little by little, the color of her scales popped. She was the same color as her egg, a beautiful pale pink. She reminded me so much of a flower I had been drawn to in the gardens at the mansion.

When we finished, she lifted her head, looking deep into my eyes.

Hello, my flame.

I choked on a sob when I greeted her back, "Hello, little Azalea."

She was so beautiful. The striking similarities in her coloring reminded me of the Azaleas I used to walk past in the gardens. Those flowers always caught my eye, so I found it fitting to name her after them.

Azalea. Thank you for my name, my bonded flame. I shall cherish and roar it to the skies when I take my first flight.

Kal and Zy huddled around me, gazing down at the youngling as I cradled her. Their relief and love flowed through as they touched any part of my body they could.

I was happy they were both here to witness Azalea's entrance into our world. Her mother would be a proud Ashix to see how stunning her daughter was.

For several days after her hatching, Azalea slept most of the time in the makeshift bedding in our room. She only woke to eat fresh, bloody meat, which usually caused a mess, which Kal gladly cleaned up. Soon enough, she was walking around and getting into trouble throughout the room, waking us at early hours by crawling into the bed and lying on top of me or pushing one of my mates over so she could curl into my warmth.

We eventually had to move her out of our bedroom and into the room across the way until we felt it was safe enough to take her to the newly built stables.

Zy spent his time in between the safe house and the mansion he took back. Constantly trying to convince me to move us all there. I wasn't ready yet. There had been so many bad memories with my father in that place. So Zy vowed to change everything before we would take up our permanent residence. He said it would be months before that happened, which was relieving because I wasn't ready to leave while Azalea was still so young.

Cassius eventually retrieved my mother from Earth, bringing her, my Gigi, and Aunt Samara back to AshFiera now that it was safe again for a visit.

Our reunion was filled with crying and laughing, and, of course, my mother scolded me for pushing her into the portal.

This was also when my mother and Cassius told me about their relationship. I was extremely happy for her. She deserved the love that Cassius gave her, and I had long considered him a father. It felt natural when their displays of affection were no longer a secret.

Zy, of course, named Kal his second. Which didn't surprise anyone since they were brothers and shared a mate. Everything was as it should have been before my father came along and interrupted the way of life in AshFiera. Peace prospered, and families were no longer starving or killed.

I giggled as Kal's lips tickled the back of my neck as we lay in bed. Zy's hands were trailing up the side of my thigh before lazily gripping a handful of my ass and pulling me toward him.

They liked to play the tug of war game with my body, usually while we were naked, which was the case at that moment.

"Goddess, you smell amazing." Zy trailed his nose along my throat, lips lightly grazing after.

"You always tell me I smell amazing, Zy." A gasp left my throat as he nipped playfully just below my ear, leaving shivering and goosebumps on my body.

"Yes, but lately, you have been smelling even more spectacular. It makes me want to drink from your cunt and never stop."

"Mhm, I agree. You smell like your usual amazing self but more." Kal lazily traced his fingers down my spine, his hand perched under his head, as he watched Zy continue to lap at my skin while moving downward.

Suddenly, I was pushed flat onto my back. Zy slithered further down my body, leaving hot kisses as he went. Kal circled one of my nipples with the tip of his finger before taking it into his mouth.

A sultry moan left my throat at the sensations my two mates brought forth. Their arousal amplified through our bond. I was so close already, and they had barely even touched me.

Kal's mouth and fingers alternated. He lightly bit one nipple while his fingers pinched the other. Zinging found its way to my core with his efforts even before Zy made his way to my center.

Hands gripped my thighs as I was spread wide for Zy to dive in between. The touch of his tongue on my clit, while Kal lavished my breasts, sent me over. Gripping both males' hair in each hand, I screamed their names as my release continued to roll over me.

They slowed their kisses, Zy leaving my center as he crawled his way back up the bed, laying next to me.

Kal slid closer, wrapping his arm around my center and pulling me back into him. His erection cradled in between my ass cheeks. I wiggled to entice him, which caused a sharp smack to one cheek and a yelp to leave my throat.

"What was that for?"

"You're misbehaving, little mate. Now, lie still and enjoy the cuddling before we tire you out in a moment." Kal sounded sleepy, while Zy didn't speak a word; he just lay there with his eyes closed.

Even with the previous orgasm, my body ramped up. I wanted to be caressed and worshipped like I always was. Only now, it was amplified, and I couldn't get enough of my mates. I needed to tell them the secret I had been keeping. They would find out eventually; now was as good a time as any.

"I have something to tell you both." I started.

"Hmm, what is it, little storm?" Zy asked, eyes still closed.

"I know why I smell better to you both," I said, waiting for them to rouse.

"Why is that?" Kal asked, nuzzling his face into my neck.

"My body is changing. It has been for a while." I said, biting my bottom lip as Zy lazily peeked at me from his slitted lids.

"Has it, my love?" Zy asked, blinking himself awake more to focus on me.

"Yes, because I am growing another life inside me."

Silence. That's all I got from them. Huffing, I began struggling to get out of their embrace. It wasn't exactly the reaction I was hoping for.

"Raine?" Zy's hands slipped into my hair, making me pause in my efforts to escape. "We're going to be fathers?" His smile broadened before descending, taking my lips with his. When he finally let up, I breathed heavily.

"Of course, you big idiot. I didn't just do it all on my own. I had help from you both."

Kal leaned over and took his turn kissing me hard. He backed away slightly only to push his forehead to mine. "You have made me the happiest male alive. Although," He pulled back, "Do I need to cut Zy's balls? Are you okay with this?"

"You don't need to cut his balls. I'm pretty sure he wasn't the only one indulging in the activities."

I squealed when suddenly hands and lips were everywhere. Both males lavished me with so much pleasure for hours I couldn't think of anything better to celebrate this new adventure we would take on besides engrossing ourselves in each other.

Epilogue

Raine

The rustle of wings fluttered in the clearing in front of the stables, where I stood watching several Ashix roam the clouds above.

The younglings scrunched in close to my legs as they watched their parents soar in the sky, unburdened, riding the waves of wind gusts, waiting for them to land.

Today, the little Ashix surrounding me would take their first flight after weeks of being watched over in the stables that Zy and Kal had specially built. My mates were too kind, and even after all these years together, they still seemed to surprise me with their generosity.

True to Zy's word, he completely redid the mansion, tearing walls down and erecting new ones. The only room he left alone was the room the three of us shared. It was the room I had stayed in while my father was still alive, and it was magically soundproofed. Zy didn't want to tamper with the spell.

Looking back over my shoulder, I noticed the smallest of the younglings hung back just inside the stable doors.

"Stay here, little ones," I said, moving toward the lone baby. When I got closer, I noticed it was Azalea's second youngling. He was a nervous little guy who didn't like to socialize with the others I watched over.

He backed further into the large enclosure, shaking so fiercely that his little claws made sharp scratches in the rhythm of his movements.

"Kyas, it's alright, little one. You can come out. Your mother is going to be joining us soon, and we don't want her to worry you're not out there, do you?" Squatting down to his level, I held out my hand for him to sniff. His hesitance was understandable. I didn't get to spend as much time with him as I did with the more sociable younglings.

He slowly approached, taking several whiffs of my fingers while keeping his eyes glued to me.

You—you are safe?

His high-pitched voice sounded inside. The fire opal was working as it always had in the last few years. Allowing me to hear the beasts who now were drawn to me in flocks.

"I'm safe. Didn't your mother impart her upbringing to you?" I asked, keeping my hand steady.

She did. But—I'm scared.

"It's okay to be scared at first, but I'm sure the others would love for you to join us. Take your time and come out when you're ready."

Okay, do you think my mother will be angry?

His question startled me. Azalea had never shown anger aside from when one of the other females got too close to her nest. "No, sweetling. She will understand. You're not ready yet."

He chuffed a trundle of smoke while I walked away, returning to the other younglings, who were beginning to get restless and waiting for guidance from either me or their parents.

It had been years since Beauty died, leaving me to raise Azalea before her father, Kovidar, came back to watch her first flight. Ever since that day, she soared with her father in the skies, and several Ashix females sought out the safety I provided. Which in turn provided trust gained between the beasts and a few of the chosen people of AshFiera.

No one could talk to the Ashix like I could. Instead, they flew in to stay at the mansion and train with me on the beast's needs. More and more, Ashix started to trust us, and it was a beautiful thing to watch develop.

"Alright, little ones, get ready. Your parents are cresting before they dive down to join us. When they swoop in low, I want you to take off and join them in the skies."

Excited trilling and yips filled the small space they huddled around. Soon, the first Ashix dove, whipping the wind to the ground before leveling out. Shortly after, a few of the younglings took off. And then it was all for one, with several impatiently leaving before their parents made it close enough. A giggle left my throat, watching their little wings flap unsteadily until they got the hang of being off the ground. And then it was a magnificent sight to behold.

"Mom!!!" An excited scream exited the back of the mansion, running through the gardens and across the extended field of grass.

When I finally spotted my daughter, who looked exactly like me and was just as obsessed with the beasts as I was, I smiled. She started running toward me. Her gaze fixated on the stunning sight above us.

She was still a little ways from where I stood when Azalea swooped down and landed in the clearing. She turned toward my daughter, and nerves frayed through our bond. Something was wrong; she was never nervous. Was it because her youngling was still clinging to his spot in the stables?

My question was answered moments later when his little body bound out towards his mother. She eyed him quickly before hissing, stopping him in his tracks and focusing on the treeline behind the stables.

Branches snapped, and a roar shook the ground beneath our feet when another Ashix came running out of the woods. This one I didn't recognize. His bright green scales shimmered under the sun while his yellow eyes narrowed in on Azalea, and then he found my daughter.

"NO! Aurora, stop!" The scream that tore from my throat alerted the male of my presence, and he sped up. My heart dropped from my chest into my stomach as I watched him approach my daughter. I couldn't see her face, let alone most of her body, and I didn't want to shadow-jump and startle him. That would have been way worse with an Ashix who wasn't familiar to me.

Kal and Zy shadow-jumped next to me while I held my breath to see what would happen. I was utterly helpless. Azalea crouched, growling low. She knew not to move either, especially since she regarded Aurora as one of her own.

"What do we do, Raine?" Kal asked, voice edged with panic.

"I'm unsure right now. He's not acting aggressively to Aurora, only towards Azalea." Holding my breath, I reached for Zy's arm and then Kal's. "Wait." I stopped their subtle movements when giggling trailed over to us.

We watched as Aurora walked around the male's side, skimming her hand along his scales as he faced Azalea. Her wide grin spread across her face.

"Goddess, our daughter is as reckless as her mother." Zy quipped.

Rolling my eyes, I focused back on what I was seeing. My

daughter was standing in between the two Ashix. Her hands stretched out, reaching for the male's face. He seemed to sense what she was doing and obliged her by tilting his head toward her. She pulled his head further down so their foreheads touched. I watched as the tension seeped out of the male's body, his eyes closing along with Aurora's.

My tension leached out, and Azalea backed away when I tugged on our bond. She could also sense a shift in the air.

"Seems our daughter has your gifts, little storm," Zy smirked, pulling me along while we slowly approached the two.

"The Goddess has blessed us with not one but two gifted females." Kal's laughter filled the silent space, making the unknown male Ashix and our daughter turn toward us.

As we made our way across the field, Aurora and the male met us halfway.

"Mom, dads, I'd like you to meet my bonded Ashix, Serth," Aurora announced. We had no idea she had been working with her own beast, and I couldn't be more proud of how much she had grown already. Aurora was only eight. It was more like eight going on eighteen with how she handled the deadly beasts.

I will always protect the female with my life, for she is my flame.

Stepping forward, I reached out a hand, letting the Ashix take in my scent. "I have no doubt you will protect my daughter as if she were your own. You are welcome to stay here." He turned his gaze toward mine, stunned.

You hear me? If that is so, I would very much like to stay around my bonded flame.

A smile tugged at my lips. "Of course, I can hear you with the fire opal bestowed upon me by the Goddess. I do hope you will get along with the other Ashix. This is their home as well." He looked around, chuffing.

Very well. I shall behave as long as no one harms my little female.

I turned toward my daughter, crossing my arms and lifting a brow. "You, little lady, will explain yourself later before bed. Until then, be careful of the younglings still working up the courage to take their first flight." I swept my hands over where Kyas still stood, shaking, watching as the others flew enthusiastically in circles around the clearing.

Everything was as it should be: this beautiful little life we built together, Watching Aurora grow into herself, and admiring my mates for being the fathers to our daughter, which I was never able to get in return from my own.

Tears sprung to my eyes, watching my family as I cradled a hand to my lower stomach. My mates approached either side, filling me with an abundance of love. Yes, this was perfect—our almost complete little life.

The End.

A note from the Author

Whew, I can't believe I wrote not one but two entire books! When I started this journey in March of 2024, I set out with only one goal in mind. Write at least one book and publish it for the world to say, "Hey, I did that." What started as one book, maybe two, has now turned into a passion for storytelling and the worlds my mind creates.

When I was working on Chapters 19 and 20, I had just helped my furry soulmate, Dane, cross the rainbow bridge. I had already planned for Beauty to die, but I wasn't planning on writing it while I was freshly grieving for my cat, who I had for over 13 years. He would sit with me while I wrote AshFiera and again while I started writing Ashix Rising. It was an incredibly hard decision to make, but his quality of life was not what an older gentleman kitty should go through. I know when it's my time to reach heaven, he will be waiting for me. To cuddle and receive endless head kisses.

I truly hope you continue to follow along in my writing journey as I learn more about the writing world, hone my writing skills, and bring you stories that give you heartache, passion, and a chance to escape, even for just a little while.

A note from the Author

Thank you so much for supporting my dreams!

About the Author

K.L. ANDERSEN is a multi-genre romance author and avid reader. Whether it's heart-wrenching or silly, she likes to write and dream up different worlds and the not-so-human men in them. She is a fierce Scorpio who lives in the Northern Midwest with her husband, two kids, two dogs, two cats, a bearded dragon, and the many chickens who roam around her home.

You can find her being a goober while enjoying writing, reading, gaming, or hanging out with those she loves.

Books By K.L. Andersen

www.ingramcontent.com/pod-product-compliance
Lightning Source LLC
Chambersburg PA
CBHW051246260626
47162CB00002B/632